THE NEUTRINO BOM

No. It was impossibl
insane....

With shaking hands, Smith quickly called up the latest image of the Radiant Grappler. He had taken over and automatically programmed the satellite.

The Spacetrack system was continuing to track the vessel. At the moment it was well past Crete. Nearing Cyprus.

The neutrino bomb.

And as his heart thudded a concert of fear in his chest, Smith knew it to be true. To the very core of his rock-ribbed New England soul.

And if the CURE director's worst fear was realized, Bryce Babcock's scheme would have awesome global ramifications.

Other titles in this series:

#95 High Priestess
#96 Infernal Revenue
#97 Identity Crisis
#98 Target of Opportunity
#99 The Color of Fear
#100 Last Rites
#101 Bidding War
#102 Unite and Conquer
#103 Engines of Destruction
#104 Angry White Mailmen
#105 Scorched Earth
#106 White Water
#107 Feast or Famine
#108 Bamboo Dragon
#109 American Obsession
#110 Never Say Die
#111 Prophet of Doom
#112 Brain Storm
#113 The Empire Dreams
#114 Failing Marks
#115 Misfortune Teller
#116 The Final Reel
#117 Deadly Genes
#118 Killer Watts
#119 Fade to Black

THE LAST MONARCH

A GOLD EAGLE BOOK FROM
WORLDWIDE®

TORONTO • NEW YORK • LONDON
AMSTERDAM • PARIS • SYDNEY • HAMBURG
STOCKHOLM • ATHENS • TOKYO • MILAN
MADRID • WARSAW • BUDAPEST • AUCKLAND

First edition July 2000

ISBN 0-373-63235-5

Special thanks and acknowledgment to James Mullaney for his contribution to this work.

THE LAST MONARCH

Printed in U.S.A.

For Kevin Howard,
who was always certain even when I wasn't.
For LOLN and IA (of the East Coast IAs),
always good for a laugh.
For RWR, with eternal thanks.

And for the Glorious House of Sinanju,
e-mail: housinan@aol.com
(After 5:00, slip gold bullion under door—
checks will be neither accepted nor returned)

It would be the his last photo op.

His wife had objected. Insisted that it would never happen as long as there was breath in her body.

Her unyielding passion on the subject would have surprised many of her harshest critics. Even a few of their oldest friends would have been stunned by her determination that the photo op not take place.

"It's not so bad," one had ventured. He had been a close family friend since the California days. His once sharp face now sagged with age. "It might even be good for him to get out."

"No," she replied with icy firmness. Sitting across from him in the sunroom, she sipped tea from a China cup.

"The kids think it's a good idea," he advised.

She laughed at this. "Why doesn't that surprise me?"

He stiffened, embarrassed at her faintly bitter tone.

"Oh, I'm sorry. I thought that was all settled."

"It *is.*" She sighed, setting cup to saucer with a

tiny click. "It's just that they don't think things through very clearly. Everyone knows that."

He tried one last tack. "Forget about the kids, then. Think about the country. Things have gotten bad in the past ten years. America needs to have its hope restored. And people *love* him."

At this, the famous ice queen's veneer cracked ever so slightly. Her eyes began to well up as she fought back the memories. All the memories—for years they had been happy. Now they were bitter, tinged with great sorrow.

She straightened her back, seemingly embarrassed by her inability to control her emotions.

"No, Cap," she replied, a steely resolve in her voice. "America or not, he's my husband, and I won't let him be used like some prop."

That was that. Or so she thought.

A few days after she'd spoken what she thought to be the final word on the subject, she flew back east for a weekend antidrug fund-raiser. Although she was reluctant to leave his side—especially now—the doctors insisted he was fine. At this point, there were no sudden changes expected in his condition. Besides, the fight against drugs had always been a pet project of hers.

Wifely concerns heavy on her mind, she left his side.

Her plane was barely taxiing down the runway before they came to collect him.

It was his daughter who betrayed him. The Goneril to his Lear. Now in her forties, she had been young when he was climbing the ladder to his great perch.

The girl had always been full of hate for her famous parents. This latest rebellion was more an act of revenge against the both of them than anything else.

Her mother was airborne—on her way to Washington. Her father was helpless to stop her. Perfect timing.

"Cowboy boots, denim shirt, jeans," she barked to the coterie of men who trailed her into her father's room. They began to dutifully raid closets and bureaus.

Clothes were tossed onto the quilt.

Through it all, her father sat there, oblivious. Perhaps a puzzled eyebrow arched as the men worked quickly. At one time the most famous face in the world, reduced now to a confused knot of sadly familiar wrinkles.

He did nothing to stop them as the strangers began to strip him of his nightclothes.

FORTY MINUTES LATER, they were on the range.

Distant mountains undulated in blue-violet waves from the ruler-flat plain. Above, wisps of clouds reflected shades of orange and red from the fire of the setting sun.

The Jeep they were in stopped beside an empty horse trailer. Father and daughter got out.

Photographers were waiting. Two wranglers stood next to the trailer, one holding the reins of a big yellow palomino. The animal snorted nervously at the crowd.

The crush of people encircled them immediately.

Her father was typically disoriented.

He had been enjoying the ride, the warm evening air sparking something in the hazy cloud that was his mind. But with the throng of people came confusion, almost a sense of fear.

Makeup was quickly applied.

"We're losing the light," a photographer complained tightly.

"Get him on it," another urged. He was clucking impatiently as he checked his light meter.

The old man's arms were grabbed. He didn't even try to fight them as they pushed and pulled him up on the horse.

It was almost a familiar sensation. This had been his experience with many things the past few years. He could almost feel, almost *remember*....

Almost, almost, almost.

He was lost in a sea of almosts. With nothing to hold on to. Nothing to keep his sanity afloat.

He had drowned long ago. Died. His mind was gone. It was only a matter of time before his body caught up.

He was in a familiar setting now—in the desert, on a horse. And he didn't even know it.

Coaxed by a wrangler, he grasped the reins.

A long-faced girl with dark hair and a lean body

looked up at him. She was the one who had orchestrated this event. She seemed very angry about something. Maybe if he smiled at her she wouldn't be so angry. He instantly forgot to smile.

Below him, the horse snorted angrily at the air.

Cameras clicked madly.

Men moved around, framing quickly.

Click, move. Click, move.

The horse snorted once more, scuffing a thick hoof at the cracked and dusty ground.

Men swirling. Skipping, sliding, twisting all around him. He was becoming dizzy.

A loud whinny.

Other men coming forward, pushing past those with the cameras. The world dropping out below him. The horse rearing, rising furiously to its hind legs.

"Hold him!"

"Get beneath him!"

Sliding backward. *Falling.* The ground racing up to him.

There was a sharp pain at the back of his head. Stars exploding behind his eyes. A flash of sudden, stark memory.

Darkness. Then light.

They were all above him, faces cast in silhouette. Behind them loomed the vast orange sky.

And he remembered nearly all of them. Those he didn't recognize, he knew he had never met before.

He *knew.* Remembered everything. And it was wrong.

Before losing consciousness once more, he murmured something to those kneeling above him. A single word. His eyes rolled back in his head, and he was gone.

Guiltily, his daughter cradled his head in her hands, less concerned with her father's health than with what her mother would do when she got back home.

"What did he say?" a Secret Service agent asked, unhappy with himself for not being more firm with the daughter of his charge.

"I don't know," his partner said.

"It sounded like 'cure,'" a photographer whispered.

"Cure? What do you suppose he meant?"

The photographer shrugged. "Who knows with Alzheimer's?" he said.

For an eternity on that dusty California desert bluff, with a soft breeze blowing down from the Santa Ana Mountains, everyone stood around in shock, not knowing what to do.

They looked down on the tired, weathered face of the former President of the United States, little realizing that their unauthorized stunt had unlocked a decades-old secret so dangerous it could very well topple the government of the nation he had served so well.

His name was Remo and from where he was standing he couldn't see a single pitchfork or burning torch.

There were no chants. No banners, per se. A few signs here and there, but these were feeble at best. The only real effort shown by the protestors was their jockeying attempts to get their faces in front of the many television cameras that whirred up at them from the sidewalk.

The Bronx police station had become a magnet for protestors over the past few weeks. More than two hundred were there today.

Leaning against a fire hydrant across the street from the milling crowd, Remo frowned. After standing in the sunlight for just a few minutes, he'd come to a single, inescapable conclusion: They just didn't make mobs like they used to.

No one paid any attention to him. And why would they?

Remo was a thin man of indeterminate age. Height, weight, hair—everything about him was determinedly average. The only things an observer might think to be outwardly abnormal about his appearance were his freakishly thick wrists, which, at times of agitation, he would rotate absently. This was not one of those times.

As he studied the crowd, Remo's arms were folded firmly over his chest.

The men and women had dressed down for the occasion. They were all meticulously swathed in sedate designer jeans and coordinating shirts. Here and there, diamond or gold accessories peeked from cuff or earlobe, but for the most part the more ostentatious signs of wealth had been checked at JFK Airport.

A line of long black limousines waited like somber sentries down the block—away from the news cameras.

Everyone wore a serious face. After all, racism and police brutality were serious matters.

It had happened again. New York City, already reeling from a simple, tragic mistake that had blossomed into a racially charged incident, was being forced to contend with the second such event in less than two years.

A cabdriver had been stopped by police. A Haitian immigrant, the man spoke little English. He pulled his wallet and jumped from the car, screaming at the officers. Sadly, the black comb jutting from his wallet was mistaken for a gun barrel. The two police officers reacted instinctively. They opened fire.

Nineteen bullets later, they realized their mistake. But it was too late.

The cabbie died at the scene. And the protests that had been dwindling in the wake of the first terrible accident had erupted anew.

The usual Hollywood horde had taken up the call to action. The socialist elite from both coasts descended like well-dressed locusts on the steps of the police precinct where the two officers worked.

And there they sat.

During the day, they chanted. At night, they lit candles. And through it all, deals were discussed and lunches scheduled. It was less a protest than a three-week-long networking session. Plus the press coverage didn't hurt their careers.

Since he'd taken up his late-morning position on the sidewalk twenty minutes ago, Remo had singled out a bunch of celebrities he recognized.

There was Susan Saranrap and her companion, Tom Roberts. Remo made a point of avoiding their line of sight.

By the looks of it, Saranrap had followed through on a threat to become pregnant yet again. But at age seventy-six, she'd had to put an entire team of Frankenstein-inspired physicians to work revving up her dusty womb. Whatever injections they were giving her made her bugging eyes launch even farther from their sockets. The ability to blink over her trademark swollen orbs had been lost somewhere in the early part of the first trimester.

The famous Afrocentric movie director Mace Scree had abandoned his courtside L.A. Lakers seat to fly in for this day's rally. His slight frame was draped in an oversize basketball jersey. A goateed face that looked as if it had been borrowed from a cartoon weasel peered millionaire malevolence from beneath the brim of his omnipresent baseball cap.

Not one, but *two* former New York mayors had joined the cause. The first was an elderly man who looked like a frog starving for a fly. He'd found time to protest in the downtime between his twice yearly heart attacks.

The second ex-mayor was dressed in a thin cotton sweater, white shorts and carried a tennis racket. Though his detractors would have found it difficult to believe, this rally seemed to interest him even less than his stint in Gracie Mansion. Sitting on the precinct steps, bored, he bounced his racket off one knobby knee.

Crowded up on the stairs, farther from the news cameras, was the usual assortment of community activists and gawkers who were always a phone call away when the evil specter of racism reared its ugly head.

And presiding over them all was Minister Hal Shittman.

The clergyman had come to national prominence back in the eighties when a young black woman claimed to have been assaulted by a group of white men. Worse than the attack was the fact that her assailants had smeared her with excrement. Hal Shittman had taken up her cause with a vengeance, screaming for justice for this poor, frightened child.

After ruining the lives of the men she accused, the girl was exposed as a liar. Although it had been proved beyond any doubt that the young woman had fabricated the entire tale, Shittman's career had yet to suffer as a result of his involvement in the fraud. Indeed, by the looks of him, he hadn't missed a single meal in the past twenty years.

A purple velour jogging suit top had been zipped over the minister's great protruding belly. Matching stretch pants were tugged up over his massive thighs. His long hair had been ironed flat and swept into a mighty pompadour.

His fingers were like ten fat, dark-as-night sausages as he raised them beseechingly to the heavens.

"How long!" Minister Shittman wailed. Diamond-and-gold rings worth tens of thousands of dollars sparkled on his pudgy knuckles.

The former mayor with the tennis-court date checked his watch. Even from so great a distance, Remo's supersensitive ears heard the man mutter, "I've been wondering that, too."

"How *long?*" Shittman cried out even louder.

As if in response, a door opened. A middle-aged police detective appeared at the top of a second set of stairs farther down from the protest site. His every move was blandly courteous as he raised a megaphone to his thin lips. His polite voice carried loudly over the crowd.

"Good afternoon," he announced in a booming, staticky tone. "The New York City Police would first like to apologize for having kept you waiting so long." He raised one hand in a beckoning fashion. "Now, those of you who want to get arrested, please move over to this door in an orderly fashion. Those of you who do not wish to be arrested today, please remain in your current protest position. The NYPD thanks you for your cooperation."

As if drawn by some hidden vocal pheromones released via the plainclothes officer's affable voice, approximately half of the two hundred people sitting around the main steps got up and moved toward the megaphone.

Like a purple Buddha, Shittman shepherded his flock of celebrities and politicians to the second staircase.

"Let's get a move on," he urged, his gloomy, sweating face always turned to the nearest available camera. "We don' want none o' that plunger action if we late."

Other uniformed officers had come out from behind the megaphone detective. As Shittman's group began to form neat queues, the newer NYPD arrivals began processing the protestors inside.

Several of the uniformed men came down into the street just to make sure there weren't any hard-of-hearing stragglers wanting to be locked up. The line was just beginning to inch its way inside the precinct when one of the youthful policemen found his way over to Remo.

"Excuse me, sir," the young officer began agreeably. He squinted in the sunlight. "Did you want to get arrested today?"

Everything about him and his colleagues was agreeable. To Remo, it seemed that *everyone* was agreeable. It was annoying in the extreme. Which was part of why he was here.

"No," Remo replied, eyes leveled on the crowd. "I'm just wondering when the jugglers and elephants are gonna join this three-ring circus."

"Sir?" the policeman asked.

His eyes were blandly noncommittal—a *Stepford Wives* replacement for the human cops of days gone by.

"Nothing." Remo sighed, shaking his head.

The officer stubbornly refused to leave. He was examining Remo's clothing.

"Are you homeless?" the cop asked sympathetically. He was careful to keep a nonjudgmental face as he nodded to Remo's navy blue T-shirt and tan Chinos.

Tipping his head, Remo seriously pondered the question for a long second.

"No," he replied at last. "I just can't go home."

It was true. It was too dangerous for him to go home right now. Not that Remo couldn't handle most dangers. But this was different.

Remo was a Master of Sinanju, an honorific so rare that only twice in a century, on average, was a single man allowed to hold that vaunted title. Remo was the Apprentice Reigning Master. His teacher was the Reigning Master.

Chiun, for that was his teacher's name, had trained Remo in the most deadly martial art the world had ever known. And all had gone well—more or less—for three decades.

But being the world's most lethal assassin was only Chiun's vocation. To Remo's eternal regret, the frail old Asian with the fatally fast hands had an avocation.

For years, the Master of Sinanju had wanted to be a writer. Since both men were in the employ of CURE, a government agency so covert its existence was known at any given time to only four men, it was problematic for Chiun to fulfill his dream.

Ordinarily, the risk of exposing the most damning national secret to exist in the country's short two-hundred-year history wouldn't have mattered a hill of beans to the wily Korean. But fortunately for CURE, for a long time Chiun's attempts at writing had been universally rejected. That had all changed a year ago.

It had all started with a trip to Hollywood, when Chiun had managed to secure a movie deal from a pair of oily film executives. Remo had been forced to keep Upstairs in the dark about Chiun's activities, lest he incur the old Asian's wrath. It was an uncomfortable time.

Luckily for Remo and CURE, the studio producing the Master of Sinanju's movie had gone bankrupt. And while the lawyers swarmed the soundstages and offices of Taurus Studios, picking whatever they could from its dead carcass, Chiun's film had been vaulted.

With the quiet demise of the movie, Remo had thought that his headaches were over. He was wrong.

Chiun had been impossible to live with since his return from the West Coast. Never the poster child for temperate behavior, the old man's attitude over the past three months had been volatile in the extreme. And the bulk of his anger had been directed at Remo.

It had gotten so bad that Remo had taken to using any excuse to get out of the house. The New York protests in the wake of the cabdriver shooting had been a godsend.

Remo was ticked off by the initial reports of the demonstrations on the evening news the previous night. It was maddening to him that the protesters seemed to care little, if at all, for the man who had been shot. It was clear to anyone with a functioning brain stem that they were merely standing on a corpse to inflate themselves. And, given his current mood, their phony sanctimoniousness was all Remo needed to set him off.

The line on the staircase before him was still annoying in its sheer orderliness. The celebrity protestors were allowing the proles to be processed first. The owner of every famous face in the crowd wanted to be last to enter that building. No one wanted to give up a single second of free camera time.

As Minister Shittman wrangled the celebrities into a manageable pack at the rear of the throng, Remo stuffed a hand deep into one pocket of his Chinos. A handful of quarters rattled obediently. He'd picked up two rolls from a bank back home. More than enough.

A hopeful face appeared before him, blocking his view of the stairs.

"There's no shame in being homeless. I can take you to a shelter," the youthful police officer offered. "Or to a counselor. Would you *like* to see a counselor? We have several inside. Free of charge, of course. The city mandated that we hire them rather than buy bullets."

Remo peeked around the man, irritated.

"What I'd *like* to see is at least a scowl on one of these cops. How much manpower are you wasting processing these nits?" He waved a thick-wristed hand at the line of filing protestors. "You should be furious."

"Oh, no, no, *no*," the young officer rapidly insisted. His worried eyes darted around, hoping no one in the vicinity had heard Remo's suggestion.

"The *new* New York police force is very responsive to the needs and difficulties of the community at large. See?"

The cop removed a tube of coiled pamphlets from the holster where his gun should have been. He peeled one off, handing it to Remo.

On the cover of the flyer, a rainbow coalition of police officers grinned agreeably. Women, Hispanics, blacks, Asians—all were represented. Missing from the group was a single white face. Beneath the men and women, a colorful banner read, It's *Your* Police Force: We Love To Help...And It Helps To Love!

Remo looked up at the officer. "I'm going to retch," he said.

"Would you like me to run down to the store and pick you up some Tums?" he offered helpfully, stuffing his remaining pamphlets back into his empty holster.

Remo ignored the offer, as well as the man's eager expression. "What do you do if you need your gun?" he asked, nodding to the flyer-filled holster.

"Weapons cause concern in poorer neighborhoods," the cop explained. "As part of the new Responsiveness to Community Issues Program, police officers are only allowed to carry firearms into those communities with a per capita income higher than thirty-two thousand dollars per year."

Remo was stunned. "What if you get shot at?" he asked.

The cop shook his head firmly. "Doesn't happen. Crime in lower-income neighborhoods is a media fabrication created to discourage investment in said neighborhoods. Page three."

He pointed to the pamphlet in Remo's hand.

"I don't know what kind of drivel they put in here, but I've *been* in those neighborhoods plenty of times," Remo said. "Any cop who doesn't go in armed to the teeth isn't likely to be coming home that night."

He spoke from experience. A lifetime ago, before being framed for the murder of a petty drug pusher and sentenced to die in an electric chair that didn't work, Remo had been a simple Newark beat patrolman. As a cop, he had taken his life in his hands every day on the job.

The young officer before him was shaking his head firmly. "You're not a protestor, are you?" he said, the light finally dawning.

"Is my head up my ass?" Remo queried.

The officer thought very carefully, surreptitiously glancing at both body parts in question. "No," he admitted finally, brow furrowed.

"Then I'm not a protestor," Remo concluded. And before the man could speak again, he pointed to the first staircase. "Ron Silver looks pissed," he said abruptly.

A look of horror sprang full-blown on the face of the cop. Knowing that there'd be hell to pay if a Hollywood activist had somehow been left out of the day's mass arrest, the young officer quickly left Remo's side. Car horns honked as he darted back across the street to the police station.

As soon as the man had stepped from the curb, Remo brought a handful of coins from his pocket. The quarters were cool in his palm. Clenching his hand into a fist, he fingered a single coin onto the tip of his thumb.

He was trying to decide who would make the best first target when a limousine roared up the street. It squealed up to the curb near Minister Shittman.

The passenger in the rear didn't even wait for the driver to run around from the front. The door sprang open, and a familiar figure popped into view.

She was six feet tall and dressed in a pair of black jeans tight enough to launch her femur marrow up into her pelvis. Her white lace blouse was chopped at her sternum to expose a perfectly flat stomach.

Remo recognized Cheri, the unimonikered rock singer and Academy Award-winning movie star, the instant she got out of the limo. He'd had the misfortune of seeing part of one of her films a few years earlier. As far as he was concerned, as an actress, she made a great singer. Unfortunately, the opposite was equally true.

In a desperate and futile attempt to remain youthful in perpetuity, Cheri had spent more time in operating rooms in the past two decades than on movie sets or in recording studios. Behind her back, friends joked that she could no longer sit next to an open fire lest she run the risk of puddling. As the years of plastic surgery took their toll, her face began to take on the elongated shape of an Easter Island statue.

Remo remembered reading somewhere that she'd had the muscles in her face paralyzed to avoid wrinkling. It had the effect of turning her immobile features into a living death's-head mask.

"Get out of my way! Out of my way, dammit!" Cheri yelled. Her warbling, whining voice rose past lips that didn't twitch a millimeter.

For Remo, her timing couldn't have been better.

"Wait your turn," a man groused.

He was an actor who had starred in *The Search for Pink November,* a movie about a defecting Russian submarine captain. In the denouement of that film, the titular sub had been able to perform acrobatics more appropriate to an aerial dogfight than an undersea battle. The only two things Remo really remembered about the movie were the ludicrous battle scene at the end and the wooden actor's flaring nostrils.

The angry star was flanked by his three untalented thespian brothers.

"I was first!" Cheri shouted. "My agent phoned ahead."

Neither the actor nor his three dull-eyed siblings seemed particularly impressed by her claim. As Cheri groused, they promptly offered her their broad backs.

It was the chance Remo had been waiting for. Across the street, he gave his thumb a simple flick.

The quarter, which had been balanced on his cuticle, rocketed forward. Only Remo saw it as it zoomed at supersonic speed across the street.

The English Remo had put on the coin made it wobble from its deadly flat trajectory somewhere midstreet. Once it reached the curb at the far side, it had slowed considerably and was zipping along heads side first.

By the time the coin struck the submarine movie actor between the shoulder blades, it had no more force than a rough shove.

The actor was launched forward into one of his brothers. They both toppled over onto the stairs.

"Hey, watch it, dude," the younger actor snarled, pushing his older brother away. He had been in the process of picking up another handsome young man.

The older brother seemed shocked. As he got to his feet, he pointed back at Cheri.

"She *pushed* me," the actor insisted, nostrils stretching to heretofore unrealized expanses of indignation.

"*What?*" Cheri's ventriloquist's dummy mouth asked. "Eat shit, you asshole."

As she spoke, she suddenly lurched forward. Arms thrown wide, she collapsed onto the falling form of the stunned actor. No one heard the clatter of coin on pavement.

"Get off me, you freaking mummy!" the actor screamed.

As he yelled, a commotion broke out in the next line.

Apparently, one of the noncelebrities in the crowd had shoved Susan Saranrap's lover. Tom Roberts had scrambled to his feet and pushed the man back. Not recognizing Roberts's standing among the unassailable glitterati, the man had promptly socked the actor in the nose.

There was blood everywhere.

Someone unseen rammed one of the ex-mayors in the back. As he fell, the man's tennis racket accidentally swatted his predecessor at city hall in the bald head. The other former mayor promptly went into cardiac arrest.

It went downhill from there.

Fistfights erupted up and down the stairs. Men screamed and swore. One man was pushed over the railing and landed with a splat on the sidewalk.

Cheri was livid as she punched and kicked the submarine movie actor. So angry was she, her eyes nearly twitched.

Minister Shittman had been propelled onto Mace Scree. Only the trademark hat of the diminutive director was visible beneath the great, wobbling purple velour mound.

For some reason, the fattest of the submarine movie actor's brothers had stripped off every last stitch of clothing. Screaming, he raced naked up and down the street.

As the riot grew, a few people begged the police to do something. Unarmed, the best they could do was read loudly cautionary advice from their pamphlets on making racist assumptions about the intentions of mobs.

Without any nudging from Remo, the protestors on the other staircase began rioting, as well.

And on the sidewalk, through it all, news cameras dutifully recorded the brawl that had broken out among the peace-loving protestors.

Remo pushed away from the fire hydrant against which he'd been leaning. The remaining coins jangled merrily in his pocket. In all, it had cost him only $2.50 in quarters.

"Now *that's* a mob," he pronounced.

While the cameras captured the true nature of the men and women on the steps of the police precinct, Remo turned away from the wrestling crowd.

He was feeling so good, maybe he'd rent a movie on the way home. Because of Chiun, he hadn't done so in ages.

Hands thrust deep into the pockets of his Chinos, he began strolling, whistling, down the sidewalk.

The August sun was warm on his face.

The somber brick building with its ivy-covered walls hunched warily amid the chirping woods and clawing night shadows. Lights from shore and the waxing moon sent ripples of shimmering silver across the undulating black waves of nearby Long Island Sound.

At the rear of the big building, one lonely light shone out from the darkness. The dull yellow glow spread thinly across the damp, midnight-black lawn that stretched to the lapping waters of the Sound.

The window through which the light spilled was made of one-way glass. Beyond the thick pane, away from the prying eyes of the outside world, a solitary figure sat at a lonely desk in a Spartan office.

Although it was well after hours, Dr. Harold W. Smith had completed his day's work only twenty minutes before.

To anyone in the outside world who might note Smith's schedule, this would not have seemed unusual. More often than not, as director of Folcroft Sanitarium in Rye, New York, Smith worked late.

However, all but a handful of people would have been surprised to learn that the work that occupied him was unrelated to sanitarium business.

Harold Smith led a dual life. To the public, he was the taciturn administrator of Folcroft, a bland man with a bland job. But in private, he was director of the supersecret government agency known only as CURE.

CURE was not an acronym, but a dream. A wish by a President—long dead—to heal the ills of a wounded nation.

At its inception, the agency was to work outside the tricky confines of the Constitution in order to protect it. A most illegal means to reach a most noble end.

Smith had toiled as director of Folcroft for the better part of his adult life. It was an irony not lost on the aging New Englander that the greatest lawbreaker in American history was also the nation's greatest defender.

He was a gaunt man, in the twilight years of his life. Smith's very being seemed to have been conceived in shades of gray. His dry skin was dead-fish gray. His thinning hair was grayish-white. Even the suit he wore was an unimaginative gray. The only splash of color was that of his green-striped Dartmouth tie, knotted tightly below his Adam's apple. Though at this time of night Smith was alone in the administrative wing of Folcroft Sanitarium, he still didn't loosen the four-in-hand knot.

Of course, in the unlikely event that anyone did stumble in on Smith, it would in all likelihood be necessary to neutralize that person as a threat to exposure. For although the agency Smith helmed had endured many dangers over the past four decades, the one thing CURE could not weather was public knowledge of its activities.

People had died who learned of CURE. Smith accepted this as an unfortunate fact of his covert existence. In his world, knowledge was danger. Not just a danger to himself or to his agency—those threats were fleeting. The danger was to America itself. For if it was learned that a succession of eight Presidents spanning much of the last half of the twentieth century had availed themselves of an unquestionably illegal agency, the very underpinnings of American democracy would be knocked loose. The country would topple.

"America is worth a life." Those were the words of an ally of Smith's, long dead. It was Smith's credo, as well. But it was a concept he applied not just to others. Smith would not exempt himself from this philosophy. The CURE director carried in his breast pocket at all times a coffin-shaped pill. In the event of exposure, he would take the bitter medicine without hesitation, insuring that knowledge of his and CURE's activities would be taken with him to the grave.

As he sat at his desk, he found that his arthritis-gnarled hand had strayed to his lapel. A gray thumb tapped absently against the poison pill in his vest pocket, pressing it against his thin chest.

Suddenly conscious of the movement, he pulled the hand away, placing it to the gleaming surface of his onyx desk.

Smith sighed, a mournful sound of rusty water trying to navigate up frozen pipes.

He knew why his hand had sought out the pill.

Although in his younger years he wouldn't have given such things a second thought, he couldn't dismiss the obvious psychological explanation for his subconscious action.

It was death. Plain and simple.

Smith was undeniably old. Part of another generation. A throwback to another era.

A few months back, he'd had a run-in with the President. In and of itself, that was not unusual. There were more times in the past than he could remember that he had come to loggerheads with a given American leader. But in this particular crisis, he had finally admitted to a basic incomprehension of this current chief executive.

Someone had twice tried to murder the President. Both attempts were halted by agents of Smith. Usually this would engender a spirit of gratitude in any man. But the President of the United States had been angry, particularly upon learning that the man who had been trying to kill him was a friend. Not just a friend, but a financial *benefactor.* In the end, the President was not so much angry that he knew his would-be killer, but that the man had contributed money to him in the past and, by dying at Smith's command, could not contribute in the future.

After the President was through screaming at him over that particular crisis, Smith had briefly contemplated dismantling CURE. His poison pill had almost seemed preferable to living in this new era of warped agendas and bizarre loyalties.

Of course, that was never a real consideration. In the end, Smith had hunkered quietly down behind his desk to do what he had always done. His job.

But thoughts of mortality continued to play at the fringes of his conscious mind. Like now.

It wasn't necessary for him to be there at this hour. If a crisis arose, the cell phone in his battered briefcase would relay the message to Smith's home.

He could have left an hour ago. Could have trudged to his rusting station wagon and driven home. Could have climbed into bed next to his sleeping wife and tried to push away the demands of his solitary life with a few hours of sleep.

But Smith was finding it difficult these days to work up the energy to do anything beyond his work.

And so he sat. Alone. In the shadows of his austere office. Embracing the dark night.

When the phone rang ten minutes later, the sharp jangle in the darkness startled him awake.

Smith didn't even realize he had dozed off. Alert now, he reached for the blue contact phone.

"Remo?"

It was a silly question. Only CURE's two field agents, Remo and, less frequently, his trainer, Master Chiun, used the phone. But Smith was not a young man any longer, and old habits had a way of dying hard.

So much a creature of habit was Smith that he didn't at first know enough to be startled when the voice that answered him was not Remo's.

"Smith?"

The older man's voice was hushed. Furtive.

For a moment, Smith thought that he had picked up the regular Folcroft line by mistake. He looked at the phone. It was blue. Remo's phone. But not Remo's voice.

The panic that had failed to materialize when he first picked up the phone suddenly manifested itself.

"Who is this?" he asked, his lemony voice straining for calm.

"Listen, I can't talk long. They're checking on me nearly every minute. Is this Smith?"

It was a demand this time.

Smith wasn't certain what to do. This had never happened before in the history of CURE.

"I cannot confirm that you have reached the party you desire. Perhaps if you gave me more information about yourself, I could be of some assistance."

The voice warmed, as if it recognized something in the tone that was familiar.

"It's you, all right. Thank God. I didn't know if

you'd still be there after all this time. The calendar in my room says it's 2000. Is that right?"

The wave of alarm that had overtaken Smith was slowly being eclipsed by worried comprehension. The voice was too familiar. The CURE director hadn't heard it in more than a decade. Certainly, he hadn't spoken to the man since the early days of 1989. But the voice was unmistakable.

Smith swallowed. "Mr. President?" he asked weakly.

There was a hint of mirth in the voice. Smith could almost see the familiar boyish grin over the line.

"Glad to see everyone hasn't forgotten about me. Guess I can't say I've returned the favor the past few years."

"Mr. President, I do not understand."

"You gave me this number years ago in case of emergency. You told me it was the contact line for those special people of yours."

"It is, Mr. President," Smith agreed slowly. "Forgive me, but you should not remember any of this."

"That's why I called." The former President's voice became grave. "Listen, Smith, we've got a problem. I don't know if you heard, but I had a little accident."

Smith's thin lips pursed. "I did not."

"You're slipping in your old age," the ex-President said with a chuckle. "Before you hear otherwise, the horse bucked me. I did *not* fall. Anyway, something happened to me when I hit my head. I remembered."

Smith felt a knot of acid sickness in his empty belly.

"How much?"

"Too much. I remember it all. Everything. You. Your group. Heck, I remembered the number to call you. Although it wasn't hard. A bunch of ones punched over and over. Not very original."

Smith was still trying to comprehend all this. "How is this possible?" he asked, shaking his head.

"You tell me. Your men were supposed to give me some kind of memory-suppression hypno-gobbledygook. Selective amnesia, and so forth."

"Didn't they?" Smith asked, not knowing whether to be hopeful that Remo had dropped the ball on this one.

"Sure. I remember them coming to me in the Oval the day before my vice president was sworn into office. I remember the old one bowing and pledging undying allegiance in that flowery way of his. I even remember him doing the whole amnesia thing to me, which I didn't before."

"So you're saying it did work until your accident?"

"Too well. I think it must have gone wrong somehow. They say I have Alzheimer's. And I know it must have looked like that. I remember getting worse. It's strange, Smith. I can actually remember forgetting. Everything's clear."

Smith was attempting to absorb what he was being told.

Of course he knew the former President had developed a degenerative brain disorder after leaving office. It had been announced by the ex-chief executive himself in a poignant letter to the American people. But it seemed as if this were only part of the story. Now Smith was learning that he might be the indirect cause of the President's illness.

"How do you wish to proceed, sir?" Smith asked after a moment of consideration.

"I think it's pretty obvious," the President replied amiably. "Your people still work for you?"

"Yes, sir."

"Even the old one?"

"Master Chiun is well."

"No kidding?" the President said with pleased surprise. "Gee whiz, Smith, whatever he's got, you should bottle it. Anyway, I expect they should pay me another visit. Fix up whatever it is that went wrong in the first place."

"I agree. Where are you?"

"Weizmann-Teacher's Hospital in Los Angeles."

"You are not in any immediate danger?"

"Only if they try serving me the cafeteria's blue-plate special."

Smith considered. "I will contact CURE's enforcement arm at once and dispatch him and his trainer to California. Expect them sometime tomorrow."

"That'll be fine," the former President said warmly. "Maybe this time, they'll get it right."

It was said jokingly. In fact, there was no rancor in the old man's voice. He didn't seem angry in the least that he'd been robbed of a good part of the waning years of his life.

"If all goes well, we should not speak again," Smith said. He was already swiveling toward the blue phone.

"Too bad. I've missed our little talks. I suppose it's necessary, though, isn't it?"

"Yes, Mr. President. If there isn't anything else...?"

It was a very obvious hint.

"No." The former President hesitated a beat. "Smith?"

The CURE director had been about to hang up the phone. He brought the receiver back to his ear.

"Yes, Mr. President?"

"It's nice to hear your voice."

Smith paused a heartbeat. In the darkness of his Folcroft office, he thought once more of how much times had changed. He took a deep breath as he thought of an earlier time, a better time.

"Yours, too, sir," he said, then hung up the phone.

As soon as Remo steered his leased car into the parking lot of the local All-Nite Bombshell Video Store, he felt his jaw drop.

A *Die Down IV* poster was taped to the interior window just beside the automatic In door.

That was Chiun's movie.

It was impossible, but there it was. On the flattened one-sheet poster was the familiar lopsided grimace of Lance Wallace, the star of all the *Die Down* films.

The sweating actor was proudly stripped to the waist, his ample belly hanging over his belt. Apparently, no one in Hollywood was willing to tell the star that he was in dreadful physical shape. Streaks of Karo blood had been applied to his slick skin. Pictured behind him were at least five separate explosions.

Remo fought waves of dread as he pocketed his keys. Head spinning, he walked into the store.

Inside, he made a beeline for the action-adventure rack. After much searching, he found a copy of the film. There were only two others behind it.

Remo went up to the counter, dropping his membership card and the plastic case containing the video before the young clerk.

"Good flick," the young man commented as he scanned the bar code on Remo's card. He slid the piece of thin plastic back across the counter.

"You've seen it?" Remo asked worriedly.

The kid nodded. "Just came in last night. A bunch of us stay and watch the movies sometimes. This is a good one."

"I heard it wasn't supposed to be released for a while."

The clerk talked as he slipped the movie into a yellow-and-blue Bombshell bag. "Lawyers worked out some deal between the estate of Quintly Tortilli and Taurus Studios. It was all done kind of quiet. Usually a movie that cost that much to produce gets at least a limited theatrical release. This one went straight to video for some reason."

He slid the bag down the counter, skirting the upright electronic sensor so that the film box didn't activate the store alarm.

"You don't have very many copies," Remo said, trying not to sound hopeful.

"Bombshell didn't order many. The demand isn't supposed to be that great. You're the first person to rent one. Too bad. Tortilli was a genius. He's like a hero to me. But we get a bunch of promotional stuff from the studios. I'm trying to get something started with the poster in the window. You know, to honor his memory."

"Yeah, I know," Remo said thinly.

He had met Tortilli. The man was responsible for a great many deaths and two situations that nearly resulted in the assassination of the President of the United States. Hardly a man who should be posthumously deified.

Remo collected his movie at the end of the counter and slipped out the door.

After he was gone, the clerk pulled out a battered movie rating guide. As he was scanning a bored eye over some of the more infuriatingly wrong reviews, he heard the In door hum open once more.

Only after a moment did he realize that no one had come into the store.

He looked up, puzzled.

It had been a slow night since the start of his shift. There was no sign of anyone near the automatic eye of the entrance.

As he looked at the door, something didn't look quite right. Whatever it was, he couldn't put his finger on it.

Oh, well. Shrugging, he returned to his book.

IN THE PARKING LOT outside, Remo used a repetitive slashing motion to reduce the twenty-seven-by-forty-inch *Die Down IV* poster to confetti. The shiny strips of paper that gathered at his feet looked as if they'd been run through a shredder. A faint breeze snagged them, blowing the long curling strands toward the street.

Gathering up the Bombshell bag from the hood of his car, Remo climbed in behind the wheel.

There was something he hadn't dared to look at on either poster or videotape. Screwing up his courage, he pulled the plastic case from the bag.

Lance Wallace's name was displayed prominently above the movie title. Remo looked below the title, at the other names listed in the fine print. He was interested in only one.

When he found the screenwriting credit, he stifled a laugh of relief.

"All I can say is, they're lucky they're all dead." He chuckled, shaking his head. "And I *still* wouldn't want to be in any of their shoes."

Grinning, he tossed the box onto the passenger's seat. Turning the key, he followed the wind-tossed poster shreds out onto the main drag.

Chiun, Reigning Master of the House of Sinanju, was absolutely, positively *not* in a snotty mood. Far from it.

Oh, considering all he had been forced to endure at the hands of idiots in the past few months, no one was more entitled than him to lapse into such a state. But it was a testament to his superior ability to cope with buffoons that he was able to rise above his snot-provoking id.

Snot. A disgustingly vile term.

It was Remo's, of course. At various times over the days and weeks since Chiun's unhappy return from Hollywood, Remo had described him as being "on the snot" or "in a snotty mood." Everything came up effluvium to that boy.

Chiun dismissed not only the term, but the accusation.

He was as happy and devil-may-care as ever. A carefree soul unaffected by the vicissitudes of life.

This was what he insisted to himself as he stomped through the empty condominium he shared with his pupil. As he slithered from room to room—

an ominous wraith in a black kimono—he slammed door after door. The echoes reached the street with the report of rifle cracks.

Who cared that he had been lied to by Hollywood producers? Such was life.

What did it matter that an untrustworthy director had ruined Chiun's first foray into motion pictures? There would be other opportunities.

Why should it matter that the film was being held from release by endless litigation? It was no skin off his nose.

Even though the world dealt him misery and abuse at every turn in his hundred-plus years of life, Chiun was happy. Happy, happy, happy.

The old Korean's tour of the house brought him back to the kitchen. He had completed this circuit a hundred times since Remo's departure that morning.

One bony hand snaked out from the concealment of a kimono sleeve. Popping the door open, he slipped inside the room, flinging the door shut behind him.

It struck the frame with a house-rattling crack.

He moved through the kitchen to the door on the opposite side of the room.

Chiun had opened this door and was about to slam it shut when he heard a familiar rhythmic heartbeat move into his sphere of detection. It came from out front.

Leaving the door to creak shut on its own, the Master of Sinanju slipped into the hallway. He deliberately lowered his own heartbeat and stilled his other life signs to avoid detection.

The front door inched open a few seconds later. When Remo tried to sneak inside, Chiun sprang like an angry feline from the shadows of the foyer.

"Where have you been?" the old Asian asked accusingly, his voice a squeaky singsong.

Remo jumped back, startled. "Geez, I thought I canceled the attack order for tonight, Cato," he groused.

"I will not be distracted by your crazed non sequiturs," Chiun challenged, hands clenched in knots of bony anger. A thread of beard quivered at the tip of his upthrust, accusatory chin. "You are late."

"I wonder why," Remo grumbled to himself. He shut the door behind him, careful to keep from turning his back on Chiun. "And you're lucky the neighbors didn't complain about all that door slamming."

"*They* are lucky they didn't complain," the Master of Sinanju sniffed, adding, "And I do not know what you are talking about."

"Yeah, right," Remo said. "I heard it down the block."

Chiun's hazel eyes steeled. "Do not 'yeah right' me," he said, his voice even. The wizened Korean tucked his hands inside the sleeves of his kimono. Placing both sandals firmly on the floor in an impersonation of a five-foot-tall colossus, he struck an imperious pose. "While you were out prancing about the countryside like a retarded grosshopper, I reached a decision."

"That's *grass*hopper." Remo sighed.

"I *know* what I said," Chiun retorted coldly.

Remo seemed eager to leave the foyer, but Chiun barred his way. For some reason, the younger man seemed to not wish to skirt the tiny Korean. Leaning carefully back against the door, he crossed his arms.

"What's the big decision?" he asked, perturbed.

"You need to show me proper respect."

"I *do* show you respect," Remo said, careful not to move.

"Saying that I am 'on the snot' is not respect. It is vulgar insolence. As well as incorrect."

"If you say so," Remo agreed.

"That is the sort of thing to which I am referring," Chiun said, stomping his feet. "Everything is 'yeah right' this and 'if you say so' that. The Apprentice Reigning Master of Sinanju should not speak thusly to his master."

Remo had a flash of anger. "I don't know why you're dumping this all on me. Ever since we got back from L.A., I've been your personal punching bag. I'm not even the one you should be mad at, but you're ticked at me because you already killed everyone who was involved. I'm your whipping boy by default."

"Do not be ridiculous," Chiun retorted. "I have already forgotten my miserable adventure in that land of lies. It matters not to me that the chimp-brained prevaricators of Hollywood snared me in their web of deception. Why should I be concerned in the least that producers and directors possessed of morals that would shame a Manila streetwalker have treated me as they would the oaf with the bucket who follows the horse in a parade? If that ever mattered to me—which it did not—it does no longer. What matters to me now is the constant scorn you show me, your father in spirit.''

''I don't do that,'' Remo said, the fight draining out of him. ''We both know that you're pretty much the only thing that matters to me in the world.''

Chiun's wrinkled face puckered in unhappy lines. ''I did not wish for you to become mawkish,'' he complained.

''So what do you want?'' Remo asked. Although his tone was exasperated, his expression was sincere. ''I'll do anything you ask.''

Remo meant it. He'd lived on edge for too long. It was like walking on eggshells every day. He just couldn't take it anymore.

He braced himself as the old man's wrinkled lips parted. He was ready for anything.

''Stop saying that I am in any way connected to snot,'' Chiun said, his face looking disgusted to even utter the word. ''It is gross. And untrue.''

The tension drained from Remo's shoulders.

''I'll try, Little Father.'' He smiled. ''Promise. Look, if that's all—''

''It is,'' Chiun interrupted, ''save one small

thing.'' He tipped his bald head inquisitively to one side. ''Tell me what you have hidden behind your back.''

Remo instantly straightened. ''Uh, what do you mean?'' he asked, a note of forced innocence in his tone.

''Please, Remo,'' Chiun derided impatiently. ''If you were any more transparent, I could *see* whatever it is you are hiding behind your back.''

''I'm not hiding anything,'' Remo challenged. ''And don't you have a kitchen door to break?''

Chiun's gaze narrowed. He didn't budge an inch.

The prickling electricity that preceded attack raised the short hairs on Remo's forearms. He braced himself, already knowing what he'd do. When Chiun grabbed for the videotape he had tucked into the waistband of his trousers, Remo would yank the movie out from the other side. While the Master of Sinanju was distracted by his own search, Remo would lob the box through the open door of the living room where it would land silently on the sofa. He could then collect it later.

A blur of movement before him. Chiun lunged as expected. The old man feinted right and darted left. A bony hand snaked around behind Remo.

Remo's own hand flew right, grabbing for the hard plastic video box. He plucked it free just as he felt the rush of displaced air from Chiun's flashing hand.

In a move so fast it was light-years beyond blindingly quick, he slipped the box up next to his head. As he'd done with the quarters at the rally in New York, he flicked his thumb. The box rocketed silently from his fingertips.

It didn't make it more than two feet on its path to the living room before another blur raced to intercept it.

As Remo's heart sank, the box jumped into Chiun's palm as if drawn by magnetic force. The old man's face was smug as he waggled the *Die Down* box.

"Predictable, as well as insolent," the wily Korean proclaimed with a superior smile.

"You don't want to see that," Remo cautioned quickly, grabbing at the box.

But Chiun held the video away from Remo. Curious eyes darted to the cover.

The rectangle of cardboard under a sheet of laminate was a shrunken version of the poster Remo had torn from the Bombshell store window. When Chiun read the title, his eyes grew wide with rage.

"What is this?" he demanded.

"I warned you," Remo replied. "Give it here." He made another fruitless grab at the box.

"How long have you known of this?" Chiun accused.

"I just found out tonight. It only came out this week."

Angry, Chiun flipped the plastic case around in his hand. Remo knew what he was looking for. He also knew that the Master of Sinanju wouldn't find it.

"Where is my name?" Chiun demanded hotly, glancing up at his pupil. His eyes were furious.

"I think that's it." Remo pointed at a name three lines up from the movie's director.

Chiun's eyes squeezed to walnut slits. "That is not my name," he said levelly. Every word dripped menace.

"It must be some kind of mistake," Remo offered with a shrug. "No one contacted you to make sure it was right?"

"Of course not," the old man spit viciously. "Do you think for one minute I would have allowed this—this *slur* to pass without my notice?" He brandished the video like a dagger beneath Remo's nose, so that his pupil could read the name on the box.

"'Mr. Chin,'" Remo read obediently.

Chiun clapped palms to ears. "Do not speak it aloud!" he shrieked.

"It sounds Chinese."

"A worse insult there has never been," Chiun lamented, hands still pressed to the sides of his head. The video box stuck out like an angry black dorsal fin. "Why did they not make me Thai, or the lowest of the low—French?"

"I think I've got an explanation," Remo said. "Did you tell them you were Master Chiun?"

The Korean's shoulders straightened. "It was a

term of respect. Something *you* would not understand."

"Oh, I understand," Remo nodded. "They thought *Master* was *Mister*."

"And this offense?" Chiun demanded, dropping his hands. His long, tapered index fingernail quivered as he indicated the name Chin.

"A simple typo," Remo suggested.

"Rest assured, simple type O will flood the streets of Hollywood when I lay hands on he who is responsible for this egregious insult," the Master of Sinanju warned.

"Before it gets that far, maybe we should check the movie itself."

"Why?" Chiun snapped. "What use is it to burrow inside a garbage heap?" He flung the box away in disgust.

"Because," Remo said reasonably, snatching up the video before it hit the floor, "it might not be wrong on the tape. I was going to check after you went to bed."

He popped open the box, removing the videotape. Chiun dogged him into the living room. Remo stopped in front of the VCR. After more than twenty years and a succession of replacements, he still wasn't sure how to use the device.

"You are saying that the mistake might only be on the case?" Chiun pressed from his elbow.

"I don't know," Remo said, frowning as he studied the VCR. ''Does that top-hat-looking symbol mean on?''

Clucking, Chiun tugged the cassette from Remo's hand. With a slap, he fed the tape into the VCR. Whirring, the machine loaded the tape and began to play automatically.

As it ran through the first of several commercials, Remo picked up the universal remote and switched on the big-screen TV. In the meantime, Chiun settled to a lotus position on the floor before the television.

''Can't we fast-forward this?'' Remo complained as the tape ran through an ad for the second *Die Down* film.

''Shh!''

Remo sank to the floor, as well, careful to stay out of hand or foot range. He braced his chin on one hand. In addition to commercials for the first three *Die Down* movies, there were ads for a soft drink, a candy bar, a minivan, two competing software companies and an upcoming animated feature from the Walt Disney company.

''I thought people rented movies to get *away* from ads,'' Remo griped as the commercials passed the twenty-minute mark.

''Leave the room if you cannot be quiet,'' Chiun ordered.

He had barely spoken before the movie finally started.

The opening credits were superimposed over a

scene depicting some sort of terrorist training camp. Apparently, it was supposed to be in Ireland if the pathetic accents the actors were attempting were any indication. To Remo, they all sounded like bad versions of the leprechaun from the Lucky Charms ads.

When the screen terrorists began to slaughter a group of drug-dealing Catholic church officials, Remo sat straighter. The scene appeared to be coming to an end, which meant the credits had to be almost over.

As a blood-smeared bishop carrying an Uzi he'd had hidden in his miter dropped in slow motion into an open grave, the thing they had both been waiting for finally appeared: "Story by Quintly Tortilli & Mr. Chin."

"Aiiee!"

The scream rose up from the wounded depths of Chiun's very soul. So quickly did the old man spring from the floor, not even Remo's highly trained eyes could follow. The Master of Sinanju materialized next to the VCR in an instant. He slammed his hand to the machine's face.

As Chiun ejected the tape, Remo jumped to his feet.

"Chiun, wait—!"

Too late.

The tape popped out into Chiun's bony hand. The other hand swung around, kimono sleeve billowing like an angry black cloud. When the hands met, the tape between them was pulverized to tiny black shards. Spools of black tape exploded out either side.

Chiun dusted the plastic fragments to the floor.

"Heads will roll!" he exploded.

Remo ignored the tirade. He knelt beside the smashed remains of the videotape.

"Dammit, Chiun, I rented that with *my* card," he complained. "Now I'm gonna have to pay for it."

"Oh, *someone* will pay," Chiun intoned seriously, his face a menacing mask. "But it will not be you."

With that, the old Korean spun on his heel and stormed from the room. When he slammed his bedroom door a moment later, the entire house shook with the vibrations. Remo felt the rattling dissipate beneath the soles of his loafers.

"At least for a change it's not me," he muttered.

Rising to his feet, he went off in search of a dustpan and brush.

The nine o'clock sun the next morning was shining warmly through the kitchen window the next morning and Remo was trying to decide what to make for breakfast when he noticed the broken telephone.

The phone sat on the counter. The plastic tab that plugged into the wall jack had been crushed. Only when he was looking at this phone did Remo notice that the one that ordinarily hung from the wall was missing entirely. A bare spot stared back at him from where it had been.

He found the phone stuffed in the trash.

Since the previous night's outburst, the Master of Sinanju had yet to emerge from his room. Remo went to the bottom of the stairs.

"Chiun! Did somebody call while I was in New York?"

"Go away!" Chiun's disembodied voice shouted back.

Remo didn't press the issue. Walking into the living room, he noted that a few black plastic videotape chips had been ground into the rug. He'd vacuum them up later. For now, he looked for the phone that was ordinarily on the lamp table.

He found it. Or what remained of it.

The phone was little more than a pile of stringy multicolored wires and broken tan plastic. Chiun had stuffed the remnants underneath a corner of the rug.

"Smith," Remo muttered with a certain nod.

He pushed the phone debris back under the carpet.

Leaving breakfast for later, he stepped outside into the morning sunlight. Enjoying the warming rays on his face, he walked down the street to a pay phone.

Humming, Remo stabbed the 1 button repeatedly. The familiar connections sounded in his ear as the call was routed to the Folcroft office of Harold Smith. The CURE director answered on the first ring.

"Hello?" Smith's tart voice asked sharply.

"Hiya, Smitty."

"Remo?" There was a cautious edge to his tone.

"Of course it's me," Remo said. "Hey, did you call me last night?"

Any relief the CURE director might have felt was overwhelmed by annoyance.

"Where the devil have you been?" Smith demanded.

The older man's aggravation was contagious.

"You're on the rag a little early this month, aren't you?" Remo asked.

"I tried calling a number of times," Smith insisted. Some of the tension drained from his voice. He seemed relieved to finally be talking to Remo. "There is something wrong with your phone line."

"Yeah," Remo dodged. "Gotta have Ma Bell look into that. What's up?"

"An unusual assignment that requires a certain level of both delicacy and discretion has presented itself," Smith said. "It involves the Sinanju amnesia technique. It would seem that a former United States President has regained knowledge of us."

Remo was instantly concerned. "Not Peanut Boy?" he asked.

The President to which he referred now worked on the Hovels for Humans program, building shanties and lean-tos for indigents. Remo had a sudden mental image of a crack-addicted, pregnant teen runaway roofer with a mouthful of nails accidentally dropping a hammer on the retired President's head.

"No," Smith replied, setting Remo's mind at ease. "His successor. The former chief executive was bucked by a horse and knocked unconscious. The accident triggered his memory."

Remo was stunned. "Smitty, he's got to be a million by now. What the hell's a guy his age doing on a horse?"

"It was supposed to be a photo opportunity," Smith answered thinly. "A foolish stunt, given his condition."

"You got that right," Remo agreed. A thought

occurred to him. "Plus, doesn't he have Alzheimer's? How do you even know he remembers?"

"He *called* me," Smith stressed. "It seems that our agency is not all that he remembers. If his conversation with me was not simply a moment of bizarre clarity, I assume that the symptoms he has displayed over the past few years have been a direct result of the Sinanju amnesia technique."

"Hmm," Remo mused. "I never heard of it affecting anyone like that. In fact, I don't know of anyone who it's ever come undone on before except Hardy Bricker. Remember that whole RX thing a few years back?"

"Of course," Smith said vaguely. "And perhaps you should discuss this with Chiun. *After* you have taken care of the President."

"Gotcha. He still in California?"

"Yes," Smith said. "I want you to visit him as soon as possible. There is no great urgency to the situation, but I do not feel comfortable having someone outside the loop with knowledge of our existence. Not even a former President."

"No sweat. We'll give him a double whammy."

"Er, Remo," Smith offered slowly, "perhaps you should handle this alone."

"Chiun's better at this than I am," Remo replied.

"But is he not the one who performed the procedure the first time?"

"Yeah," Remo replied. "But you can't say this

is his fault. By my tally, he's four and one with retired Presidents."

"I understand that," Smith agreed. "But news of the accident has leaked. The press has staked out the hospital. It will not be easy for you and Chiun to get in undetected. If I had been able to contact you last night—"

"But you didn't," Remo interrupted. "Guess you dropped the ball there." Before Smith could bring up the trouble he'd had calling, Remo asked, "What hospital is he in?"

Smith sighed. With practiced patience, he gave Remo not only the hospital's name, but the top-secret room number of the ex-President.

"Relax, Smitty. This'll all be a memory by tonight," Remo promised once the CURE director was through. "And don't worry. All follow-up visits are freebies."

Smiling, he hung up the phone. Hand still on the receiver, he turned toward his house.

"Now comes the tricky part," he muttered.

Leaving the pay phone, he headed back down the sidewalk toward Castle Sinanju and its stewing occupant.

The former President of the United States could not believe how much he had forgotten. Nor how much he now remembered. It was as if for the past six years he had been in a long, foggy twilight from which he was only now emerging.

The sunlight that shone through the tinted glass of his private hospital suite was brilliant. The blinds were partly angled to keep out prying eyes.

Touring the rooms in his blue pajamas, hands stuffed in the pockets of his terry-cloth robe, the President paused at a bedroom window. He used his fingers to crack two blind slats.

Reporters were on the street eight stories below. Camped out like vultures. Most had accepted the assignment gleefully, thinking they were on a death watch. It wasn't surprising. The press had never had a kind word to say about him.

"You fellas are in for the shock of your life," the ex-President whispered in the soft, playful tone that was at one time familiar to all Americans.

He checked the digital clock on his nightstand for what seemed like the millionth time.

It was 6:00 a.m., Pacific Standard Time. He had called Smith late the previous evening.

He wasn't concerned that Smith's men wouldn't show up. Smith had always been reliable. The lemony voiced man had gotten America out of more than a few scrapes during the former President's tenure in office.

Once Smith's people got here and worked their magic, the ex-President could get on with what remained of his life. He would lose his memory of CURE, but that was as it should be. It wasn't right for more than four people to know of the agency at one time: Smith, his two special people and the current U.S. President. That had always been the way with CURE. Four was enough. More than that would risk exposure.

He tried to think of how many ex-Presidents were still alive.

One had died a few years back, he thought. If memory served, there were four remaining, including himself. If those men who were retired hadn't been given amnesia, that would make eight men total to know of CURE. Far too many. Smith was right to make departing Presidents forget.

The President released the blinds. He wandered back across the room, taking a seat at the foot of his bed.

It was difficult to reconcile some bits of memory. His mind had struggled to record some things over the past few years, but it seemed as if they hadn't been properly filed. Everything before the onset of his brain disease was crystal clear, however.

Smith told him on the phone the previous evening that both of his operatives were still with the agency. Things were still fuzzy last night, so soon after the accident. But the more he thought of it, the more he knew that wasn't right.

The young one was dead. That's what Smith had told him years ago, during the waning days of his presidency. Not only that, but the old one had supposedly quit CURE over a contractual clause.

For some reason, Smith had lied to him. It didn't trouble the former President in the least. If there was one thing he remembered about the taciturn Smith, it was that he was a good man. The kind America used to turn out like good, solid reliable cars or black-and-white two-reelers where the black hat always lost and the white hat always, *always* won. The former President trusted that the director of CURE had a reason for keeping him in the dark back then. Just as he trusted that Smith would send his men as promised to right their mistake.

As he sat patiently, hands upon his knees, the door to his bedroom opened. A doctor in a white coat and green surgical scrubs entered. The blue stitching on his coat identified him as Dr. Kahler.

For an instant, the former President saw the familiar black suit of one of his Secret Service guards standing stoically in the hallway.

The doctor frowned as the door swung shut.

"You should be in bed, Mr. President," he said seriously.

"Do you have any idea how much sleep I've gotten the past six years?" the President asked with a wry smile. "That sandman fella and I are on a first-name basis."

The doctor's expression remained somber. "Be that as it may, you're going to have to lie down while I examine you. Please."

Dr. Kahler tried to ease the former President onto his back. Although he was much older than the doctor, the President didn't budge.

"I know you're just trying to do your job, and that's fine," the ex-President said, his voice firm. "But I've been examined all night long. If you want to poke and prod me again, you're going to do it while I'm sitting up."

The doctor pursed his lips. "Yes, sir."

When he tried to unbutton the blouse of the President's pajamas, strong hands pushed him away. Mouth twisted in mild displeasure, the President opened his own shirt.

Dr. Kahler saw at once that his famous patient was in amazingly good shape for a man his age. Some old, faint scarring around the chest from an assassination attempt nearly two decades before. A stethoscope showed that lungs and heart were fine. His pulse rate would have put to shame a man a quarter of his age.

"How's the head this morning?" the doctor asked as the President buttoned his pajamas once more.

"On straight," the former President replied.

"Headache?"

"A little. It hurts behind my eyes."

Dr. Kahler nodded. "We were worried about a concussion, but everything looks okay today. X rays don't show any fluid build-up like the last time you fell off your horse."

"I was *bucked*," the President insisted. "And if it was a concussion, why didn't you folks keep me awake? Isn't that what you're supposed to do?"

The doctor hesitated. "Actually, we kind of thought under the circumstances...ah..." His voice trailed off.

"My daughter, right?" the President said, eyes level.

The physician shifted uncomfortably. He cleared his throat. "She thought it would be best."

"To let me just drift off." The President shook his head. "She was always so worried about everyone else's shadow, she never really tried to cast one of her own." He exhaled loudly. It was a sigh of regret. "What about my wife?" he asked, looking up suddenly.

"According to the news, she's on her way back from Washington," Dr. Kahler said.

At the mention of his former residence, a wistful smile drew up the deep crags of the old man's face.

"The shining city on a hill," he uttered softly.

The doctor's brow furrowed at the words. The

man on the bed obviously hadn't been to Washington in quite a while.

The ex-chief executive's tan, wrinkled face had taken on a contented expression as he stared into space.

This wasn't right, Dr. Kahler thought. Everyone knew that the former President was suffering from Alzheimer's. He had a degenerative brain disorder that was incurable. There was no way the man should ever have been this lucid for this long so far into his bout with the disease.

But he seemed fine. He recognized faces of family members when shown pictures of them. The same for people from his days as governor of California and as President. Even though he'd only awakened a few hours ago, he already knew many of the doctors and nurses on staff at Weizmann-Teacher's Hospital by name.

Never in his thirty years as a physician had Dr. Kahler heard of an instance where a blow to the head restored memory in an individual with Alzheimer's. Even if one threw all logic out the window and accepted the premise that the former President's fall had somehow miraculously healed him, it still should only have arrested the progress of the disease, locked it in at its current level. Not only had that not happened, but somehow the irreversible process had been rolled back. It was impossible. Yet…

In his head, Dr. Kahler was already sketching the rough outline of the paper he would publish on this remarkable case when he heard the first sounds of commotion beyond the closed hospital-room door.

There were muffled shouts, followed by something that sounded like firecrackers going off.

"What's that din?" the doctor asked, taking a step toward the door.

Behind him, the President stood slowly, a worried look on his deeply furrowed face. "It doesn't sound good," he answered. The noises were familiar. He remembered similar sounds from a March day years ago.

"Well, this *is* a hospital," Dr. Kahler said, marching briskly to the door.

The President lunged. He tried to grab him. Tried to *stop* him. But Dr. Kahler was too far away. The physician flung open the door and marched into the hallway.

As the President held his breath, there came another pop. This one much louder than the rest.

The doctor stumbled back into the room a moment later, a thin line of blood dribbling from a spot dead center in his pale forehead. Black powder burns surrounded the bullet hole.

Sightless eyes turning to the horrified former President, the doctor dropped to his knees. He flopped forward, a look of dull incomprehension on his face.

The President was already moving, propelled by shock. He raced past the body and over to the door.

A closet was beside him as he pressed his back against the wall.

Shouts issued from the hall.

The Secret Service men who'd been guarding the door were dead. Otherwise, they would have swarmed into the room to protect him. His detachment was small. Only a few men. Not like the old days. Not enough against an all-out assault.

Footsteps coming closer. Pounding up the hall.

Holding his breath, the President fumbled behind him, curling one hand around the cold steel handle of the closet's door. The instant he did so, a face poked into the room. Furtive eyes darted over to the bed. A paisley bandanna covered both mouth and nose.

The intruder was armed.

Automatic rifle balanced before him, he took a cautious step into the room, not seeing the former President plastered against the wall to his right.

A sudden creak.

Eyes turned away from the unmade bed, opening in shock at the sight of the ex-chief executive.

Something else cut into view. Fast. *Hard.*

The closet door slammed full force into the intruder's face. Forehead cracked and bleeding, the man fell backward into the hallway. His gun dropped, useless, to his chest. The President jumped forward and grabbed the man by the ankles, struggling to drag him back into the room. If he could just get his gun…

Other shouts. Running footsteps. A shadow falling over him. Crouching, the President froze. He glanced up.

Two terrorists towered above him. Like the first, bandannas obscured their features. Still more intruders ran up the hallway, jumping over the bodies of his Secret Service detachment.

"We got him, man!" a nearby voice exulted beneath a flowery bandanna. Sweat had broken out across the visible portion of his face. His pupils were pinpricks.

Still squatting, the President reached a rapid decision. If he was going to die then, dammit, he'd die like a man.

He lunged for the nearest man.

In his younger days, he'd been strong and spry. But he was old now. Slow. *Too* slow.

In a panic, the gunman sidestepped the old man's awkward attack, stumbling hard against the door frame. As he dropped back, another intruder jumped forward, swinging the butt of his rifle down against the side of the President's head.

The old man saw a brilliant explosion of light...followed by a shroud of pure enveloping darkness.

The fog was thick and impenetrable. The President's last thought before he toppled onto the cold hallway floor was of his wife. He hoped she could forgive their daughter. The final light of reality flickered and was gone.

THE OLD MAN at their feet was a lifeless mannequin.

The masked men swarmed around the weather-beaten body.

"You *hit* him!" one accused.

"Is he dead?" another asked.

"Get the tranq," commanded a third.

A syringe was brought forward. The needle was jabbed into the ex-President's arm.

"Should we get his clothes?" the man who had administered the injection asked, his bandanna sopped with sweat. He tossed away the syringe.

"Yes! But hurry!"

As one man dashed into the room, the others grabbed the former President under the armpits. He was deadweight. Grunting, they began to drag the old man rapidly down the hall past the bloodied bodies of the Secret Service agents.

"He's gonna be in for one hell of a surprise when he wakes up," one of them enthused, the outline of his mouth quivering wetly beneath his multicolored bandanna.

"*If* he wakes up," cautioned another. "We were just supposed to use the tranquilizers on him."

The man who had bashed the elderly ex-President in the head shrugged. "It's a *kind* of tranquilizer," he snarled. "Besides, *he* doesn't deserve any better."

They dumped the ex-President into a laundry cart near a nurses' station. Behind the desk, two RNs were sprawled on the floor, glassy eyes staring blindly at fluorescent lights. Crimson stains seeped from their bellies onto crisp white uniforms.

Two men helped up the groggy terrorist the President had coldcocked. Running now, the group wheeled the cart away from the desk and onto a rear service elevator.

A moment later, the silver doors slid across the bloody scene of carnage with barely a whisper.

Chiun didn't kill anyone on the long cross-country plane trip from Boston to Los Angeles. Remo considered this not only a blessing, but a surprise.

At first, Remo was worried that the Master of Sinanju wouldn't even want to accompany him to California. The old Korean's troubles with Hollywood were far too fresh. But Chiun had agreed readily.

The flight had been surprisingly peaceful. On their way through the crowded LAX terminal, there were no sudden and mysterious bloody noses or severed ears on anyone they passed. In fact, as they headed off in search of a cab, Chiun even managed a sympathetic smile for a harried young woman hauling two crying children.

His teacher's uncharacteristically placid behavior made Remo intensely uneasy.

Chiun was building to something. The Master of Sinanju was planning to use his time on the West Coast to wreak some sort of terrible vengeance against those who he thought had perpetrated injustices against him. But to Remo's knowledge, there wasn't anybody left for the old Korean to kill.

"Quintly Tortilli is dead, Little Father," Remo reminded Chiun in the cab on the way from LAX to the hospital.

"And rightly so," Chiun replied calmly. "He was a foul-mouthed liar who endangered Emperor Smith's charge, the corpulent marionette. However, that is all water under the bridge."

"We're not stopping by Taurus," Remo warned.

"That studio no longer exists," Chiun answered.

"Neither do Bindle and Marmelstein," Remo suggested, naming the studio chiefs who had betrayed Chiun during the making of his film.

"This is true," Chiun mused. He tipped his head to one side, considering. "Perhaps I will visit their graves to pay my respects."

"You're not going to dig them up and try to kill them again, are you?" Remo asked worriedly.

Chiun raised a thin eyebrow.

"Now, Remo, you are being silly."

"Can you blame me?" Remo asked. "Last night, you were ready to tear all of Hollywood a new A-hole. Now you're acting sweeter than a Prozac pixie stick. It's scary as all hell."

"Meet the new me," Chiun announced airily, waving a long-nailed hand. "I am like a duck."

"Short and greasy?"

Chiun frowned at his pupil. "Everything runs off my back," he explained.

"Yeah?" Remo said doubtfully. "We'll see."

When they arrived at Weizmann-Teacher's Hospital, they found a gaggle of reporters standing in an unhappy knot in front of the main parking area. Dozens of news vans emblazoned with station call letters blocked the ambulance entrance. Satellite dishes from the network and local news vehicles pointed skyward.

Cables snaked from trucks to videocameras and lights.

Hoping to avoid the newspeople, Remo instructed the cabdriver to drop them off down the street. As the taxi drove away, he and Chiun walked up the sidewalk to the hospital.

Only a few reporters stood before cameras to offer taped digests for hourly news updates. The rest lounged around the area, bored expressions on their plastic-surgery-tightened and makeup enhanced faces.

There were several card games in progress.

Smith had been worried that Chiun might call attention to them, but Remo saw as they approached that only a few faces looked in their direction. These quickly turned away in disinterest. A kimono in L.A. just wasn't news.

As Remo and Chiun slipped behind one cameraman, a female reporter was summing up her taped spot.

"Few have shown up here outside the hospital to wait out the end of the former President. No doubt, most have realized the damage his monster deficits and hate mongering caused this nation. The most evil man in American history, or just a misguided old fool? You be the judge. Konchacata Badadada reporting."

She waited a few seconds before dropping her microphone. The woman seemed very pleased with her unbiased work.

As the reporter handed off her microphone to an intern, Remo tapped her cameraman on the shoulder. "Did she just say they're waiting for him to die?" he asked.

"That's what we've been hearing," the cameraman said.

Remo frowned, assuming he'd just wasted his time coming all the way to California to give selective amnesia to someone who was already knocking on death's door.

"Who's saying it," he asked, "the hospital?"

The cameraman shook his head. "Him," he replied, pointing to a spot closer to the main hospital doors.

The Big Three networks had bullied their way to the front of the line as soon as they'd arrived on the scene, staking out the prime reporting real estate. Remo saw a giant *A* peeking out from one of the parked network vans. The other two letters were obscured by a bizarre-looking man in a dark blue suit and fire-engine-red tie.

He looked half vulture, half Vulcan and all Satan. Demonic eyebrows—painted black—rose at crooked angles above eyes that were twin lasers of focused malice. The mouth was twisted back in a constipated rictus. Worst of all was the hair. The man wore a ghastly jet-black toupee that was so flat it looked as if it had been run through a clothes wringer and secured in place with shellac.

Remo recognized the hairpiece even before he saw the man. Stan Ronaldman. Longtime political reporter for one of the big networks.

While the ex-President inside the hospital was in office, Ronaldman had been the White House correspondent. The reporter had a hatred for the President that was so obvious and so visceral it was almost as if he blamed the chief executive for the genes that had cursed him with his own hairless pate. His infamous bile was on full display as Remo and Chiun approached.

"Isn't he confirmed dead yet?" Ronaldman was complaining to a harried producer.

"There's still a news blackout," the woman replied. "I think something might have happened."

Ronaldman clapped his hands together ecstatically. Dull eyes bugged out over a corpselike smile.

"*Dead.* That's the *only* explanation," he enthused.

"I'm not sure, Stan," the producer warned. The woman was listening to something on a headset that ran into the open back of the news van. "There's lots of weird radio stuff going back and forth. All kinds of yelling and code words that aren't in any of our source books. I think all those cars that showed up early this morning were Feds or something."

"More government waste," Ronaldman complained, shaking his toupeed head. "*He* specialized in that." His happiness at the thought of the former President's death shifted to anger, a change in expression so subtle it was barely discernible. "So I suppose now we'll have a big state funeral at taxpayer expense. Why don't we just throw him in a landfill somewhere and spend all that wasted funeral and B-1 bomber money where the people want it? On follicle-stimulation research and sheep-ranch subsidies."

"What's national defense or honoring a beloved political icon when you could be getting mohair aid from Washington?"

"Exactly," Ronaldman enthused. His tight smile returned as he sought out the source of the voice behind him.

The reporter was surprised at the very odd couple he found. One was an Asian who was as old as the hills around Ronaldman's own Arizona sheep ranch. The other was a thin Caucasian in a white T-shirt and black Chinos.

"Is the President okay?" Remo asked, noting the many news vans.

"*Ex*-President," Ronaldman stressed. "And he's dead. Dead as a five-hundred-dollar Pentagon toilet seat."

"*Possibly,*" his producer cautioned from her post

on the van floor. The woman turned away, grateful to have Ronaldman distracted, even if only for a moment.

"Don't listen to Madame de Gloom over there," Ronaldman insisted. "*I* say he's dead, and I should know. After all, I have been interviewed extensively on the subject by my colleagues in the press."

"Interviewed?" Remo asked. "Aren't you supposed to be reporting on this thing?"

"I have a history with the late former President," Ronaldman replied. "People are interested in what I have to say."

The reporter glanced momentarily at Chiun.

The Master of Sinanju had sidled up to Ronaldman. Hands behind his back, he was standing on tiptoes, the better to see the glistening black wig plastered to the man's skull. He dropped quickly to the soles of his sandals when Ronaldman looked his way. Chiun whistled casually.

"Forget about the fact that it's supposed to be your job to report, not offer commentary," Remo said, tearing his own eyes from Chiun. "What was the last *official* word from the hospital on his condition?"

"Of course I don't trust them to give the *real* story," Ronaldman sniffed. "But they claim he only bumped his head. There were early reports that his brain condition had somehow been miraculously healed, but I don't buy it. Propaganda. Plain and simple. Everyone inside the Beltway knows he had

Alzheimer's when he was in the White House. If they *don't* know, *I* tell them."

As the reporter was speaking, Chiun surreptitiously signaled Remo. Pointing at Ronaldman's toupee, he covered his mouth with one hand, stifling a silent laugh.

"Knock it off, Chiun," Remo groused.

Sensing movement, Ronaldman twisted sharply to Chiun. He found the Master of Sinanju standing placidly, hands clasped behind his back. Face growing even more suspicious, the reporter turned back to Remo.

"So, as far as you know, he's fine," Remo pressed.

"He's *dead,*" Ronaldman insisted. "About a hundred of those government cars showed up here around seven this morning. They're part of his funeral procession."

"Government cars?" Remo asked. "Are you sure?"

"I've been in Washington long enough to know what G-men drive," Ronaldman replied aridly. Satanic eyebrows rising in disdain, he turned from his insulting visitor.

Remo frowned at that information. Would so many government vehicles show up in the wake of a simple accident for a man who hadn't been President for more than a decade? Only if he had something important to tell them.

Remo's worried thoughts were of CURE as he

turned to Chiun. "Let's go, Little Father," he said tightly.

Walking briskly, Remo and the Master of Sinanju headed for the hospital doors. They had gone only a few paces when Remo noticed something in Chiun's hands.

It was flat, black and shiny. And hairy.

"What are you doing with *that?*" Remo demanded. He nodded to Stan Ronaldman's wig, which dangled like a harpooned rat from one of the Master of Sinanju's long fingernails.

"He annoyed me," Chiun replied flatly.

"Dammit, Chiun, he annoys *everybody.*"

Remo shot a look back to the news van.

Ronaldman was as bald as a plucked chicken. He fussed around the open door of the van, pale head slathered in dry glue, oblivious to what had transpired. The reporter had yet to notice the draft on his scalp.

A crowd of smiling gawkers was beginning to form.

"Is this some kind of latent hostility from this whole *Die Down* fiasco?" Remo whispered harshly.

"Latent?" Chiun asked blandly. "Forgive me, Remo. I thought I was being obvious."

"Har-de-har-har," Remo said, voice hushed. "Now get rid of that thing before we have to spray you for chiggers."

"It *does* look diseased," Chiun said, examining his prize. "Very well. But I do not want to hear a complaint when you get nothing on your next birthday."

With a snap of his wrist, he launched the toupee back in the direction from whence they'd come. The hairpiece soared like a flung Frisbee. It ate up the distance in an instant. With a thick splat, it attached itself like a remora over the *C* in the network logo on the side of the news van.

When Ronaldman turned toward the odd sound, he saw what looked like a giant, flattened tarantula glued to the truck's side. Only after he saw his own reflection in the glistening black surface of the nylon hair did he realize what it was. His eyes grew as wide as fried eggs.

"Aaaaaaaaaahhhhhh!" the reporter screamed.

Desperate, he flung one hand, his arm, his necktie, *anything* he could up over his head, even as he unstuck the wig from the side of the truck. Wilted toupee in hand, he dove inside the van amid a chorus of laughter from the gathered media.

Remo turned from the rocking van, his eyes flat.

"This an example of the *new* you?" he asked dryly.

"Do not worry, Remo," Chiun assured him. "Deep down, I am still the same person I always was."

Spinning on his heel, the old man marched toward the main entrance.

"That's what worries me," Remo muttered.

He trailed the Master of Sinanju through the throng of press to the hospital.

According to Smith, the former President was in a private east-wing suite on the eighth floor. Remo intended to ride the elevator up to eight, but the car had other plans. It stopped on the sixth floor. The doors slid open on the solemn face of a muscular Secret Service agent. A thin white cord ran from jacket to ear.

"I'm sorry, but you can't go any higher," the agent insisted.

"Sure, I can," Remo said.

He pressed the button for the eighth floor, and the doors began to slide shut. The Secret Service agent pushed them back open.

"The eighth floor has been evacuated."

"But Aunt Iggy's expecting us," Remo informed him.

"There's been an emergency," the agent explained. "A gas leak."

"Sounds like Aunt Iggy." Remo nodded to Chiun.

"Stop being stupid," Chiun said. He jabbed a nail

into the eighth-floor button. The doors slid silently shut...and promptly opened once more.

"The elevators will not function above this level," the agent informed them. "Because of the gas leak, floors seven through ten have been completely evacuated. If you're looking for a patient, I'd advise you to try the main desk."

Remo shook his head. "Nothing's ever easy," he mumbled. "And next time, I'd suggest the brain trust at Treasury come up with a better cover story. If the Secret Service is worried about gas leaks, you could've stayed in Washington. After his regular six Big Mac breakfast, the guy in the White House has it coming out both ends."

At Remo's mention of the Secret Service, the agent was instantly alert. A hand darted beneath his jacket.

Before the man even touched the butt of his automatic, Remo's own hand flew forward. He pinched a spot at the agent's elbow, locking the man's arm in place.

Desperate, the Secret Service man clamped on the wrist microphone in his other hand. It wasn't there.

Trailing wires, the unit had been plucked from his belt. The earpiece came loose with a loud pop. When the agent glanced up, Chiun was examining the radiomicrophone.

"Are you able to hear *The Jack Benny Program* on this device?" he asked.

"You men are in deep trouble," the Secret Service agent threatened in reply. He yanked at his frozen arm. It wouldn't budge.

"No, Little Father," Remo supplied.

"A shame," Chiun said, shaking his head. "I used to listen to his program many years ago in Sinanju. He was quite amusing. Although Rochester was the true star."

With a blur of tapered fingers, he smashed the entire radio transceiver to shards.

"There's no way out," the agent warned. "Give it up."

"In a sec," Remo promised. "Questions first."

As the Secret Service agent complained, Remo used his elbow grip to bounce the man into a nearby room. Two vacant beds with crisp white sheets were pushed against the wall.

"Okay, what's the deal?" he demanded after the Master of Sinanju closed the door behind them. "The guy bumped his head. I'm assuming you aren't all here to deliver aspirin."

The agent refused to reply. Screwing his mouth tightly shut, he leveled his eyes on the closed door.

Remo pinched the agent's elbow.

Bolts of white-hot fiery acid burst from the joint, exploding out into his extremities. He gasped in pain.

"The old President was kidnapped," the man blurted.

Remo's stomach tightened. "Kidnapped? When?"

"Hours ago. Early morning." The agent's eyes were watering.

Remo glanced at the Master of Sinanju. "Looks like this is bigger than we thought," he said grimly.

"Why is that?" Chiun sniffed. "If one of your rulers is missing, vote yourselves another. Every time I turn around, you people are anointing a new one. What this nation needs is the stability only a lifelong despot can bring."

Remo wished he could share the old Korean's cavalier attitude. He turned his attention back to the Secret Service man. "Any leads?" he pressed, squeezing tighter.

"None that I'd be privy to." The agent winced. "The President's detail was shot. Lot of other people, too. Doctors, nurses. No witnesses. They got away scot free."

Remo's brow was dark. "What about all those ditzes out front with cameras?"

"Kidnappers used a back exit. No press there."

"Security cameras?"

"I don't *know*." The agent was pleading by now.

He had given up everything he knew. Wordlessly, Remo tapped a single finger dead center in the man's forehead. The Secret Service agent stiffened as if in shock, then the air slipped from him and he slumped forward. Remo dumped the unconscious agent onto one of the empty beds.

"So much for the simple assignment," he groused as he flung a blanket over the man.

"Do not complain to me," the Master of Sinanju warned, folding his arms. "You were never called Chinese in a major film franchise. Everything else pales in comparison."

"I thought we weren't talking about that," Remo said, only half listening. He was trying to think what their next move should be. "And this is much worse. Smith said the old President remembered all about us."

"Good," Chiun retorted with a satisfied nod. "Let the aged one sing our praises from the rooftops of the nation he once led. Maybe I will finally get some proper recognition."

"Smitty'd love that," Remo grumbled. "Speaking of which, I'd better call him. He's gonna want to know about this if he hasn't already heard."

Cruel face etched in lines of deep concern, Remo reached for the room phone.

HAROLD SMITH HAD LEARNED of the former President's kidnapping an hour earlier. Although the news had not yet filtered out to the mainstream press, it was spreading like wildfire through official government channels. It was only a matter of time before the public learned of the abduction.

A blue bottle of antacid sat on Smith's desktop. He had opened the bottle three times in the past sixty minutes. Given the nature of the crisis, there was no sense putting it away.

Each new report Smith read added to the growing

tidal wave of nausea welling up within him. Someone possessed with knowledge of CURE was in the hands of an unknown force.

The kidnappers were vicious and ruthless. They had killed more than twenty people in their murderous route from the hospital subbasement parking area to the ex-President's eighth-floor room.

Their identity was still a mystery.

Smith's mind reeled as he considered the possible suspects. As a result of this President's very public convictions, the list of potential enemies was vast.

The massive mainframes hidden behind a secret wall in the sanitarium's basement had been working overtime since the start of the crisis. Dubbed the Folcroft Four by Smith in a rare display of creativity, the computers had compiled a detailed list of the most likely suspects.

Smith had always found organization to be the key to every successful operation. To this end, he had initiated a program that divided the huge list into two separate sections: homegrown threats and those from abroad.

It was a coin toss to decide which category of potential culprits he should begin sifting through first. In the end, Smith decided to go with those at home, for the simple fact that the former President was kidnapped while on American soil. He would expand the search as circumstances dictated.

Alone in his drab office, Smith lowered his hands to the special capacitor keyboard buried beneath the lip of his gleaming black desk. Casting a final, longing glance at his antacid bottle, he began to sift through page after electronic page of likely suspects. He had barely gone over a dozen names when the familiar jangle of the blue contact phone cut through the tomblike silence of his office.

Behind his desk, Smith froze.

The ex-President had called on that very phone the night before. It was possible that this was him once more. This time in the hands of an unknown enemy.

Realizing that the ringing phone might be sounding the death knell of both himself and the organization he led, Harold W. Smith wrapped an arthritic hand around the receiver. With great deliberateness, he answered it. Blood pounded in his ear.

"Yes," he said, his voice totally devoid of any inflection.

"The President's been kidnapped."

At the sound of Remo's voice, Smith released a mouthful of bile-scented air. He hadn't even realized he had been holding his breath.

"I have heard," Smith said. He spoke in precise, measured tones. "You and your associate should return to home base at once."

Remo sounded puzzled. "My associate? You mean Chiun?"

"Please, no names!" Smith insisted sharply.

"Cheez, what's wrong with you, Smitty? Somebody spike your Maalox?"

The CURE director's heart did a somersault at the mention of his own name. "I am sorry, sir, you have the wrong number," Smith spluttered, lamely covering. Fumbling, he quickly hung up the phone.

It rang within three seconds.

Smith did his best to ignore it.

Remo obviously didn't appreciate the gravity of this situation. If the former President had given away even a small bit of information to his captors—Folcroft, Sinanju, Smith—the organization could already be compromised. Right now, maintaining simple security protocols was more important than ever.

As the phone continued to squawk unanswered at his elbow, Smith attempted to concentrate on his work. Remo's persistence was greater than he'd expected. After a full five minutes of solid ringing, the blue phone finally fell silent. Smith breathed a sigh of quiet relief.

Head swimming with concerns, he threw himself back into his work. Smith had only time to scan a dozen or so names of potential kidnappers when there came a timid knock at his closed office door.

He lifted his hands from the keyboard. The amber keys faded to black. The special computer monitor beneath the surface of the desk was angled so that only the person seated behind it could see it. Confident that everything was in order, he lifted his head to the door.

"Come in."

Eileen Mikulka, Smith's secretary for the past twenty years, sheepishly rapped a single knuckle against the heavy door even as she pushed it open.

"I'm so sorry, Dr. Smith," the matronly woman apologized. "I *know* how you hate to be disturbed while you're working."

"What is it?" Smith asked, hurrying her along.

Her lopsided smile was uncertain.

"Your friend Mr. Remo is on the phone," she explained. "He says that the fate of the nation is in your hands." She gave a little apologetic shrug.

By colossal effort, Smith fought down any hint of a reaction. "Put him through," he said levelly.

Nodding, Mrs. Mikulka backed from the room.

When the primary Folcroft line sounded, Smith depressed the blinking light and picked up the phone. "Use the other line," he ordered. He promptly hung up the phone.

This time when the blue contact phone rang, Smith answered it.

"You are behaving recklessly," the CURE director accused.

"Relax," Remo replied. "Your secretary's clueless. And *you're* acting paranoid."

Smith leaned an elbow against his onyx desk, cradling his patrician nose between thumb and forefinger. His rimless glasses bit into the bridge. "If we *must* have this conversation, we will make it brief," he said wearily.

"Fine with me. Why do you want me and—"

Remo caught himself "—my *associate* to come back there?"

"It would be best during the current situation."

"Don't you want us to try to find you-know-who?"

"Possibly," Smith suggested. "Eventually. But as I understand it, there are no leads at present. It would be unwise for you to stay in the vicinity, given the knowledge that he has recently displayed."

"You think he might finger me to someone?"

"It is a possibility."

"No biggie," Remo said. "We can take care of anyone who comes our way."

"We do not know that," Smith replied. "This is a deadly serious situation, and we are dealing with a faceless enemy."

"You really think this is that big a deal?" Remo asked. "Aren't there about twenty ex-Presidents kicking around right now? Who's going to miss one?"

"This conversation is getting too specific," Smith cautioned. "Any more so and I will terminate it."

"Okay, okay," Remo relented. "Here's what I'll agree to. The two of us will do a little snooping on this end. If we come up empty, we'll hightail it back home."

"That is not wise," Smith stressed. He was thinking of all the FBI and Secret Service people already on the scene—not to mention the local police and national press who would swarm into the Los Angeles area once the story broke.

"Call me unwise," Remo said. "'Cause that's what we're doing. Toodles."

As the dial tone hummed in his ear, Smith released the grip on his nose. Adjusting his glasses, he slowly hung up the blue phone. If neither he nor Remo was successful in their respective efforts, it might be the last time he used the special contact phone.

His head had begun to throb.

Smith took two baby aspirins from a childproof bottle stored in his left hand drawer. He washed them down with a healthy swig of antacid.

Forcing the grimmest of scenarios from his orderly mind, Harold Smith focused his attention back on his computer. With a steely resolve, he threw himself into his work.

The *Radiant Grappler II* was a fishing boat that had never fished. Designed and constructed by a French shipbuilding company, the high-tech vessel was promoted as the inevitable future of all commercial firms that plumbed the depths of the sea for their fortune. The ship was truly one of a kind. Unknown to its builders, it would remain such.

Although it had planned to reap great rewards on its new boat, the company that built it hadn't counted on the ensuing protests. On the day it was unveiled, a collection of environmental groups held a rally at the shipyard gates, denouncing the vessel, as well as the wholesale destruction of ocean life it represented.

They were torpedoed before they even set sail.

As a result of waging its losing battle with the rabid environmental groups in the French press, the shipbuilding company found itself without a single buyer. It was a marketing disaster. Already millions of francs in debt, the company was forced to come to a final, reluctant decision. It declared bankruptcy.

When the company's assets were sold off at auction, first in line with a bloated checkbook were agents for Earthpeace, the primary environmental group responsible for putting the company out of business.

The *Radiant Grappler II* was snatched up as the Earthpeace flagship, a replacement for another, ill-fated ship of the same name.

The *Grappler* was both functional and ceremonial. The activists could sail to environmental crisis points and—thanks to the way in which they'd acquired the vessel—gloat along the way.

The ship was large and menacing. At just under 450 feet long, it weighed nearly twenty thousand tons. Its hundred-thousand-horsepower engine propelled it through ocean waves at speeds in excess of sixty knots. It didn't so much break through the swells as crush them beneath its merciless hull. It was an awesome, frightening spectacle to behold.

Anyone viewing the *Grappler* now, however, would see an entirely different, much more helpless image.

At the moment, the ship's mighty engines idled softly. The ship was stationary between the Miraflores Locks on the Pacific side of the Panama Canal.

The locks outside the ship had already been sealed. Once the *Grappler* was in place, water was allowed to flood into the artificially created basin. With a steady movement that was so gradual it was nearly imperceptible, the ship rose slowly above the level of the ocean it had just left.

Inside the rusty hold of the huge vessel, two Earthpeace activists listened to the creak of metal as the ship began to reach equilibrium with the water level of Miraflores Lake.

"Yo, Jerry, dude. You know how long this'll take?" the first asked.

His torn jeans and flannel shirt looked as if he'd mugged them off a scarecrow. Although his button-down Madison Avenue, Rotary Club-loving parents had named him Ralph, he liked to be called Bright Sunshiny Ralph.

"This part, or the whole trip?" Jerry asked absently.

Like his companion, Jerry Glover was dressed in rags that seemed held together by grime and stink. Unlike Ralph, Jerry was preoccupied. Bent at the waist, he was peering through the iron bars of a zoo transport cage.

The vast hold around them was otherwise bare. Rats scurried and squeaked in distant shadows.

"Through the canal," Sunshiny Ralph said.

"Seven hours," Jerry replied.

Sunshiny didn't seem thrilled at the prospect of being stuck in the canal so long. Standing beside Jerry, he wrapped weak arms around his own chest, hugging himself the same way women used to during the Summer of Love. It had been a long time since a female had touched him that way. Such caresses had stopped around the same time his hairline and belly began their middle-age race in opposite directions.

"I feel I'm, like, *trapped,* man," he complained.

"Yeah, but how does *he* feel?" Jerry grinned, nodding to the cage.

Sunshiny glanced through the barred door.

In the shadows at the rear of the sturdy box, a familiar figure slept. The infamous face was visible in silhouette. Straw hung from steel-gray hair.

When he looked at Jerry, Sunshiny's face was filled with contempt. "He don't feel nuthin'. What's wrong with you?"

He seemed disgusted at Jerry for ascribing human emotions to their prisoner.

"*I* know that," Jerry said, backpedaling rapidly. "But if he *could* feel? Dude, *imagine* how he'd feel."

Sunshiny wouldn't hear it. "You're anthraxpromotizing," he insisted.

"Huh?"

"You know. It's when you give animals, like, human characteristics."

Jerry took a horrified step back. "I'd *never* do that!" he exclaimed. "Why would I want animals to behave like *humans?* Humans make, like, H-bombs and nuclear war and stuff. If we could only learn from animals, Earth would be, like, a real cool place to live. And pot'd be legal."

Sunshiny wasn't listening to Jerry's passionate defense. He was looking back inside the cage.

"He looks even more evil in person," Sunshiny Ralph commented softly.

"You hit him awful hard," Jerry said. "Are you sure he's even still alive?"

Another glare at the sleeping form of the former President of the United States. They couldn't tell if he was breathing.

"Maybe we should poke him with a stick," Sunshiny suggested.

Jerry shook his head. "Sticks ain't allowed, remember? Gotta protect old-growth timber and the rain forest."

"Oh, yeah. How 'bout a pipe?"

"Hash pipe or pipe pipe?"

"Pipe pipe," Sunshiny said.

"That'd be okay. You got one?"

There ensued a fruitless search through their ragged clothing, during which the only sounds were of the creaking boat and the swelling water outside the hull of the *Grappler*. They turned up three hash pipes and zero pipe pipes.

It was finally decided that Jerry would watch the maybe-dead prisoner while Sunshiny went off in search of a good, solid poking pipe.

Sunshiny Ralph scaled the ladder at the side of the hold up to the cabin level. He had just struck off down the narrow corridor where he and the rest of the *Radiant Grappler II* crew bunked when he bumped into a man in a dark blue double-breasted suit walking in the opposite direction.

On the man's left lapel was a familiar pin: a single dove wrapped its wings around a lone fir tree. Everyone on board the *Grappler* wore the same insignia. Sunshiny sported one on the collar of his grimy shirt.

The instant the man in the suit saw Ralph, his jowly face drew up into an angry scowl.

"What are you doing up here again?"

Sunshiny opened his mouth wide. It remained agape even as his brow collapsed in utter confusion.

"Um..." Sunshiny said. He scratched his bald pate.

The suited man emitted a hissing sigh. "Get back below," he ordered.

He had to guide Sunshiny by the shoulders to start him off in the right direction. He stood in the narrow corridor and watched to make sure Sunshiny didn't accidentally wander into one of the cabins and fall asleep. Again.

"And to think we're saving the planet for the likes of *that,*" America's secretary of the interior, Bryce Babcock, muttered to himself.

Still scowling, Secretary Babcock headed down an adjacent corridor.

There were no portals so deep in the *Grappler*. Not that it mattered. Babcock knew precisely what was going on outside. He could feel the watery displacement taking place beyond the hull.

In spite of the small difficulties he was having with the Earthpeace crew, Bryce Babcock had to admit, everything else was going perfectly. No, better even than that. *Flawlessly.* The complex plan he had developed was unfolding without a single major error.

As he walked through the ship's maze of narrow passages, his drooping scowl re-formed into a sagging smile.

Once they passed through the Miraflores section, they would move on to the Pedro Miguel Locks. The eight-mile Gaillard Cut would bring the *Grappler* and its precious cargo across the continental divide to Gatun Lake. On the other end of the canal, the three flights of Gatun Locks would lower the water level by eighty-five feet, easing them gently into the Atlantic Ocean. They would then sail past Colón and into the Caribbean Sea.

And, Secretary Babcock thought with a giddy shiver, into history.

Still smiling in his sad, drooping way, Babcock pushed open the door of an unmarked cabin. The room beyond was small and dimly lit. A dull fluorescent light shone down on a workbench against the distant wall.

A lone man sat on a stool before the bench, the sleeves of his white dress shirt rolled up to his elbows. His underarms were stained yellow with old perspiration. On the lapel of his discarded jacket was the familiar dove-fir pin.

Dr. Ree Hop Doe didn't even look up as the interior secretary stepped inside the muggy room.

With a tiny click, Babcock closed the small door.

The air inside was fetid. Hours of human sweat and ripe body odor clung to the walls. The only ventilation passed through a small metal grate near the ceiling.

At the bench, Dr. Doe's hunched shoulders obscured much of the large, shiny object with which he continued to tinker even as Babcock crossed over to him. Tired hands used tweezers to lay out strings of multicolored wires.

For several giddy moments, Babcock watched in silence as the Asian scientist worked. He finally couldn't contain himself any longer.

"How's it going, Doctor?" he said eagerly.

Dr. Doe almost fell off his stool, so startled was he by Babcock's voice. He had been so engrossed in his work that he hadn't heard the secretary enter. Eyes that had been staring too long at miniature components attempted to blink back into focus.

"I arr set," Doe said, his accent thick. He lay his tweezers on the bench. "It ready for arming."

At the news, an excited grin flickered across Babcock's saggy face. It disappeared almost in the same instant.

"It won't go off now?" he asked, suddenly worried.

"No," Dr. Doe insisted. When he shook his head, the greasy black hair plastered to his scalp didn't budge. "That not problem."

"Because *now* won't do any good," Babcock stressed. "We need the optimal location."

"Do not worry, Mr. Secretary," Doe said. It came out *wolly*. "Nothing happen till I make it happen."

The secretary's smile returned.

This was the precious cargo. Not the former United States President. That old fossil was just gravy. The real reason for this trip sat on the oil-stained bench before him.

On the workbench, the stainless-steel casing of what appeared to be a small nuclear warhead reflected the wan light of the room. But even though it had the appearance of a standard nuclear device, Secretary Babcock knew that it was much, much more.

The smile on his flaccid face broadened as he considered what this one piece of hardware would mean for the world. Humankind was finally going to get its comeuppance. And it was about damned time. Bryce Babcock would bear witness to the event that would have global repercussions for generations to come.

Far below, the engines suddenly rumbled to life.

The ship had reached equilibrium. Slowly, the *Grappler* began to move forward into the final set of Miraflores Locks.

Bryce Babcock felt a trickle of warmth at his groin.

It was a problem he'd had since he was a toddler. All the excitement, the movement of the ship and so much water all around had tickled his nervous bladder.

"I'll be on the bridge," he said quickly.

Hoping Doe hadn't caught a whiff of his very pungent urine, he excused himself from the room. Usually if he hurried fast enough, he had to change only his underwear.

As he hustled up the hallway, Babcock hoped he'd brought along enough spare pairs. This trip promised much excitement. It would be very risky for him to attempt to witness the event that would end Man's technological age without the backup safety of a good, thick pair of Hanes.

Remo had left most of the IDs Smith regularly issued him on the dresser back home. He was worried that he'd have to try to bluff his way past the Secret Service with his blue Bombshell Video card when he found a spare ID next to his passport in the back of his wallet. As luck would have it, it identified him as Remo Blodnick, an undersecretary of the Treasury Department.

The laminated card got him and the Master of Sinanju through most of the security checkpoints between the sixth and eighth floors. Only on their way down the eighth-floor hallway toward the suite in which the former President had spent the previous night were they finally stopped.

The Secret Service man on duty inspected Remo's ID with great care. When he looked up, he nodded crisply. "You're okay, Mr. Blodnick," he said. "But he doesn't have clearance." He nodded to Chiun.

"It's okay," Remo assured the agent. "He's with me."

"No, I am not," Chiun interjected.

The man raised an eyebrow. "Sir?"

"*He* is with *me,*" Chiun explained.

"Be that as it may, I can't allow you to pass without clearance."

Remo sensed a troubling stillness about the old Korean. Fearing a repeat of the Stan Ronaldman wig incident, he quickly stepped between the Master of Sinanju and the agent.

"It's okay, Chiun," Remo said. "I won't be long."

The Master of Sinanju gave each man in turn a vaguely dissatisfied glare before turning away. The drab wall suddenly became infinitely more fascinating to him than Remo.

Taking this for approval, Remo left Chiun in the care of the Secret Service agent and hurried down the hall to the President's hospital room.

At several points along the way, he spied bloodstains on the floor. The bodies of the slain had been removed—only very recently, it would seem—but there was evidence of a battle all around.

Black scuff marks marred the floor. Bullet holes outlined in pencil crayon pocked the bland green walls.

The deadly activity had come to a head in front of the suite itself. Here, the bullet-and-blood trail stopped.

When Remo stepped inside, he found an FBI forensic team methodically searching through the hospital rooms. They were being watched with great suspicion by a team of Secret Service agents. Most of the men were huddled near the door inside the bedroom. A man in an FBI windbreaker was lifting a fingerprint off the door of the closet.

"Let me guess," Remo said to the ten men near the door. "The stateroom scene from *A Night at the Opera,* right?"

The faces that turned his way were annoyed. Most were too engrossed in the single fingerprint being lifted to even bother to look at him.

One man separated from the rest. His face was angry as he approached Remo.

"You can't be here," he announced. A Secret Service emblem was emblazoned on the back of his blue windbreaker. His clip-on tag identified him as Agent John Blizard.

"Can," Remo disagreed. "Am." He flashed his ID. "Blodnick, Treasury. What have you got so far?"

Agent Blizard inspected Remo's credentials carefully. When he looked back up, his narrow face was pinched.

"Since when do undersecretaries get involved in investigations?"

"You haven't heard of me?" Remo asked. "I'm like the Miss Marple of Treasury. They put me on all the really big stuff. Every time the VP gets lost in the woods or needs help shaking down Buddhist nuns, I'm there."

The glint of mistrust in the agent's eyes sparkled

more brightly. "I better call Washington," he said suspiciously.

The others had returned to their duties. No one was even looking their way. Remo nodded to the agent.

"Be my guest," he said, smiling tightly.

"Be back in a minute," Agent Blizard announced to no one in particular.

As soon as they stepped into the hallway, Remo frowned. The Master of Sinanju was nowhere to be seen. Nor, it seemed, was the agent Remo had left him with.

"Swell," Remo griped to himself.

"What's wrong?" Agent Blizard asked.

"What's *always* wrong?" Remo grumbled as they headed down the hall. "He's got a bug up his ass and he's taking it out on me."

"Who?" Blizard asked. He suddenly wasn't interested in a reply. He had just noticed that there was no longer an agent posted near the stairwell door. "Hey, where's—"

It was all he could manage to say before he felt a strange tightening sensation at the small of his back. His spine instantly went rigid.

"This is just like him," Remo muttered as he guided Secret Service Special Agent John Blizard down the hall. "Doesn't give a damn about me or anyone else. It's all the time him, him, him."

Agent Blizard tried to yell for help, but found he couldn't even speak. There was no pain, just Remo's hand and the knot of tense muscles in his lumbar region.

"He says he's turned over a new leaf," Remo stated as he kicked open the fire door at the end of the hall. "But that's bullshit," he added, hauling Agent Blizard into the stairwell. "And I *know* it's bullshit," he insisted, kicking the door shut with his heel. "And *he* knows *I* know it's bullshit. He's this frigging Korean volcano, and I wish he'd just erupt already and get it over with."

Alone in the stairwell, Remo released the agent.

"You know what I mean?" he asked, spinning the man so that they were face-to-face.

Up until now, the only responses Agent Blizard had been capable of consisted of frantic, Morse-code blinks. The instant Remo's hand fled his spine, Blizard grabbed for his side arm. Remo pulverized it in its holster. Thick metal fragments clanked to the concrete landing. The Secret Service man's face registered shock.

"I'm tired, I'm cranky and I can do the same thing with skulls," Remo warned. "*Plus* I'm on your side. So why don't you do us both a favor and tell me what I want to know?"

Agent Blizard wasn't buying it. He fumbled in his pocket for his retractable truncheon. Desperate fingers had just closed around it when he felt a fresh sensation in his back. This time, it wasn't like before. This time, there was pain.

The Secret Service man sucked in a shocked gulp of air.

"We've got nothing so far," Agent Blizard gasped. "Couple of fingerprints. Could be from anyone. Witnesses all dead. Kidnappers wore masks."

Remo's face clouded. "If the witnesses are dead, how do you know what they wore?"

"Surveillance cameras," the Secret Service agent explained. Beads of sweat had erupted on his forehead.

"They got a good look at them?" Remo asked.

"For what it's worth, yeah."

Remo considered. If the only evidence available was the security tapes, he'd better look at them quick. For all he knew, Chiun was somewhere in the hospital doing something that would insure they both wound up on the Treasury Department's most-wanted list.

"C'mon, Eliot Ness," he said, sighing.

Hand firmly in place, he guided the Secret Service agent down the stairs.

WHEN REMO PUSHED open the door to the security room, he was surprised to see a familiar wizened figure.

Chiun stood before a bank of television monitors, arms folded imperiously over his narrow chest.

Seated near the old Korean was the Secret Service agent that had stopped them in the eighth-floor hallway. The man held a blood-speckled handkerchief firmly against his left ear. He and another man—this one wearing an FBI tag—were operating the equipment.

"Where have you been?" Chiun asked blandly as Remo entered the small room in the basement. "We have been waiting hours for you."

"You've been waiting all of ten minutes," Remo replied, pushing Agent Blizard into the room before him. "And you could try giving me a little warning when you take off like that. I figured you were in some other wing of the hospital terrorizing Liz Taylor."

"And why would you think something so foolish?" Chiun asked, all innocence.

The seated Secret Service agent interrupted. "This is it," he offered, glancing up. He leaned back to allow the Master of Sinanju a better view of the monitor before him.

The camera that had collected the footage was stationed at the end of the eighth-floor hall beyond the former President's room. The image was in color, but grainy, as if the tape had been reused many times. The sharpness was washed out.

Their own conversation forgotten, Remo and Chiun stepped forward. Alert eyes watched the recording of the morning's events.

At first, little happened. A pair of Secret Service men stood at attention outside the former President's room. A doctor entered the room, closing the door behind him.

"This is dead space," the FBI agent said. He fast-forwarded through five minutes of footage, during which nothing at all happened. He stopped when the first sign of trouble appeared.

Men swarmed from both directions. Some came from down the hall near the elevators and others from the stairwell beneath the surveillance camera itself.

Bandannas masked their faces. Hats were pulled low. Even given the condition of the tape, the guns were obvious. With eerie silence, they fired.

The Secret Service agents near the door didn't have time to draw their own weapons before being cut to shreds. The doctor emerged in the doorway briefly, only to be blown back into the President's room.

A masked man hurried into the President's room. He collapsed back out into the hall almost instantly, legs jutting, unseen, inside the room. The unconscious man's body shook, as if someone were trying to drag him into the room.

The three agents in the security room were drawn in by the silent, unfolding drama. They watched alongside Remo and Chiun, grimly fascinated.

A kidnapper wielded his gun like a club against an unseen target in the room. Afterward, the former President made his first appearance, toppling into the hallway.

The kidnappers flocked around. A needle was injected into their captive's arm. Once empty, the syringe was flung away.

Remo's face was severe. "What did they give him?" he demanded.

"Three distinct compounds," the sole FBI man volunteered. His voice was hollow as he stared at the tape. "Methohexital and a diazepam variant. That's a barbiturate and a heavy-duty tranquilizer. They're still working on the third compound, but I'd guess it's more knockout juice. They didn't want him waking up for a while."

Smith would find some small comfort in that. Whoever had grabbed the former President wouldn't be getting anything out of him anytime soon.

Remo shot a glance at the Master of Sinanju. The old man's expression was unreadable. Flickering images from the monitor lent his face a ghostly cast.

When Remo looked back to the screen, his face hardened.

"Freeze the tape," Remo ordered urgently.

The seated FBI agent glanced furtively to his Secret Service colleagues before pressing Pause. The image locked in place. The kidnappers were struggling to lift the former President.

"It's no good," Agent Blizard grunted unhappily. "Too blurry without enhancement. Whatever you think you see, it's nothing."

Remo ignored him. "You see it, Little Father?" he asked Chiun.

The Master of Sinanju nodded. "However, it is unfamiliar to me."

"What's unfamiliar?" Blizard asked. "What do you see?"

"I'm pretty sure I've seen it before," Remo mused, brow furrowed.

"Seen *what* before?" Agent Blizard demanded. He leaned forward, examining the monitor, trying to see if there was something new, something he could possibly have overlooked.

He saw only a blurry jumble of disguised kidnappers and the ex-President limp in their arms.

"There's nothing to see," the Secret Service agent insisted. Face a sour mask, he turned back to the man who claimed to be an undersecretary of the Treasury.

He was stunned to discover the guy who had dragged him down here was gone. So was the old Asian.

The door to the security room was closed tightly. It was as if they were never there.

With deliberate slowness, Agent Blizard turned back to the other two men. They were glancing around the room, surprise and relief visible on their faces.

"We better get somebody after them," the FBI man said, clearly not thrilled with the prospect of crossing Chiun. He reached for the phone.

A hand quickly pressed on the receiver, holding it firmly in the cradle.

"Whoa," Agent Blizard said, his voice soft. His hand never left the phone. "I think we should keep this one quiet."

A puzzled expression formed on the FBI man's face as Blizard dragged his own gaze back to the surveillance video.

On the monitor, the scene remained unchanged.

Agent Blizard had a gut feeling that these guys were on the level. But no matter who they were, they were wrong. The image on that tape hadn't changed one iota since Blizard had first laid eyes on it that morning.

"Shut it off," the Secret Service agent commanded, a note of fresh revulsion in his voice.

Possessed as he was of normal human eyesight, Agent John Blizard could not have hoped to see what Remo and Chiun had noted pinned to the shirt of the man who held the ex-President.

When the tape was shut off, the grainy white insignia depiction of a snow-white dove with wings wrapped around a lone fir tree disappeared from the monitor, and was gone.

Remo and Chiun swept back out the gleaming front doors of the prestigious hospital, sliding easily into the throng of patiently waiting reporters.

"Why didn't you wait for me back there?" Remo complained as they glided through the thick cluster of cameras, lights and reporters.

"Forgive me, Remo," Chiun replied dryly. "I was not aware that it was my duty to be tethered at inconvenient moments like some mangy canine."

"It's your own fault," Remo said. "Where did you put the Treasury ID Smith gave you?"

"The dog ate it," Chiun said blandly.

"Can we can the fido motif?" Remo said. "And if you're going to blow up, I wish you'd hurry up and get it over with, for crying out loud."

"Blow up?" Chiun queried. "Whatever do you mean?" The Master of Sinanju's wrinkled face was chillingly serene.

"That. *That's* the sort of thing that scares me," Remo insisted, pointing to the old Asian's tranquil expression. "You're a ticking time bomb just waiting to blow, and I'm sick of cringing every time I think you're gonna go off."

"I do not know why you persist in this," Chiun said.

"Twenty years of mood swings is why," Remo muttered.

Remo had been searching the crowd as he walked. He found whom he was looking for near the line of news vans.

Stan Ronaldman had plastered his shiny black toupee back onto his scalp. The reporter was scrupulously checking his hair in the side-view mirror of his network truck when Remo and Chiun sidled up to him.

"What whacko group uses a pigeon hugging a Christmas tree for its logo?" Remo demanded.

Ronaldman jumped, cracking his forehead on the mirror. When he spun to face the voice, his eyes opened wide in horrified recognition.

"*You!*" he gasped. His jet-black devil eyebrows formed frightened triangles alongside a freshly swelling forehead bump.

"C'mon, c'mon," Remo encouraged, snapping his fingers angrily. "I don't have all day. What's the group?"

"*I'm* calling the *police,*" Ronaldman proclaimed.

When he tried to bully past them, Remo reached out and plucked the toupee from the reporter's head.

Ronaldman shrieked like a woman. Even while he threw the tail of his suit jacket over his shiny bald scalp, he was making desperate grabs for his wig. Remo held the clump of nylon hair at arm's length.

"*What* group?" Remo repeated.

"I don't know!" Ronaldman pleaded. "You said a pigeon?"

"No," Chiun interjected. "It was a dove."

"What's the difference?" Remo asked.

"For some, the dove is a misguided symbol for peace. A pigeon merely symbolizes filth."

"Hugging a Christmas tree?" Ronaldman's worried voice asked from beneath his jacket.

"Yes," Remo said.

"No," Chiun stated firmly. "It was a simple fir tree. There was no Druidic ornamentation."

"That sounds like Earthpeace," the reporter volunteered.

Remo snapped his fingers in sudden recognition.

"That's it," he announced. "I *knew* it was from some nutbar group."

"Oh, Earthpeace isn't nutty," Ronaldman insisted from the recesses of his jacket. "They're very concerned with issues dealing with the environment and disarmament."

"And the people who dedicate their lives to either are *never* complete flakejobs," Remo said dryly.

He dangled the reporter's toupee in front of the shadowy opening of his jacket. Far in the back of the Brooks Brothers cave, a pair of eager, bloodshot eyes opened wide.

"Their address gets you back your Woolworth's tresses."

Stan Ronaldman couldn't speak quickly enough. "San Francisco!" he said. "Somewhere near Golden Gate Park. I don't know where exactly. I could check. Hell, I'll *drive.*"

"Pass," Remo said, tossing the limp wig into the jacket hollow.

By the sounds of the ensuing happy growl, Ronaldman had snagged his hairpiece in his sharp teeth. Coat still draped over his head, he spun and ran straight into the side of his news van.

As Stan Ronaldman sprawled, unconscious on the ground, wig drooping from his mouth like a furry, distended tongue, Remo turned away.

"Let's get a move on," he announced.

"Should you not first call Smith?" Chiun asked.

"Not this time," Remo replied, shaking his head. "He's worked himself up into too much of a lather already. I don't want to talk to him until we have something concrete."

"Where you go, Remo Williams, I will follow," the Master of Sinanju proclaimed. "After all, I am agreeable." His dry lips curled to form a mummified smile.

"Stop *doing* that," Remo groused.

The two men walked away from the gathered reporters, who persisted in their death watch even though the man whose death they were so eager to report was no longer there.

In the San Francisco headquarters of Earthpeace, located south of Golden Gate Park in a small office complex off Lincoln Way, Brad Mesosphere smiled the oily, superior smile he'd perfected as a PR flak for the world's most famous environmental organization.

His five-pack-a-day cigarette habit had turned his once yellow teeth a dirt friendly brown.

"My allies," he announced to the five Earthpeacers arranged around the grubby conference table, "I have just learned that phase one has been a complete success."

The faces that looked back at him were eager.

"They made it to South America?" one man asked, awed. His filthy clothes looked as if they'd been used to mop out the monkey house.

"According to what I just heard, they're through the Panama Canal already and are heading into the Atlantic." Brad's grin broadened. "Tomorrow, the world as we know it will be changed permanently and irrevocably."

There was a quaver of pride in his voice.

It was a quaver well-earned. Man was about to be hoist on his own petard. The blind worship of technology would be his undoing. And the deindustrialization cause would be advanced as never before.

Brad was a man who lived his life for the Cause. He had even changed his surname from the hideous white Anglo-Saxon "Hayward" to the more enviro-conscious "Mesosphere," in honor of the late great scientist-activist Dr. Sage Carlin. In one of his many groundless theories, Carlin had claimed that methane released from overbred beef cattle was depleting the mesospheric layer of Earth's atmosphere.

In taking the name, Brad felt as if he were honoring Sage Carlin's memory. Even though lately there were rumors that Carlin's death was greatly exaggerated, Brad thought that this was neither here nor there. The fact was, Carlin—dead or alive—had *cared.* Brad cared, too.

He'd cared even when he'd worked at NASA as a legitimate scientist—the kind who seemed to diligently struggle at squandering all professional credibility on every half-baked, fly-by-night environmentalist scheme to come down the pike.

In the seventies, Brad had screamed about the coming Ice Age. In the eighties, it was nuclear winter. The nineties brought fresh, frightened tantrums about global warming.

That in the geologically insignificant span of twenty years he'd gone from claiming Earth would soon become a freezing ball of ice to a burning ashen cinder was perfectly acceptable in his job at NASA. Hell, most of the folks who worked there had made the same cold-to-hot journey with nary an eye blink from the higher-ups.

His performance at his space-agency job had been without a single complaint. Until one fateful day just a few short years earlier.

NASA had just landed a small probe on the surface of Mars. The pictures taken by the miniature robotic dune buggy had captivated the world.

On a tour of mission control, Congresswoman Shirley Magruder-Jacklan was impressed by the images displayed on the large suspended screens. Dull eyes earnest, she turned to her guide, the soon-to-be-unemployed Brad Hayward.

"This is amazing," Congresswoman Magruder-Jacklan said of the grainy pictures being broadcast from the red planet. Cameras flashed images of her for newspapers and magazines. Spools of videotape whirred for the nightly news.

"Truly amazing," she repeated. When she turned to Brad, her face was deadly serious. "Now, can your little car thingie drive on over to where our brave astronauts planted our proud American flag?"

It was the earnestness of her tone that did it. Although he was in political lockstep with everything the congresswoman stood for, her supreme ignorance in that single moment was too much for Brad to endure.

Before he knew it, he laughed right in her face.

He laughed and laughed and laughed some more, even as it was explained in hushed tones to the congresswoman that man had never set foot on Mars. He laughed as she was ushered hastily away, scowling back at her tour guide. He laughed until he cried, right up until the point he was fired.

Only then did reality set in.

As a former NASA scientist, Brad was employable in two fields: the environmental movement or the food-service industry. He chose the former.

After a quick name change and a move to the West Coast, Brad found a new home at Earthpeace. And, as luck would have it, he was blessed to be a member of the movement during its greatest hour. The moment that would get them all written up in the history books. Assuming it was even possible to *print* history books after the following day.

At the head of the Earthpeace conference table, Brad could barely wrangle in his idiot's grin.

"No longer will Homo sapiens rape Mother Earth for sport," he proclaimed grandly. "We're on the cusp of a great new age. Thanks to us, mankind will finally be made to understand his true place in the natural order."

Although use of the masculine was universally frowned on within the Earthpeace organization, Brad's usage here was clearly acceptable. When talking about the destruction wrought on the poor, pitiful, defenseless little blue planet, male pronouns were not just encouraged—they were *mandatory*.

"Nothing in the press *yet?*" a grossly overweight woman in a paisley dress asked, her rapid-fire voice quivering. She'd been a pop diva twenty years and two hundred pounds ago. As her weight rose, her career had fallen. Over the past two decades, she'd been forced to resort to gimmicky big-band and Spanish-language albums.

A nine-by-thirteen-inch cardboard tray filled with greasy French fries sat on the conference table before her. As she listened to Brad, the singer continuously stuffed fries into her bloated face.

"Not yet," he admitted. "The media's still treating it like the old fascist is in the hospital."

"Shouldn't we call them and tell them?" one of the men asked.

"Absolutely not," Brad stated firmly. "Anyway, he's only window dressing. The real cargo is too important to let them know about our involvement just yet. We can't risk them intercepting the *Grappler* before it reaches its destination."

The pop singer belched loudly. A hail of half-eaten fries splattered the table. She swept them up with greedy, fat fingers, stuffing them back in her maw.

"So what do we do now?" one of the men asked, one eye on the pop singer. She was sucking half-chewed fried potato from her chubby fingertips.

"Nothing we can do now but wait," Brad replied, shaking his head. "Except—" he threw his hands out wide, a grand expression on his beaming face

"—this is a cause for celebration!" he yelled. "Fruitopias all around!"

And as a cheer rose up from the gathered Earthpeacers, a jubilant Brad Mesosphere marched to the minifridge that chugged away in the corner. Freon-free, of course.

INCENSE BURNED in smoldering tin dishes that resembled battered bedpans. Potpourri smells wafted from genuine Native American and Mexican clay pottery that looked to have been made with diligence by an ungifted preschooler.

The desks and chairs within the office had been recycled from the nearest landfill. To conserve water, they hadn't been rinsed off. The scent of coffee grounds, slimy banana peels and rotten eggshells filled the air.

Remo's nose was bombarded with competing noxious aromas the instant he stepped through the front door of Earthpeace's San Francisco headquarters.

"Pee-yew," he griped. "What the hell died in here?"

Behind him, the Master of Sinanju's face puckered in intense displeasure.

"It stinks of rotting garbage," the old Korean complained. The air seemed to have curdled his button nose. He pressed one broad kimono sleeve over his face. The other, he fanned frantically before him.

"I've smelled *better* garbage," Remo disagreed. "Let's get this over with before our noses drop off."

They kept their breathing shallow as they stepped over to the reception area.

Behind a filthy desk, a middle-aged woman with a bandanna tied around her hair sat reading a copy of *Mother Jones,* a pair of tinted granny glasses perched on the end of her nose.

She lowered her magazine as they approached, a perpetual scowl on her blotchy face.

"Can I help you?" she asked.

"Not unless you've got a can of Lysol stashed up your caftan," Remo said. "Just get me your boss."

The woman instantly frowned at the term. "There is no *boss* here," she said frostily. "We're a collective. Everything is voted on and done for the good of all."

"Vote yourself a bath," Remo suggested. "Look, somebody's in charge here. Get him."

"I feel ill," Chiun's muffled voice announced through his kimono sleeve. He started to lean against the woman's filthy desk for support but at the last minute thought better of it. He opted for swooning in place.

The receptionist ignored Chiun. Her dagger eyes glared malevolence at Remo. "Why do you automatically assume a man is in command?" she asked, bristling.

Remo rolled his eyes. "Lady, I don't care. Him,

her, it, *you.* I don't care. Just get them. This place reeks like sweaty hockey equipment."

Her severe frown lines deepened. A long, dirty fingernail unfurled. "Take a seat," she commanded.

Remo looked at the nearest chair. Some unidentifiable viscous goo dripped down the plastic back.

"I wouldn't sit on that with *your* ass," he said.

Her face was stuffed back into her magazine. "Sit, stand, hop on one foot. It doesn't matter to me."

"How about if I kick?" Remo suggested.

Before she could protest, he skirted the desk.

There was a closed door beyond. He brought the heel of his loafer into the warped wooden surface.

The door exploded from its frame, skittering in thick fragments into the hallway beyond.

Behind him, the woman leaped to her feet, chair toppling backward onto the floor.

"What are you doing?" she shrieked.

"Giving someone an excuse to kill another tree," Remo offered.

It was a split second before she realized what he meant. Only when he took his first step through the shattered remnants of the door—the door that would now have to be *replaced*—did the truth dawn.

"You're one of *them!*" the woman screeched behind him.

"If by 'them' you mean people who've figured out that Right Guard works on both sides, guilty as charged," Remo called over his shoulder.

She wasn't listening. As he and the Master of Sinanju slipped into the corridor, she was wrenching open her desk drawer. Remo could hear her fumbling frantically even as his finely tuned senses honed in on the cluster of six heartbeats dead ahead.

The smell wasn't as bad in here. An open window carried fresh air into the corridor.

"You want to do the honors?" Remo offered, pausing before the closed conference-room door.

"Just be quick about it," Chiun urged, his face still firmly planted in his sleeve of brocade silk.

Remo nodded sharply.

The inner door surrendered to his kicking heel. When the two Masters of Sinanju breezed inside, they were greeted by half a dozen shocked faces.

The room was a continuation of the squalid decor of the lobby. Colorful posters thumbtacked to the pressboard walls expressed such sentiments as Have You Hugged A Seal Today? and No Nukes Is Good Nukes.

At the appearance of the intruders, Brad Mesosphere's Fruitopia bottle slipped from his fingers. It cracked, spraying its contents across the grimy linoleum floor.

"Oh, my God," he gasped, his voice tremulous with soft disbelief. "They're *here.*"

"The dirt mother in the lobby had the same reaction," Remo mused. "Looks like we were expected."

Brad blinked at his words, a hint of terrified realization in them.

"What do you want?" he chirped, frightened.

"My ability to smell back," Remo said. "But thanks to the cavalcade of stench out there, that seems out of the question right about now, so I'll settle for the President." His eyes got suddenly very cold. "Where is he?" he demanded.

The jaw of one of the younger group members jutted defiantly. "In Washington, man," he said, sneering.

"You wanna get this one, Little Father?" Remo asked.

Chiun impatiently removed the sleeve from his face. "If only to hasten our departure," he snapped.

The arrogant young Earthpeacer was fouling the air a few feet from the Master of Sinanju.

His face was a cast of youthful disdain. A curling, contemptuous mouth snarled within spotty patches of goatee and mustache. Eyes glistened with wet malevolence.

The man didn't seem to find Chiun a threat, directing his contemptuous attitude solely at Remo. He was stunned, therefore, when he felt a sudden sharp pain in his chest.

Sucking in a shocked gasp of air, he looked down.

The fingertips of one bony hand were pressed against his grubby Green Day sweatshirt. Only four long fingernails were accounted for. When the pain exploded within his chest, he realized where the fifth had gone.

Chiun whipped his hand away, his curving index nail slipping out through the incision it had made between ribs.

Pulsing blood erupted through the tiny snick the Master of Sinanju had made in the man's pulmonary artery.

With a sudden surge of crazed energy, the Earth-peacer clutched both hands desperately to his chest. Face turning ashen, his eyes bugged wildly as his mouth opened and closed in pained confusion. As the last powerful squeeze of his heart pumped blood into his chest cavity, the man pitched forward, landing spread-eagled on the conference table.

A final twitch, and he didn't move again.

Brad Mesosphere watched the scene with growing horror. When he tore his gaze away from the body, he found that he was staring into Remo's dead eyes.

"*Where?*" Remo repeated.

"Halfway across the Atlantic by now," Brad blurted. "He was flown down to Central America after we snagged him. We put him on the *Radiant Grappler.*"

Remo felt his entire body tense.

Out of the country. More great news for Smith.

"The *Radiant Grappler?*" Remo snarled. "I thought the French sunk that barge."

"That was *Radiant Grappler I.* This is the *RG II.*"

"Great," Remo complained. "Now I have to schlepp all the way out to the middle of the ocean. Do you even care how big a nuisance that's gonna be? The guy isn't even in office anymore. Why'd you kidnap him?"

Brad gulped. He seemed like a death-row inmate who was only just beginning to come to terms with his fate.

"He was taken as an example to all the fascist warmongers in the world," the Earthpeacer offered. "As the greatest living illustration of oppressive capitalist imperialism, it's only fitting that he be present at the first outbreak of true peace."

Remo turned to the Master of Sinanju, a blank expression on his face. "Okay, I'm lost. Do you know what the hell he's babbling about?" he asked.

Chiun had taken up a sentry position next to the doorway. "Do not ask me," he sniffed. "I speak English, not American."

"The peace bomb, man," Brad insisted. "The final ironic twist to humanity's adoration of technology."

Remo had heard enough nonsense. "Okay, here's where it gets painful, Maynard G. Krebs," he said.

He took a single step toward Brad. It was as far as he got.

"Long live Gaia!" a voice screamed from the hallway.

All eyes in the room turned to the corridor.

Lumbering up the hall, an automatic clutched in

her filthy hands, was the woman from the reception desk.

Remo assumed the gun was for him and Chiun. But when she squeezed the trigger, the first rounds slammed into Brad Mesosphere's chest with meaty thuds.

The Earthpeace member was thrown backward, crashing from chair to floor.

She whipped around the weapon to target another Earthpeacer.

At the table, the 1970s pop singer had moved on to dessert. She continued to shove brownies into her mouth even as the bullets ripped into the back of her head. She fell face first into her plate.

"Stop her, Chiun!" Remo yelled to the Master of Sinanju, even as the woman swept around to the last remaining environmentalists.

"Who, *me?*" the Master of Sinanju called.

But it was too late. The final three were ripped to shreds in an instant.

Quickly, the woman turned the weapon on herself. Her grin was one of vicious, gleeful victory as she yanked the trigger. Her head popped like a dirty red balloon.

A few feet away, Chiun had to step back to avoid the grisly spray. The body collapsed near his sandals.

Far across the room, Remo's face collapsed into a scowl.

"Dammit, Chiun, why didn't you stop her?" he snarled.

Chiun looked at the body at his feet. When he looked back up, his eyes were bland. "You were closer."

Remo threw up his hands. "I'm sick of this passive-aggressive crapola," he snapped. "Thanks to you, we don't even know where that dingdong boat of theirs is heading. Now if I want to find out from this guy, I'm gonna have to use a Ouija board. I hope you're happy." Scowling, he kicked Brad Mesosphere's leg.

"I am *always* happy," Chiun replied placidly. "In fact, there are times when I am positively ecstatic."

And, stepping over the receptionist's lifeless body, the old man slipped back into the hallway. As he disappeared from sight, his wrinkled face was a mask of utter calm.

Alone in the Earthpeace conference room, Remo slowly shook his head. It seemed to take all his effort.

"And I thought you'd be insufferable if your movie was a *hit,*" he muttered.

Still shaking his head, he trailed the Master of Sinanju outside.

Smith's voice on the phone was fraught with tension.

"Report."

"What do you want first," Remo asked, exhaling, "the bad news or the really bad news?"

He was on an outdoor phone in a small park. Behind him, the Golden Gate Bridge with its garishly painted cellular steel towers rose red from the Golden Gate Strait, the waterway linking San Francisco Bay to the Pacific Ocean.

Smith was instantly wary. "What went wrong?" he asked.

"Chiun and I are in San Francisco," Remo explained.

"No names, *please,*" the CURE director pleaded.

"Yeah. Right. Anyway, Earthpeace is behind the kidnapping. Assuming it's all right to say 'kidnapping.'"

Smith didn't respond to the sarcasm. His lemony tone took on a hopeful edge. "You're certain of their involvement?"

"Sure as shootin'," Remo replied.

"Where is the, er, package they collected?"

Remo knew he was referring to the former President.

"Now this is where it gets a little tricky," he said.

At the pay phone, Remo glanced around for the Master of Sinanju.

Chiun was standing several yards away down a gravel path. The old Asian had a handful of pebbles that he was tossing—one at a time—into the air. A flock of eagerly circling seagulls, which assumed the old man was throwing pieces of bread, dove for each stone. Each time at the last minute the birds would discover they'd been had. As the pebbles dropped back to earth, the seagulls would break away, flying back up to join the swirling flock.

It was a cruel trick, Remo knew, but it could have been a lot worse. So far, none of the birds had bought the farm.

"We tracked them to their headquarters," Remo said, turning his attention back to the phone. "I barely started to question them before one of their own members gave them all 9 mm enemas."

Behind him, the seagulls began to squawk in greater agitation. He did his best to ignore them.

On the phone, hope had drained to hollowness.

"Then this is the end." Smith's voice was perfectly level. "I will make the necessary arrangements. Remo, you and Chiun are relieved of your contractual obligations. Good luck and Godspeed."

Remo's eyes shot open. He pressed the phone

more tightly to the side of his head. "Are you out of your mind?" he whispered. "If Chiun hears you, I'll be picking melons in Persia by next week. And what happened to all that 'no names' garbage?"

"It no longer matters," Smith explained. "This will be our last phone conversation. I will initiate the shutdown procedures that will make tracing impossible."

"Keep it down, will you?" Remo said.

He shot a glance at the Master of Sinanju. Fortunately, Chiun hadn't heard Smith. He was still taunting the flock of seagulls.

"Smitty, there's got to be something we can do," Remo insisted. "From what I saw on the security tapes, they pumped him full of knockout juice before they carted him away. He's in no position to talk."

"But how long will he remain unconscious?" Smith asked reasonably. "This is a security risk like none we have ever faced. There is someone out there who knows of much more than our existence. He knows specifics of our operation, as well as details of events to which we are tied. That information could topple our form of government."

"No one listens to ex-Presidents, Smitty," Remo insisted. "Hell, half the people in the country probably couldn't name the *current* President. Not that I'd blame them for pleading the Fifth."

"They would listen to this. Even you must see

that," Smith said patiently. The older man was infuriatingly calm.

"Okay, okay," Remo said. "It's big and it's bad. *Possibly.* But before we take down the tents and move on, why don't we wait until we've exhausted all our options? One of the Earthpeace freaks told me they've got the former President aboard the *Radiant Grappler.*"

"The *Radiant Grappler?*" Smith interrupted sharply.

"Yeah," Remo said. "It's the boat they use whenever they want to nudzh out on the high seas. Guess they're not content to just pester people on dry land."

"Why didn't you mention this before?" Smith asked, annoyed. "Wait a moment."

In the background, Remo could hear the dull, persistent drumming of Smith's fingers as he typed. When he returned to the phone a minute later, his voice was tight.

"Remo, the *Radiant Grappler* passed through the Panama Canal several hours ago. It made it into the Atlantic without incident. If the President was on board, he was not discovered."

"Can you say 'big fat bribe'?" Remo asked thinly.

"That is possible." Smith's voice was distant, as if he were having difficulty digesting this new information.

Across the country, the CURE director gripped the edge of his desk with one hand, knuckles white. He felt light-headed. His acid-churned stomach clenched in knots of growing fear as a wave of concern swelled within him.

"You still with me, Smitty?" Remo asked after a moment of silence.

Smith was trying to will himself calm. The air he drew into his abdomen was ragged and searing; his breath was labored.

"The President is no longer in the country," Smith said at long last.

"Yeah..." Remo said leadingly. "I think we determined that."

"Since the outset, I had assumed this was either an old enemy seeking vengeance or a simple kidnapping for ransom that had taken place at an unfortunate time for us. It is likely it is much more than either now. I doubt they would take him out of the country if they desired only ransom."

Smith was trying to force his reeling mind back into focus. Since learning of the President's abduction, he had been preoccupied with both the risk to CURE and the search for the former chief executive. He had been so busy that he had not contemplated a more sinister reason to the abduction than those he had initially assumed. Now it seemed as if it could be for a larger purpose.

"Remo, the *Radiant Grappler* is en route to South

Africa,'' Smith said. ''According to my information, it will be in Cape Town in three days.''

Remo nodded. ''Okay. Great,'' he said. ''Chiun and I can head them off, no sweat.'' He was relieved when Smith didn't argue.

''I am curious as to what possible motive Earth-peace could have. Why kidnap a former United States President and take him to South Africa?''

''Don't put too much hope in finding a why with these nudnicks. They said something about having him around for the outbreak of peace. I figured it was another dog-and-pony show for sixties rejects to plant daisies on Siberian missile silos.''

''Outbreak of peace?'' Smith sounded puzzled.

''Don't read too much into it, Smitty. Everyone in that place was probably looped on something. My guess'd be a contact buzz from whiffing the lobby seats.''

There was a sudden loud squawk behind Remo. Phone in hand, he spun.

The Master of Sinanju stood below the flock of seagulls, no longer tossing pebbles. The wizened Korean's bony hands were tucked inside the wide sleeves of his kimono.

Remo frowned. Did the flock seem thinner?

''Okay,'' he said into the phone, still eyeing Chiun. ''So what's the story? We still in business, or what?''

''For now,'' Smith replied. ''But we must act

quickly. I want you in South Africa before their arrival. You must be there to greet that ship. If they manage to sneak their cargo off before you arrive, the risk of exposure multiplies to unacceptable limits. So far, we can only hope that their passenger has remained unconscious."

"Gotcha," Remo said. "Light a candle in the window."

He hung up. Turning from the pay phone, he struck off toward Chiun. As Remo headed down the gravel path, the Master of Sinanju made a point of keeping his back to his pupil. The seagulls had begun to disperse, flying in ever widening circles around the old Asian.

As the birds began to separate and fly away from one another, Chiun's bald head bobbed appreciatively. The smile on the old man's face was a disconcerting sight.

"Looks like the avian population's been made to pay for Hollywood's transgressions," Remo commented dryly once he'd caught up to his teacher.

Chiun's face was perfectly calm. "I do not know what you are talking about," he said. "A refrain, I might add, that I have been forced to use far too often in our interminable association."

"Yeah, right," Remo said, deadpan. "Let's go."

On the way to their rental car, Remo glanced once at the sky. The fleeing seagulls were black specks against a tapestry of brilliant blue.

As they climbed in the car and drove away, Remo briefly wondered what Chiun had done with the missing birds. He knew enough not to ask.

Ten minutes after they were gone, the first wispy seagull feathers began floating gently to the ground.

15

At the edge of the Columbian Basin, before the *Radiant Grappler II* had even passed the divided island of Hispaniola on which sat the tiny countries of Haiti and the Dominican Republic, a change was taking place aboard the huge vessel.

Potbellied men in tie-dyed shirts swarmed up from belowdecks, hauling buckets and heavy burlap bundles. Thinning hair blew wildly in the warm breeze; breath came in rasping puffs as they ran through their arranged routine.

Knives were produced. As the heavy sacks were dropped to the deck, frantic hands sliced them open. Thick fishing nets spilled out, the smell of the salt ocean already strong in their fibers.

The buckets held drab gray paint. Screwdrivers pried the tin lids. Another burlap bundle yielded paintbrushes. The men shouted encouragement to one another as they raced along the deck, buckets and paint in hand.

Some stayed behind with the nets. These were hooked into the trawling arms that had been left affixed to the deck after the ship's conversion from its original purpose.

As the men were fastening their nets, Secretary of the Interior Bryce Babcock stepped from the *Grappler's* bridge into the brilliant Caribbean sunlight. He surveyed the activity on deck.

It was all going according to plan.

The men worked quickly, efficiently.

They appeared not to notice the secretary as they hurried past him on the broad deck, each lost in the minutiae of his own assigned duties. Here, men painted. There, nets were unfolded and hooked into place.

As he viewed the activity, Babcock felt the familiar excited tingle in his bladder. He dared not take a bathroom break. Not now. Not when the most brilliant part of his plan was coming to life right before his very eyes.

As the ship picked up steam for its trip past Puerto Rico and the Leeward Islands, Babcock could not avoid congratulating himself.

The scheme was flawless, masterful. He had hoped it would go well, but he hadn't dared *dream* that the plan would be executed with such exacting precision.

They were moving fast now. Barreling through the waves at sixty-two knots. The massive, intimidating form of the *Radiant Grappler* pummeled ocean beneath her enormous, merciless prow.

They would be out in the Atlantic in no time. And then…

Another tingle. Standing, Babcock crossed his legs.

"Mustn't get ahead of ourselves," he murmured, resisting the urge to squeeze his privates like a three-year-old. "We have to get there first."

But the fact was, they were on their way!

Salty spray pelted Babcock's basset-hound face. An observer would never have guessed he was ecstatically happy. Judging by his face alone, it looked as if he'd just come back from putting his dog to sleep. Bryce Babcock had always had that same hangdog expression. Even in grammar school, the other kids had called him Droopy, after the cartoon character. Even when he was elated, Babcock looked dejected. But he was absolutely not unhappy. Not now.

His sagging face drawn up in what, for him, was the closest thing to delighted he could manage, Babcock strolled along the deck.

All around, men worked and yelled. And beyond them all, the beautiful blue ocean.

"Water, water everywhere," Babcock said. He tried to avoid looking at the sea.

He walked a little farther, each droplet of salt water that collected in the worry lines of his hanging face reminding him of the heaviness that was swelling beneath his belly.

The bathroom was enticing, but the view here was

too splendid. All of the men working on the plan. On *his* plan. He couldn't go now. He'd tough it out a little longer.

Bryce Babcock tried not to think about the pressure that was building in his bladder as he made his way down the deck.

In the stern, he noted the sadness on the faces of the men near the trawler arms. Unlike the others who were still hurrying to complete their chores, these sailors were sitting around. Waiting. They were staring into the churning white wake of the *Grappler*.

The men back here knew what their next task would be. And they did not revel in it. They looked up with sad eyes as Babcock approached. Fat tears streamed down long faces. Squatting on the deck, Bright Sunshiny Ralph sniffled.

"Tell us again why this is necessary?" the Earthpeacer asked the secretary when he'd stopped beside them.

"You know why," Babcock replied. "We've got to make this as authentic as possible." He placed a firm hand on Sunshiny's shoulder. "It's the only way."

"I know," Sunshiny Ralph said morosely. "It just seems so—so *human*." He used the word like a curse.

Babcock couldn't argue the charge. His face reflected deeply somber sympathy. It was an expression identical to his delighted look of a moment before.

"I feel your pain," Babcock intoned. "But remember, what we do here today we do for a higher cause."

There were nods among the sniffles. Though most still fought back tears, they sat more proudly, shoulders forced back, chests thrust forward.

Babcock flashed the men a dyspeptic wince that might have been a smile of encouragement before turning away.

It was time to deal with more pressing matters. The endless churning water had had a negative effect on his already full bladder. The pressure was too great to ignore any longer.

Turning from the men, he began to hurry back along the deck. He had taken barely a step before something far above caught his eye. It was framed against the azure sky of the Caribbean.

He stopped dead.

On a lone mast high above the giant ship fluttered a green flag. On it was embroidered the familiar dove-and-tree symbol of Earthpeace. Bryce Babcock's sour face collapsed as he watched the flag snap crazily at the sky.

He wheeled back on the men.

"What is *that* still doing up there?" he demanded, jabbing an angry finger mastward.

"Uh, dude," Sunshiny said, "we thought, you know, fly the colors till the bitter end."

"That's the *first* thing that should have gone, you idiots!" Babcock snapped. "Get it down from there! *Now!*" His baggy eyes suddenly widened. "Oh, *no.*"

Face sick, the interior secretary glanced down at his trousers. A seeping wet stain was easing over his crotch. As he gasped in anger, warm rivulets began the remorseless trickle down the front of his thigh, dampening the band of his black dress socks.

"Dammit," he griped. "I *knew* I should have lined with plastic."

Shaking the growing wetness from his leg, Bryce Babcock hustled belowdecks on squishy shoes.

BY ORDER of the interior secretary, the Earthpeace flag was lowered. It was folded reverently and placed in a simple cardboard box in the hold. At the same time, the last white lapel pins were collected.

Jerry Glover had the honor of bringing the shoebox containing the insignias down below. He hid it behind the former President's cage. Sneaking a peek at the prisoner, he found that the ex-chief executive was still snoring, oblivious to all that was going on around him.

"You're gonna be in for one mother of a shock when you wake up," Jerry whispered. "This ain't no bourgeois *National Review* cruise."

Leaving the old man in the darkness of the damp hold, he hurried back up on deck.

The catwalk door closed with resounding finality. The noise echoed through the shadowy hold.

For several long seconds, intense silence filled the rusty belly of the ship. The only sounds were those that filtered through the *Grappler's* thick hull. Waves crashing. Creaking metal. Muffled shouts. Muted, distant.

Another sound. Closer. This one originating within the hold itself. So soft was it that it could have been mistaken for background noise.

A soft, urgent scratching noise. Very faint.

And this new sound issued from out of the dark cage interior.

AT THE PUERTO RICO TRENCH, the *Grappler* made an unexpected course alteration. Instead of turning south for the run to the southernmost tip of Africa, the ship veered northeast, aiming for the wide expanse of the Atlantic.

Scaffolding was lowered over the sides. Paint strokes removed the last of the *Grappler's* identifying marks. New identification numbers were stenciled in large white letters on the gunmetal-gray hull.

The men in the stern were given word to begin the task that had caused them such grief.

Nets were lowered from heavy steel arms into the churning ocean water.

Sonar in the helm was quick to locate a school of fish. In a matter of minutes, the dripping nets were hauled back up to the deck, laden with bluefin tuna. The fish were dumped unceremoniously onto the deck.

Men who had held themselves together until now broke into tears at the sight of the hundreds of fish slopping out around their ankles.

"The carnage!" Sunshiny cried. "The viciousness! Oh, the *humanity!*"

"Humanity is right," another Earthpeacer blubbered, wiping at his runny nose. "Fish would *never* kill one another for food. They don't have it in them."

Sunshiny Ralph steeled himself. "We're supposed to be a fishing boat now. We need to have something in the hold if we're stopped."

Jerry Glover sniffled, nodding agreement. "This is necessary. For the greater good."

The men waded into the pile of live fish and began to load them, as gently as possible, into a special metal sluice. The tuna disappeared down the chute, flopping moments later into the hold of the big ship.

The work went on for only a few minutes. The cries of the men, which had died down after a time, grew frenzied once more when the last of the dumped nets revealed the familiar shape of a large dolphin. The creature was dead.

Gasps went up all around.

"Oh, my God!" Sunshiny shrieked. He hopped up and down in front of the dead mammal.

"This is *awful!*" Jerry echoed, clutching his own throat.

Another man dropped to his rear end on the deck, knees pulled to his chin.

"Greater good...greater good...greater good..." he muttered over and over as he rocked back and forth.

As Sunshiny attempted mouth-to-blowhole resuscitation, buckets of ocean water were hastily brought up in a futile attempt to revive the animal. To no avail.

The mood went from frantic to funereal. No one seemed to know what to do with the dead creature. A burial at sea seemed the most fitting, but someone argued that this was just a fancy term for dumping the poor creature overboard.

"These are the *geniuses* of the deep," Jerry wept. "We can't just chuck it out like garbage."

"If they're so smart, why do they keep getting caught in nets?" one timid Earthpeacer asked.

The rest joined Sunshiny and Jerry in pelting the blasphemer with a dozen flapping, undersize tropical fish.

Afterward, they wrapped the dolphin's corpse in a spare Earthpeace flag and lowered it gently into the sea.

There was no joy aboard the transformed *Radiant*

Grappler II after this incident. The dark mood remained with the crew like a stubborn black cloud on the remainder of their uneventful trip across the Atlantic.

The summer sun was dying long and slow across the reddening New York sky. As the afternoon blurred into dusk, a palpable sense of loss seemed to rise with the gloaming—the sort of wistful malaise that began to set in on the last full month before the start of autumn and the winter it presaged.

A soft breeze off Long Island Sound touched the shadow-smeared leaves of ancient oak and maple.

Alone in the drab confines of his Folcroft office, Harold W. Smith noticed neither the sigh of leaf nor the encroaching darkness.

Fingers moved with perfect efficiency of motion, striking silent keys. Smith was lost in his element. As he surfed the Net, page after electronic page reflected in his owlish glasses.

For the moment, he had put aside his greater concerns. Even so, while it was not yet an actual crisis, it remained a far worse *potential* crisis than any he'd ever faced.

The situation as it was playing out was clearly an unfortunate quirk of fate, rather than part of some deliberate scheme.

The former President hit his head and regained his memory of CURE. An ecoterrorist group saw the opportunity his hospitalization presented and abducted him. The group ruthlessly seized the moment, oblivious to the damning potential of the information that had surfaced in the ex-President's mind.

A series of unfortunate coincidences. Nothing more.

Under other circumstances, Smith might have hesitated to use Remo and Chiun against Earthpeace. After all, other agencies would certainly be involved in the search. They would find him eventually. And even if they did not, well, the truth was that, lamentably, ex-Presidents were expendable.

But the CURE information this President possessed made this situation unique. In having the President, Earthpeace had CURE. Whether they realized it now or not.

A potentially disastrous situation. Smith had tried for several hours to put it from his mind as he worked, with varying degrees of success. At the moment, as he studied his monitor, concern had been eclipsed by confusion.

At his keyboard, Smith paused.

"Odd," he said quietly. So engrossed was he with the information on the computer screen he did not realize he had spoken the word aloud.

On the monitor buried below the dark surface of the desk was a photograph. Taken from a satellite, it showed the area of the Atlantic where the Earthpeace flagship should now be, given its reported course and likely speed.

But the *Grappler* wasn't there.

At best, the *Radiant Grappler II* wasn't due in Cape Town for another twenty-nine hours. Remo would arrive before that. All any of them could do in the meantime was wait.

To fill the idle time, Smith had been doing research on the Earthpeace organization. At the same time, he had logged on to a military satellite in geosynchronous orbit over the Atlantic. Efficient to a fault, Smith wanted to be certain the ship was on schedule. He farmed out the task of actually locating the *Grappler* to the CIA.

It was a procedure he had used in the past. Analysts at CIA headquarters in Langley, Virginia, were assigned the job of finding the Earthpeace ship by some unknown superior. Taking a break from his own work, Smith had just checked the satellite images to see if the CIA had made any progress.

They had not.

Smith's gray eyes were hooded by his frowning brow as he studied the latest real-time image.

There were red circles on the map. Tiny boats—like miniature bathtub toys—threw up frothy wakes of white within the small circles. Some of the vessels were labeled. None was the *Grappler*.

"Very odd," Smith said aloud.

This time, he realized he had spoken the words to his empty office.

Smith leaned away from the computer. He adjusted his glasses with one hand, even as he tapped the other on his desk.

They should have found the ship by now. He had issued the order almost two hours ago.

It was taking far too long. Even by CIA standards. Even if it was traveling at half speed, they should have found the Earthpeace vessel by now.

Assuming it was where it was supposed to be.

A fresh tug of concern.

Empty belly grumbling, Smith leaned forward, his chair creaking. A scrambled phone line gained him entry to Langley. The young voice that answered was bored, but efficient. A low-level functionary not yet disinterested enough in his work to be indolent.

"Imaging analysis."

"This is General Smith," the CURE director said, using the cover ID that had gained him access to both the military satellite and the CIA. "To whom am I speaking?"

The voice grew tighter, bored tone fleeing. "Mark Howard, General. I'm afraid you're not going to be happy with what I've got."

Though he labored to subdue it, Smith's worry deepened.

"Explain."

"We've searched the corridor you gave us, but we're coming up empty. There is no ship remotely resembling the *Radiant Grappler* in Atlantic waters from Antigua to the Cape of Good Hope."

"Is it possible you are in error?"

"No, sir," Howard insisted. "The *Grappler* isn't an ordinary tug. It's as big as a small cruise liner. If she was there, there'd be no missing her."

"Widen the search parameters," Smith instructed.

"We *have*. Three times already. I'm sorry, General, but your boat isn't out there."

Smith thought of the former U.S. President. Held captive on a phantom ship, lost somewhere in the Atlantic. Even now, he could be speaking to his abductors about CURE.

"Widen them again," Smith ordered with forced restraint.

"You know, General, Spacetrack probably followed that ship through the Panama Canal. It might be smarter to review their older satellite photos to get a positive locate on her. Like, say, from six hours ago. If she veered off any other way, we could extrapolate a route from there. *Maybe*."

Smith pursed his thin lips. "Do it," he said.

"The satellite I'm using now is real-time. I'll need current Spacetrack access and the full day's records."

Smith entered some rapid commands into his computer.

"The access codes have been sent to your terminal."

Howard seemed impressed. "That was quick," he said.

Smith ignored him. "If there is nothing more you require, I will be in touch," he said crisply.

"General, you should consider another alternative," Mark Howard said quickly before the CURE director had a chance to break the connection.

"What is that?"

"It's possible your boat went down."

In his Folcroft office, Smith's expression remained unchanged.

"I had already entertained that possibility," he replied as he replaced the phone.

DEEP IN THE BOWELS of the CIA's Langley headquarters, Mark Howard scowled. The sleek white phone in his hand released a steady hornet's buzz from its earpiece.

"You're welcome, you old buzzard," he griped.

In the privacy of his drab, gray cubicle, he briefly considered dragging his feet on the search. It would be a fairly easy thing to do, considering the work it entailed. The volume of information he'd been given access to by the mysterious General Smith was vast.

After a moment's blank hesitation, Mark Howard blinked hard. "Ah, the hell with it," he muttered. "Better to get him off my back fast."

Rubbing his tired eyes, he turned back to his worn keyboard.

On the flight from San Francisco International Airport, Chiun took his usual seat on the left-hand side of the plane above the wing. Remo settled in next to him. Only when they were safely in the air and Chiun was thoroughly convinced that the wing wasn't going to fall off did the old man turn away from the window. His face was disturbingly calm.

The sunlight that glinted off the fuselage streamed through the small window, surrounding the old Korean's vellum-draped skull with an almost ethereal nimbus.

It was the halo effect that did it for Remo. The damnably serene expression on the Master of Sinanju's wrinkled puss didn't help.

"You know you don't have to keep this up," he snapped, annoyed.

"Keep what up?" Chiun asked blandly.

"This phony tranquil front."

Chiun regarded his pupil with hooded hazel eyes. "I am going to take a nap. Please wake me if you intend to make sense."

"Don't pretend you don't know what I mean. I

know for a fact you're ticked as all hell about this movie thing. The only thing keeping you from splattering all over this cabin is the fact that you don't have anyone left to disembowel. You're this close to blowing your top."

"Will you be comforted, Remo, if I tell you my top is secure?"

"Tell it to the seagulls," Remo said. He shook his head resignedly. "I just wish you'd get it over with already. This waiting for you to erupt is driving me nuts."

"Your feeble grip on sanity notwithstanding, I am truly not upset. I have implored the gods to grant me the serenity to accept the things I cannot change, the courage to change that which I am able and wisdom to see the difference."

In spite of himself, Remo snorted. "Where'd you pick that one up?"

Chiun raised a haughty eyebrow. "I do not pick up. Remember, I am a writer."

"Well, you didn't write that. That's an AA prayer."

"Is it?" the old Korean asked vaguely. He settled back in his seat. "They probably stole it from me. Doubtless the rum-soaked walls of Triple-A offices throughout this fetid nation are adorned with my poignant words. Credited to Mr. Chin, of course."

Chiun closed his eyes, indicating that he was through speaking. He folded his hands neatly across his belly. After a moment he was fast asleep.

Remo watched the Master of Sinanju's calm, rhythmic breathing. It was as if he didn't have a care in the world.

It was irritating to Remo. He knew Chiun was pissed, yet Chiun wasn't displaying any signs of being pissed. And that had the practical effect of pissing *Remo* off.

"No matter what you say, I *still* think you're upset, you old faker," he whispered to Chiun's softly sleeping form.

"Think quieter," Chiun squeaked.

IT HAD TAKEN several hours, but he'd finally found her.

The contours were right, and it was certainly the right size. Mark Howard had enlarged the image just to confirm.

He copied the photo to a ROM disc and brought it down to a screening room. Once he'd doused the lights and displayed the image against the white wall, he'd removed all doubt.

The *Radiant Grappler II.*

Alone in the shadows of the small room, Howard compared the computer-enhanced image to the file photos he'd dragged up from the CIA archives. It didn't quite match.

By the looks of it, the vessel had undergone some modifications to make it look like an innocent fishing boat. A waste of time. The ship was so distinctive, there was no mistaking it, no matter what was done to its exterior.

"You can't paint stripes on a cow and call it a zebra," Howard whispered in the darkness of the empty room.

The cosmetic alterations weren't the only odd thing about the *Grappler.*

Howard glanced at the longitude and latitude displayed at the bottom of the picture. On the screen, the enlarged numbers were three inches high. Unless the pilot was high or a complete idiot—both possible, given the Earthpeace rolls—the vessel had deliberately changed course. No simple navigational error could possibly put the ship five thousand miles away from where it was supposed to be.

Flipping on the lights, he popped the disc from the CD-ROM drive.

Howard left the room, returning to the seclusion of his cubicle. The phone rang the instant he sat in his swivel chair.

"Imaging analysis," he said, tucking the receiver between ear and shoulder. The smaller satellite image of the *Grappler* was still on his monitor.

"Mr. Howard, General Smith. What have you learned?"

The voice was as sour as a sack of squeezed lemons. Howard placed the silver disc softly on his desk.

"For starters, your ship didn't sink, General," he said.

"You have located it?"

"Yes, sir. And not at all where you expected it to be."

"Where is it?" Smith demanded.

"Right about now, it's southeast of the Azores and tearing through the ocean like a bat out of hell. It should be passing through the Strait of Gibraltar by morning."

"Are you certain?" Smith asked.

"I've got the real-time satellite feed on my monitor right now," Howard said. He spun his feet into the footwell of his desk. The image of the *Grappler* updated at twenty-second intervals. As he spoke, the old picture was eclipsed by the newest snapshot. "If you can get access to Spacetrack, you'll see what I'm seeing."

Howard heard some rapid tapping from Smith's end of the line. It was more precise than drumming fingers. If he was typing, he didn't have a standard keyboard.

The tapping stopped.

"This is not clear enough," General Smith complained.

"I enlarged the image, sir. It *is* your boat," Howard insisted.

As he spoke, Howard was stunned to see the image on his own screen enlarge. The larger image of the *Radiant Grappler II* came into starkly clear focus, much clearer than any photographic reproduction.

Howard stared at his computer in disbelief. Not only had he not touched his keyboard, his system shouldn't have been capable of enlarging a real-time satellite feed.

General Smith was accessing the Spacetrack data through Howard's own computer.

On his monitor, the bird's-eye photo of the *Radiant Grappler II* showed the ship continuing its remorseless trek across the cold Atlantic.

Howard bit the inside of his cheek. This was all too weird. "General, may I ask what this is all about?" he ventured hesitantly.

But the nasal voice on the phone acted as if he hadn't even spoken.

"Thank you for your assistance, Mr. Howard," General Smith said.

The line promptly went dead. A moment later, the image of the Earthpeace ship vanished from Howard's computer screen. When he checked, Howard found that his uplink to the Spacetrack system had been severed.

Howard leaned back in his seat, crossing his arms thoughtfully. He stared at his monitor for a long time without actually seeing it. Even when the screen saver came on, he didn't notice.

"Interesting" was all he said after many pensive minutes. The word was a soft murmur.

He picked up the CD on which he'd downloaded the satellite data. Fingering it for a few lingering seconds, he finally slipped it into a plastic jewel case. When he stored the disc far back in his desk drawer, there was a thoughtful expression on his pale face.

He closed the drawer with a muted click.

REMO'S PLANE from San Francisco had taken them as far as New York. He and Chiun had boarded the first direct flight from JFK to South Africa.

They were well into the second leg of their journey when Remo felt a gentle tap on his shoulder.

Since the start of his Sinanju training, he'd had a problem with women finding him irresistible. Flight attendants were always the worst.

Although he had discovered a few years ago that shark meat was a natural inhibitor to his pheromones, he hadn't had any in days. Obviously, the effects of his last shark meal were wearing off.

As the stewardess persisted in tapping his shoulder, Remo feigned sleep.

"Excuse me, sir?" she pressed. Her breath was warm and close and smelled strongly of peppermint.

Remo kept his eyes twisted shut. "Can't talk. Sleeping."

It didn't work. She gripped his shoulder and shook.

"Sir?"

From the seat beside Remo, the Master of Sinanju snorted impatiently.

"Answer it or it will not go away."

This irritated Remo even more. He was already

ticked at Chiun for taking so long to get upset about the whole Mr. Chin fiasco. Now, after pretending to sleep practically the whole way from California to the middle of the Atlantic, the old crank roused himself just long enough to drag Remo into a conversation with some sex-crazed flight attendant.

"Thanks a heap, Chiun," Remo growled.

Thinking foul thoughts of the Master of Sinanju, he turned a baleful eye on the woman.

Everything about her that would traditionally be considered attractive in the female form had been inflated to near-comic proportions. Her lips, hair and nails were huge. As she leaned into his seat, her massive breast implants threatened to put out his eyes.

"In the event of a water landing, do those things double as flotation devices?" he asked, his voice devoid of any trace of enthusiasm.

"Hmm?" she smiled. She didn't seem to hear him. "I'm terribly sorry to wake you, sir," the woman cooed in a sweetly Southern drawl, "but you have a call." She nodded apologetically to the seat phone in front of Remo.

"Oh," Remo grumbled, inwardly relieved.

But when he reached for the phone, a pair of soft, scented hands grabbed hold of his.

"Why, was there something *else* you wanted?" the stewardess asked coyly. She caressed his wrist lovingly.

"The use of my hand will be just fine," he replied.

"In due time, sugar," she purred. "When I'm through with it."

"I am going to be ill," the Master of Sinanju said from the adjacent seat.

"No comments from the peanut gallery," Remo growled. He pulled his hand from the woman's strong grip.

The flight attendant's face clouded.

"But it's my job to make you happy," she said, pouting.

"I'm plenty happy," Remo said, snapping up the phone.

Chiun snorted.

"I don't want to lose my job," the woman whined. "I refuse to leave till you let me do what I'm paid for." She crossed her arms over her massive, artificial pontoons.

"Remo?" the confused voice of Harold Smith asked over the seat phone.

"In a minute, Smitty," Remo said. He clapped the phone to his chest. "You know what I want?" he asked the morose stewardess.

Her cloud of dejection broke. Hope sprang anew on her makeup-slathered face.

"Me?" she sang. "You know, these seats recline."

She bent to show him.

Remo shook his head. ''Peanuts,'' he insisted. ''All you can get.''

She crinkled her nose and bit her lip. ''Huh? Why?''

Remo pitched his voice low. ''They get me in the mood,'' he said with a conspiratorial wink.

It was all she needed to hear.

The woman made a mad dash up the aisle to the service area. As she went, she plucked the complimentary packets of nuts from the trays of the other passengers. A few she yanked right out of people's hands.

''That should buy me about ten seconds,'' Remo muttered as he brought the phone to his ear. ''Okay, Smitty, what's up?''

After waiting so long, the CURE director seemed ready to explode. ''There has been a change of plans,'' he announced breathlessly. ''The *Radiant Grappler II* is nearing Portugal.''

''Portugal? That's in Europe.''

''I doubt the emperor phoned to administer a geography quiz,'' Chiun's squeaky voice said blandly. When Remo glanced over, the Master of Sinanju's eyes were open. He was casting a bored eye out the window.

''Why don't you go back to sleep, Rip van Winkle?'' Remo suggested, agitated.

''I have tried. But the tawdry soap opera that is your life has murdered sleep for me.''

"You were doing a good job faking it the first fifteen thousand miles."

"It is not clear where the *Grappler* is now heading," Smith persisted, interrupting Remo. "The likeliest route, however, would bring it into the Mediterranean."

"You said it was heading for South Africa."

"That was the stated destination. It altered course en route."

"Smitty, *we're* heading for South Africa," Remo pressed.

"Not any longer. I have issued an emergency course alteration to the pilot. Your new destination is Gibraltar."

"Gibraltar." Remo frowned. "Spain, right?"

"Actually, it is a colony of Great Britain," Smith said. "By the time you land there, we should have a clearer picture of where the Earthpeace vessel is heading. I will make arrangements for you to be picked up and transported to proximity with the *Grappler* when it arrives at its ultimate destination.

"Has anyone else gotten wind of who's on board?" Remo asked.

"No," Smith said. "Fortunately for us, the efforts of other agencies thus far have been limited to the United States. However, that could change very quickly. I will continue to monitor the domestic situation and phone you when you land."

"Okeydoke," Remo said. He replaced the phone.

"Where will this goose chase take us next?"

Chiun complained before Remo had sat back in his seat.

"You mean seagull chase," Remo said dully.

"I mean what I mean," Chiun sniffed.

Remo sighed. "Wherever these Earthpeace whackos go, we follow. They're the ones with the President, remember?"

A hint of a scowl touched the Master of Sinanju's weathered face. "He is not even your nation's current leader," he clucked. "Why does anyone even care?"

"Most people don't," Remo admitted honestly.

"Then why not just forget him? The bloated nitwit who now rules from the Eagle Throne has the makings of a fine despot. He lies, cheats, betrays his closest allies and is as libidinous as a monkey. All are qualities endemic to the greatest dictators. Be content with him."

"A compelling argument," Remo said dryly, "but I think we'd better stick with the mission as outlined. We'll get the old President and bring him home."

"President." Chiun spit the word as if it were a curse. "Pah! What good are Presidents? Idiots appointed by fools to reign for but a few scant years. Every civilized nation knows that the only true leader is a monarch who is born and bred to rule. Preferably a tyrant."

"Presidents have paid your salary for more than twenty years," Remo pointed out.

"*Smith* pays me," Chiun stated firmly.

"Only because a President started the agency."

"And not even the one for whom we now search. To say that this is a fool's errand is an insult to fools." As he spoke, his eyes suddenly narrowed to slits. "I see your lunch is ready."

Chiun nodded to the front of the plane.

Remo's stewardess was coming up the aisle, arms laden to overflowing with tiny bags of peanuts. The small plastic-wrapped packets that fell to the carpet in her wake were gathered up by two more flight attendants. All three women wore perky, hopeful expressions.

"I think I'll lock myself in the cockpit for the rest of the flight," he said, turning to the Master of Sinanju.

Chiun's eyes were already closed tight.

"Can't talk. Sleeping," the old man said just before he started to snore.

The hot, white Mediterranean sun that poured in through the bridge windows of the *Radiant Grappler II* washed warmly over the dripping chest of Bryce Babcock.

Even though Earthpeace had lobbied against the use of air conditioners, no one in the group thought the ban should extend to themselves. After all, they were changing the behavior of countless millions in their fight for Mother Earth. They above all others should be rewarded for their years of tireless effort.

Although the air conditioning aboard the ship chugged relentlessly, it wasn't enough for Bryce Babcock.

"My goodness, it's hot, isn't it?" he commented to the skipper. "It's global warming, right?" He used an already damp handkerchief to mop the sweat from the back of his neck.

The captain, who was a hired hand and not an Earthpeace member, smiled tightly. "This is the Mediterranean, sir," he explained thinly. "It was hot like this long before hairspray and shaving cream."

The handkerchief came back soaked. Babcock had to wring it out before returning it to his pocket.

"Almost makes you wish for the days when science swore we were entering a new ice age, hmm?" he commented.

The captain didn't respond.

As the sailors went about their busy routine, Babcock found himself being shunted off to a corner of the bridge.

The camouflage had worked perfectly. No one had given the *Grappler* a second look as it sailed through the towering rocks that lined the Strait of Gibraltar. They were already well past the Gulf of Tunis and in the Strait of Sicily near the Island of Pantelleria. Malta was already 120 miles away. At the rate they were traveling, they'd pass the Maltese Islands in under two hours.

Babcock was actually surprised at the lack of resistance the *Grappler* was encountering. They had sighted commercial vessels and warships from dozens of nations on their journey thus far. All had been supremely disinterested.

It was as Babcock had hoped. The *Grappler* was now a commercial fishing boat with a Greek registry. As long as it wasn't fishing in the territorial waters of any of the countries it passed, who cared?

From his small corner near a window, Babcock spotted another vessel far across the unusually calm, sun-dappled waters. It was like an overturned skyscraper floating in a sea of scattered diamonds.

The skipper was peering at the new ship through a set of big binoculars. It seemed to be on a course parallel with that of the Earthpeace ship.

"American." The captain frowned. He lowered the binoculars.

"What is it?" Babcock asked worriedly. Even from that distance, the ship was huge.

"Aircraft carrier," the captain said. "Not many of them left these days."

The interior secretary allowed a flutter of fear to creep into the pit of his stomach.

"Let me see those," he hissed, holding out a hand for the captain's binoculars. Brow furrowing, the sailor handed them over.

They were as heavy as lead. Palms sweating, Babcock trained the glasses on the distant ship.

The binoculars enlarged the carrier to a frightening degree. As he ran the glasses along the ship, it seemed almost close enough to touch.

Sailors peppered the deck, their trousers flapping in the gentle breeze. There was no sense of urgency as far as the interior secretary could detect. No one was even looking in the direction of the *Grappler*.

As he followed the sharp contours of the dull gray hull, Secretary Babcock saw the ship's name. USS *Ronald Reagan*.

"Are you all right, sir?"

The voice rang hollow in his ears. Babcock pulled the binoculars away. The captain was staring at him, a concerned expression on his face.

"What?" Babcock asked, gulping. His heart was thudding like mad.

"That gasp you just made," the captain began, "it sounded— Are you okay?"

"Yes. *Yes,*" Babcock snapped. He stabbed an anxious finger to the aircraft carrier. "Are they onto us?"

The captain shook his head. "They're in no hurry," he replied. "If they hold speed, we should begin to outpace them in the next ten minutes or so."

"So they're on routine maneuvers," Babcock suggested hopefully.

"That would be my guess," the captain nodded.

Babcock exhaled relief, handing back the glasses. "Can you get us away from it any faster?"

"We're practically full out now, but I'll see what we can do." Turning to his men, he began to issue commands.

Bryce Babcock melted into a corner of the bridge until the *Grappler* pulled abreast of the aircraft carrier.

In spite of the intense heat, he'd felt an involuntary shudder the moment he laid eyes on the American warship. It was a bad omen. He hoped he'd feel better once the ship was in their wake. However, the chill remained even as he watched the aircraft carrier begin to fall slowly behind.

Even when they had outdistanced the U.S. Navy

vessel, Bryce Babcock couldn't shake a feeling of intense unease.

A sense of dread weighing on his slight shoulders for the first time in days, the secretary of the interior quietly left the bridge.

Terror hadn't worked.

He wished for all the world it had, but it had not.

Nossur Aruch liked terror. *Lived* for terrorism. In his day, he had found it to be a mighty weapon. A sword that could be brandished from the dead of night against an unsuspecting enemy. An arrow that always struck its target. A bullet fired with unerring accuracy.

Of course, few in the so-called civilized world agreed with Nossur Aruch, leader of the Palestine Independence Organization and director and chairman of the Free Palestine Authority. In the soft capitals of the Western imperialist nations, terrorism was soundly condemned. Practitioners of the art of terror were even hunted down.

They thought it sloppy. A bomb lobbed onto a bus, a grenade tossed into a crowd, a foreign leader shot.

But Aruch knew better. These acts only *seemed* haphazard. Terrorism was a precise game. But, lamentably, the game had been lost. Practically before it got started.

"Timing is everything," Aruch said, sighing wistfully.

"Sir?"

On the vine-enclosed balcony of his Hebron office in Israel's West Bank, Nossur had thought he was alone. He had forgotten about Fatang, the young PIO soldier who was assigned to protect him. If Nossur Aruch's beloved terror campaign had worked, he would not need such a guard.

Aruch smiled sadly as he glanced at the young man.

"I am a man out of time," he said. "The great war of terror could have been fought a century ago. Two would have been even better." There was sadness in his voice. He sighed into the warm evening air. "Do you know why the Americans won their independence from the English, Fatang?"

"I do not, sir," the youthful soldier replied. His olive face was earnest, his eyes burning with the intensity only the very young and very idealistic could muster. That flame had long ago winked out for Nossur Aruch.

"They fought a terrorist campaign. The British soldiers of the time were used to fighting armies that lined up on one side of an open field. Obeying the laws of civility, the British would line up on the other. Once everyone was in place, each side would shoot and shoot until the last man standing was declared the winner."

"That is foolish," Fatang volunteered.

Aruch nodded sagely. "The Americans thought this, as well. That is why when the British formed their skirmish lines, the American colonists did not. They hid in trees and behind rocks. They used guerrilla tactics. They were most uncivilized in the way they fought their war. And because of this, they won their independence."

The soldier seemed surprised. "Is this true?" he asked.

"Oh, there were other factors to be sure—" Aruch waved "—but this contributed to their victory." The PIO leader's face took on a faraway look. "Of course, they did not go far enough. Had I been there to guide them, the Americans could have fought a *real* war of terror. With my knowledge, London would now be the capital of the United States. I could have been a colossus in another era, straddling the globe. But thanks to an accident of birth, I am a man out of time."

A morose expression on his face, Aruch turned away from the much younger man.

The FPA chairman wore the plain olive drab fatigues that had become his sartorial trademark. They were so wrinkled it looked as if he balled them up and stuffed them under his mattress every night.

A deep gray mustache scuttled from beneath his large nose, fading into a scruffy white beard.

His eyes bordered on psychotic. They were so wide they gave the impression of a man who didn't blink. Dark irises floated in circular seas of white.

A black-and-white-checked kaffiyeh adorned his head. To foreign observers, it seemed to get larger with each passing year. This was obviously a false impression. The fact was, Nossur Aruch had been shrinking for much of the past thirty years. By his calculations, if he lived longer than another decade, he would disappear into his black army boots.

Many people thought that he was an uglier, hairier, dumpier version of Beatles drummer Ringo Starr. Not Nossur Aruch, however. When he looked at himself in a mirror, he saw a Palestinian matinee idol. Although, granted, a *depressed* matinee idol.

Lost in thought, Aruch sighed deeply at the growing dusk. His forlorn exhalation of air seemed almost like a recrimination. Knotted hands rubbed the rough concrete of the balcony rail. Tangles of grapevines ensnared the railing. He stared off into the distant twilight.

Less than thirty miles to the north of his secluded balcony sat Jerusalem, a fat target waiting to be struck. Yet it was out of reach.

Actually, that was only true in the metaphorical sense. In point of fact, it was *infinitely* reachable.

Nossur pushed away from the rail.

Fatang stayed at silent attention just outside the French doors that led into the PIO leader's office. He watched as his superior squatted near the edge of the balcony's sturdy inner railing.

In the early nineties, the Nobel committee had awarded the former terrorist its coveted Peace Prize.

To Nossur Aruch, the million-dollar award had been found money. Splurging, he had blown it all on a single special item.

A vast section at the center of the balcony seemed to be overgrown with vines. Aruch grabbed hold of a chunk of what appeared to be branches, tugging them aside. They folded with a plastic-sounding crinkle, exposing a heavy black base hidden beneath.

Aruch pulled back farther, exposing a single white fin.

The young soldier wasn't surprised by what he saw. Often on nights like these, Aruch's trips to his balcony would end in a maudlin moment like this. The ex-terrorist would pine over the road not traveled.

The camouflage netting Aruch peeled back revealed the rocket boosters of a slender missile. Nossur had used the "mad money" granted him by the Nobel Committee to purchase a surplus British long-range Bloodhound Mk2 missile.

It was aimed at the heart of Jerusalem.

Obscured by trees and vines, the balcony was set back in an alcove at the center of the private courtyard. The yard itself was surrounded by a high wall. The missile was well hidden from prying eyes.

Aruch had bought the missile on the black market and had it smuggled into the West Bank piece by piece.

An impotent gesture. For, although Nossur Aruch

loved terrorism almost more than life itself, he would never use his weapon. He had employed terror tactics in his younger life, but he was a diplomat now. And diplomats did not drop bombs on the heads of their enemies. No matter how strong the desire to do so.

Tears welled in the corners of his crinkling eyes as he studied the magnificent lines of his beautiful prize.

It was a giant paperweight. Nothing more.

He drew in a mucousy sniffle as he pulled the camouflage back across the missile's exposed tail section.

As he headed across the balcony to the open French doors, Nossur blew his big nose on the sleeve of his fatigues. A honking, wet bray. By the look of the splotches up and down the arm, it wasn't the first time.

Fatang marched in behind him.

The leader of the Palestine Independence Organization stepped over to his cluttered desk. The weight of the world on his drooping shoulders, he slumped into his chair.

Although the desk was a jumble of half-crumpled papers, Nossur knew where everything was. He spotted an unfamiliar sheet atop the pile the moment his gaze fell upon the desk.

He scooped up the note.

"What is this?" the PIO leader asked.

"It came while you were napping," the soldier

said from his sentry post near the open balcony doors. Sounds from the deepening Hebron night filtered in across the dark yard.

Aruch frowned as he quickly scanned the paper. He groaned before he'd even finished.

"Yahrak Kiddisak man rabba-k," he cursed softly.

"Is something wrong, sir?" Fatang asked.

Aruch glared up at the young man, a sour expression on his face.

"Things could not be better," he spit sarcastically. He crushed the paper in his hand, dropping it to the clutter on his desk. "I am to meet with the American secretary of the interior tomorrow morning."

"The Americans?" the guard asked. He seemed disgusted at the very prospect.

"Not *the* Americans. *An* American. The fool contacted me several weeks ago. He said something about a secret mission that only I would appreciate. The man is irredeemably stupid. He is what is called an environmental activist."

"Ah, I have heard of these." The soldier nodded. "Is it not their desire to have men live in caves like beasts?"

"That is true," Aruch said. "And I am told this Bryce Babcock is one of the worst. In settling their West many years ago, the Americans slaughtered every last wolf in an area known as Yellowstone Park. Babcock actually had wolves flown in from

Canada and set them loose in the preserve. This is a spot where families vacation, mind you, Fatang."

The young soldier was incredulous. "Were the people not outraged?" he asked, stunned.

"Americans are apathetic," Aruch explained with a wave of his hand. "As long as it is not their child that is mauled, they do not care."

Fatang shook his head in disbelief. "Americans will forever remain a mystery to me, sir."

Aruch nodded. "To me, as well. But I must deal with them, for such is the life of a diplomat." As he spoke the contemptuous word, he cast a longing eye beyond the soldier at the shadowy contours of his precious Bloodhound. His eyes grew watery as he studied the tangle of vines painted on the plastic sheet that concealed his balcony missile.

The truth was, he didn't really care what Babcock had to say. The meeting was just another in a long line of pointless summits he had attended since renouncing the use of terror.

"More of the same," he muttered, thinking of the following day's meeting with Bryce Babcock. "The fool mentioned something about ushering in a new era of peace. The Palestinian people are doubtless about to be asked to capitulate once more."

Fatang smirked. "The Americans still believe that Muslim and Jew can live together in harmony."

Aruch tore his eyes away from his beloved missile.

"They can," he said softly. "As long as the Muslim stands above the ground and the Jew lies below it.''

The former terrorist rose to his feet. Shuffling wearily on his black boots, he headed out the office door.

He didn't cast a backward glance at his cherished Nobel missile. The thought that it would never be launched against Jerusalem brought him far too much pain.

20

The plane touched down at the airport that had been constructed on the mile-and-a-half-long sandy isthmus that separated the crown colony of Gibraltar from the Spanish mainland.

The complaints had started the instant the pilot announced that they were being rerouted. They had continued unabated throughout the flight and were still going strong even as the passenger jet taxied to a stop in the shadow of the great limestone mass that was the Rock of Gibraltar.

Before the plane had stopped, Remo and Chiun rose from their seats. They waded through an ankle-deep pile of unopened peanut packets on their way down the aisle. At the front, Remo's flight attendant was just opening the door when they arrived.

"Oh, *now* you're up." She pouted as the ramp was rolled to the side of the plane. "I tried to wake you a bunch of times."

"Peanuts make me sleepy," Remo explained.

The woman's eyes widened. "You said they put you in the mood," she accused angrily.

"Yes." Remo nodded. "The mood for sleeping. But if it's any consolation, I dreamed only of you."

"Fat lot of good that did me," she snapped.

She practically shoved him onto the ramp.

The air outside was cooler than Remo expected.

The airport extended out into the Bay of Gibraltar. A stiff wind blew in across the bay, causing the wisps of hair above the Master of Sinanju's ears to twirl madly around his bald scalp.

"Smitty was gonna call," Remo said as he and Chiun descended the ramp.

"I do not even see a telephone," the old Korean commented. The tarmac was deserted. A few buildings speckled the distance in the direction of the Rock.

"Guess we walk till we find one." Remo shrugged.

They struck off together toward the control tower.

"He could have at least had a car waiting," Remo said as they strolled across the windswept field.

"Add it to the list of insults heaped upon us by our current employer," Chiun replied. "A true monarch would have arranged for proper transportation."

"A while back you were saying you liked working for Smith," Remo said.

"Bite your tongue," Chiun retorted. "I merely said I work for Smith, not some temporary occupant of the Eagle Throne. The madman provides the stability of a paycheck. That is all. In spite of our association with the lunatic Smith, a true king is always preferable to any alternative."

"Not for me, Little Father," Remo said. "I kind of think Smitty's okay."

Chiun struck a bony fist against his own chest. "Go ahead, Remo," he insisted. "Stab the knife farther into your poor, poor father's heart."

Remo was surprised to detect the shadowy flicker of a light undertone. Barely perceptible. He didn't have time to press it.

He'd been aware of the great mechanical cry of a helicopter almost since they'd deplaned. The aircraft was sweeping toward Gibraltar from the harbor. Remo had assumed it was part of some routine British naval operation, until the helicopter slowed to a hover above their heads.

"You order a chopper?" he asked the Master of Sinanju over the roaring wind of the downdraft.

As displaced air swirled around them, the bluish-green Westland Naval Lynx settled on three fat wheels to the tarmac before them. The main rotor didn't stop its chopping whir as the side door slid open.

A British Royal Navy officer stuck his head out. "Gentlemen, I've been sent to collect you!" he shouted.

Remo glanced at the Master of Sinanju. The old Korean's face was blandly curious.

"I don't think so," Remo called back to the RN officer.

The man shook his head firmly. "Your Aunt Mildred sent us," he yelled over the wind.

Remo recognized it as one of Smith's code names.

"He came through after all," Remo commented to Chiun. "This make him a true monarch?"

"Not at all," the Master of Sinanju replied. "And in spite of that, he is *still* head and shoulders above any mere President." Hiking up his kimono skirts, he scurried inside the belly of the Lynx, slapping away the offered hand of the British officer.

Remo climbed in behind him.

The door slid shut. A moment later, the helicopter was pulling up into the sky, screaming a metallic protest.

Nose dipping, it soared away from the airport, flying over the small isthmus and out across the brilliant blue waters of the Mediterranean Sea.

"OUTBREAK OF PEACE." In death, Remo's Earthpeace contact had provided Harold W. Smith with the posthumous clue that had finally revealed the frightening power in the hands of the environmental group.

Smith had ignored the enigmatic phrase for much of the past two days, but with the *Radiant Grappler* located and Remo and Chiun's plane rerouted to intercept it, he had finally found time to investigate its possible meaning.

The time spent researching Earthpeace while the

CIA was locating the missing boat had yielded much information.

Earthpeace had been founded in the late 1960s by a group of Canadian environmentalists whose credo was confrontation. The group was active in its approach, whether it was blocking fishing boats, stopping Eskimos from hunting seals or blowing the whistle on companies for illegal ocean dumping.

It seemed clear to Smith that, as a group, Earthpeace thrived on both confrontation and sympathetic media attention. That sympathy had reached its peak when, in 1985, French agents had sunk the first *Radiant Grappler* in the harbor at Auckland, New Zealand, while it was on its way to protest nuclear testing in French Polynesia.

Earthpeace representatives screamed bloody murder, and as a result of this blessing in disguise, donations to the group had risen along with its public profile. The infusion of cash allowed them the opportunity to hire more high-profile spokesmen. One of these mouthpieces was none other than Bryce Edmund Babcock.

At the time, Babcock was between positions. He had been governor of Arizona for a number of years, but had recently left office to pursue other career opportunities.

Everyone knew that Babcock had an eye on the Oval Office. With his days as governor behind him, it was important for him to find a position that kept him in the public eye. Earthpeace came with its offer at just the right time. The joining together of the two-term governor and the environmental organization had been a perfect fit.

Babcock was a firm believer in the rights of the state over those of the individual. If you had an endangered rat in your cornfield, you plowed somewhere else. If you had a slug living on the basement walls of your waterfront home, you vacated the premises to the invertebrate. If you had a slimy, mosquito-filled puddle in your backyard, it was an untouchable wetland.

The former governor and presidential hopeful relished his Earthpeace power. When he shook an admonishing finger in the Northwest, hundreds of lumberjacks were thrown out of work. When he frowned in New England, generations of fishermen were forced to scuttle their boats along with their livelihoods. Men who tilled the soil or toiled at sea shuddered and swore when they heard his name.

When the 1988 presidential race came along, there was no question that Bryce Babcock would throw his hat in the ring. The two years he'd put in at Earthpeace had been but a stepping-stone to the ultimate position of power to all environmentalists. The presidency of the United States.

Bryce Babcock ran.

Bryce Babcock lost.

His showings in Iowa and New Hampshire had been pathetic. In both contests, he limped in as an also-ran.

The loss was devastating to Babcock, as well as to the rank and file of Earthpeace.

The timing couldn't have been worse for Earthpeace. The group's influence had waned in the years following the sinking of the *Grappler.* The public had begun to view its rolls as a bunch of hemp-worshiping loons. And on top of everything else, the world had maddeningly started to adopt the organization's message.

The whaling industry was dead in most parts of the world. Toxic dumping was nearly extinct. A moratorium on atomic testing was accepted by almost every nation on Earth. The Russians and Americans had even begun to roll back their nuclear stockpiles.

The fact of the matter was, Earthpeace *needed* a sympathizer like Babcock to win the presidency in order to boost its waning celebrity. When he lost, the group lost, too.

It was touch and go for a few years after the former governor's primary loss. Fortunately for Babcock and Earthpeace, all politics were cyclical. The party that had gone on to beat Babcock's in 1988 found itself on the outside looking in in 1992. With his impeccable liberal environmental credentials, Babcock was tapped by the new President to head up the Department of the Interior.

During the two terms of the current President, Babcock made his allegiance to Earthpeace clear in both attitude and policy.

Since Babcock's ties to Earthpeace had remained strong throughout his tenure as a cabinet secretary, Smith had decided to try a more private search. In perusing the interior head's e-mail, the CURE director had found a note from the Treasury secretary, under whose auspices the Secret Service fell. In it was mention of the former President's horseback-riding accident.

A red flag instantly went up for Smith.

The note had been sent before the event had become public knowledge. A follow-up letter from Babcock to the Treasury secretary very casually questioned the whereabouts of the old President, including hospital and room number.

Certain of the link now, Smith had checked the rest of Babcock's outgoing e-mail. Sure enough, the information had been forwarded to the Earthpeace cell in San Francisco.

Babcock *was* involved.

Further checking revealed that the interior secretary had purchased a plane ticket to Panama more than a month before. His arrival time coincided with the passage of the *Radiant Grappler* through the canal.

But surely Babcock could not have known about the ex-President's accident a month before it happened. There had to be yet *another* explanation for his trip.

Smith had uncovered the reason, once more, in Babcock's e-mail.

Dr. Ree Hop Doe. When Smith saw the name, he blinked in shock. The name was infamous in intelligence circles—*should* have been despised throughout the country.

Doe was a naturalized American citizen of Taiwanese birth. A scientist at Los Alamos National Scientific Laboratory, he had been indicted on charges that he had betrayed his adopted country by selling decades' worth of nuclear secrets to the Chinese. Thanks to Doe, the People's Republic of China had leaped a generation ahead in its offensive nuclear capability.

Doe was currently out on bond and awaiting trial. But his legal difficulties had not prevented him from corresponding with the secretary of the interior. And when he saw the topic of their hundreds of e-mail notes, Smith's very marrow froze.

The neutrino bomb.

Three of the most frightening words the CURE director had ever read. Mentioned *dozens* of times by both men.

When first he saw those words, Smith's mind reeled. So shocked was he, his ulcer medications were all but forgotten.

Although he knew of the preliminary research on the beta decay-causing neutrino bomb, the details since then were few and sketchy. Part of the military buildup of the 1980s, it was thought that the project hadn't progressed beyond the drawing board before the cutbacks at the end of that decade put an end to the research. Apparently, this was not the case. And this realization was almost more than Smith could comprehend.

Outbreak of peace.

No. It was impossible. They would have to be insane....

With shaking hands, Smith quickly called up the latest image of the *Radiant Grappler II*. He had taken over and automatically programmed the satellite so the Spacetrack system would continue to track the vessel. At the moment, it was well past Crete. Nearing Cyprus.

An outbreak of peace. In the Middle East.

The neutrino bomb.

And as his heart thudded a concert of fear in his chest, Smith *knew* it to be true. To the very core of his rock-ribbed New England soul.

And if the CURE director's worst fear was realized, Bryce Babcock's scheme would have awesome global ramifications.

FROM THE BRIDGE of the USS *Ronald Reagan*, Admiral Jason Harris watched the British Lynx glide a perfect line of descent for the aircraft carrier's flight deck.

Rotor blades swished with blinding ferocity as the helicopter set down.

Before rubber touched deck, Admiral Harris was already off the bridge and clomping down the steep metal companionway to greet the helicopter. As he climbed to the lower level, he wore a deeply unhappy expression on his ruddy face.

A barrel-chested man in his late sixties, the admiral was a no-nonsense type who didn't cotton to the sort of shenanigans that were going on around his boat today.

The worst thing that could possibly happen in a military man's life had taken place. Admiral Harris was being given orders by civilians. His superior had spilled the beans when he called to inform Harris that a British helicopter out of Gibraltar would be bringing aboard two passengers.

"He claimed to be an Army General," the commander of the Atlantic Fleet had said. This was the admiral to whom the officers of the Second Fleet in the western Atlantic and the Sixth Fleet in the Mediterranean were answerable. "But he sounded like a spook to me."

"CIA?" Admiral Harris had asked, annoyed.

"Probably. But don't quote me on that, Jason. Whoever he is, he's got top security clearance. He arranged the thing with the British before he even contacted me."

"You mean they're *already* on their way?"

"They should be on your radar by now."

Harris checked. They were.

"Do *I* have any say in this?" he snarled.

"Not if you want to keep your command."

Admiral Harris had grown fond of the commanding view from his bridge. He decided to hunker down and take whatever came his way.

On the carrier's flight deck, Harris began to regret his accommodating nature the minute he got a load of the pair who jumped down from the helicopter.

One was a skinny white guy dressed casually in a white T-shirt and Chinos. His pants flapped wildly in the gale-force wind of the chopper's downdraft.

The other passenger looked like a soft breeze should have tossed him into the sea. He was a hundred if he was a day and wore a flaming orange brocade kimono.

The pair of them headed straight for Harris as he approached from the opposite direction across the deck.

Behind them, the Lynx was already rising back into the air. The British officer in the chopper barely had a chance to salute before the door slid shut.

The helicopter was soaring back across the water in the direction of Gibraltar by the time Harris met with the two strangers.

"Welcome aboard, gentlemen." Harris smiled tightly. He stuck out his hand to the arrivals.

The older man lifted his nose and pretended he didn't see the offered hand. When the younger one accepted it, Harris noticed that his wrists were unusually thick, as wide around as fat tomato-sauce cans.

"Mind telling us what the hell we're doing here?" Remo asked.

"Don't *you* know?" Harris said.

"No," Remo admitted, glancing around. "Except we're supposed to be looking for a boat. From what I can tell, this ain't it."

"I'm not sure of any of the specifics," Admiral Harris admitted, "but I was told to inform you that your mission has become more urgent."

"This isn't like Smith." Remo frowned at Chiun.

The Master of Sinanju had turned his attention to Admiral Harris. "On the contrary," the tiny Asian sniffed. He was examining the admiral's uniform as if its occupant were no more than a department-store mannequin. "He has only become more insane with the passage of time. As far as I am concerned, this is in lunatic character."

"Smith?" Admiral Harris asked Remo. "That'd be *General* Smith, I presume?"

"That what he's calling himself today?" Remo asked, uninterested. He nodded up to the bridge. "I'd better call him. This tub have a radio?"

It was a supreme effort for the admiral to not lose his temper at the insulting term. Adding to his agitation was the fact that the old man seemed to have taken an abnormally keen interest in Harris's uniform. The Asian's wrinkled face puckered as he examined the admiral's epaulets.

"I'm sorry, sir. No can do," Harris said through

clenched teeth to the younger man. "I was given very specific instructions not to let you use any equipment that runs any risk whatsoever of being monitored. Once you're on the ground, you may call." His frown lines deepened. "Though that's odd to me. We've got some of the most sophisticated equipment in the world on board this ship. You're far more likely to run the risk of being heard from a public phone."

Remo waved a dismissive hand. "My boss majored in scrambling with a minor in bugging the hell out of me. Where's the nearest phone booth?"

Before the admiral could reply, Chiun interrupted.

"Do not pester the man, Remo," he admonished before turning attention back to the seaman. "What is your station?" Chiun asked pointedly.

"What?" Harris asked.

"What?" Remo asked, as well. "Chiun, we don't have ti—"

"Shush," the Master of Sinanju insisted. "What station do you hold?" he pressed Harris.

The sailor towered over the old man. He looked down at the wizened figure, a strange expression clouding his ruddy face. "I'm an admiral," Harris said, unsure whether to be insulted or confused.

"Ah." Chiun nodded knowingly. "*Amir-al-bahr.*"

Harris's face registered surprise. The old man's Arabic pronunciation was flawless.

"You know about that?" the admiral asked, an unintentional smile cracking his hard veneer.

"Of course," the Master of Sinanju replied. "Who would not?"

"Well, actually...*most* people," Admiral Harris said. "Not many do in this day and age."

Standing between them, Remo frowned. "A mere what?" he asked the Master of Sinanju.

"It means 'prince of the sea,' O ignorant one," Chiun answered with thin impatience. "The leader of the Muslim fleet in these very waters was known by that name eight hundred years ago."

Admiral Harris suddenly found himself warming to his Asian passenger. After all, anyone who knew about *amir-al-bahr* couldn't be all bad. The young one, however, was still a vulgar landlubber. And seemed to go out of his way to prove it.

"Whoop-de-do," Remo said, twirling a finger in the air.

The admiral ignored him.

"Do you know about admirabilis, sir?" he asked Chiun.

Chiun made a displeased cluck. "The Christian corruption for the purer Arabic," he intoned. "And before you ask," he said to Remo, "they brought back the term during one of their silly Crusades, thinking it was analogous to the Latin word for admirable."

"I wasn't gonna ask," said Remo, who had been about to. "And who gives a crap in a hat?"

Harris was finding it easier to ignore the young man. He was positively beaming at Chiun. "Are you a sailor, sir?" he enthused.

The old man took a deep breath of clean Mediterranean air. "In my long life, I have spent much time on the sea." He nodded.

"Complaining every minute," Remo pointed out.

"*You* strike me as the nautical type," Harris said to Chiun, his smile interrupted for the briefest of glares at Remo.

Remo had had enough. "Listen, Captain Crunch, unless you want me to strike *you* as the nautical type, I suggest you get me to a freaking phone."

With great reluctance, Harris turned away from the delightful old man. "Yes, *sir,*" he said icily. "I was told to inform you that your quarry has landed in Lebanon."

"Perfect," Remo groused. "More traveling."

"You need not be concerned," Chiun said. "For we are in the capable hands of Amir-al-bahr." He lowered his head in a slight bow to the Navy man. The wind threw his tufts of hair in crazy directions.

The old seaman smiled warmly. "You flatter me with the title, sir," Admiral Harris said, returning the bow. "But I don't think it's deserved. Why not just call me Jason?"

"Very well, Jason, Prince of the Sea," Chiun replied, a smile cracking his parchment face.

"Where do you stow the barf bags?" Remo asked.

From the back seat of his bulletproof sedan, Nossur Aruch watched the countryside race past in shades of brown.

The sky above Lebanon was a thin pastel blue. The car's tinted windows made it seem much darker. A rich texture of color foreign to much of the sun-bleached Middle East.

The shaded windows—also bulletproof—enabled Aruch to see out while preventing others from seeing in.

It wasn't vanity that put the one-way windows on his car, but *survival.* With so many people thirsting for his blood, the last thing he wanted was for someone to spot him on one of his infrequent trips to the countryside.

Fanatical Jews wanted him dead.

Fanatical Muslims wanted him dead, too, but only after they'd punished him. Knives, stones and boiling oil always topped the lists. Even after they killed him, the indignities would not end. The reformed terrorist didn't even want to *think* about what they'd do to his battered old corpse once he was dead.

Although fear for his life kept him hiding in his West Bank compound, death was the last thing on Nossur Aruch's mind at the moment—unless one counted being *bored* to death.

His driver turned onto the road that would take him to the port of Tyre in Lebanon, twenty miles from the Israeli border. Behind, a truckload of armed guards followed suit.

"I hate this," Nossur muttered.

"Sir?"

It was his driver's voice on the speaker. Aruch had raised the partition between the front and back seats but hadn't shut off the intercom.

Reaching a lazy hand for the control panel, he powered down the smoky privacy partition. Fatang was behind the wheel, a bodyguard seated beside him.

"Are we not there yet?" Aruch complained.

"Ten minutes more, sir," Fatang said.

Aruch leaned an elbow on the handle and braced his chin in one hand as he stared outside. The scruffy white whiskers felt like steel wool against his wrinkled palm.

"He had better be there," Nossur grumbled.

The message from Secretary Babcock had been cryptic. He had mentioned Aruch's conversion to the peace process several times during a number of his rambling telephone calls and insanely long letters. The unhappy decision of the people of Israel to elect a prime minister from the conservative Likud party had soured Babcock on that country's commitment to peace. Even though they had recently corrected that mistake at the ballot box, the notion that they would do so in the first place was something he had found unforgivable. Only Nossur, Babcock had said, would appreciate the gift he was bringing to the Middle East.

Aruch wasn't certain what exactly to expect. But a clandestine mission for Washington likely meant that the current American President was trying yet again to secure a positive place in future history books. Aiding the Mideast peace process would somehow help everyone forget about his numerous personal and political failings.

Thinking of the words that would be written about him by the future histories of a free Palestinian state, Aruch sighed loudly. Whatever gift the interior secretary was bringing, it wouldn't be what Nossur *really* wanted.

As the car drew close to the Mediterranean shore, the houses grew more densely packed. Pedestrians crowded the streets. Many women wore the traditional black robes and veils. The men sported Western-style pants and boots. Shirts were opened to the third button, revealing dark skin.

The sheer number of guns slung over sweaty backs made Aruch all the more thankful that the people couldn't see beyond the closed window of his speeding sedan.

They arrived at the port of Tyre at the appointed time.

The streets gave way to huge docking areas at the rocky coast. Flocks of awkwardly ambling gulls scattered from their speeding path. Fatang guided the car to the proper berth, slowing to a stop beneath the great looming shadow of the *Radiant Grappler II*.

Aruch frowned at the famous Earthpeace vessel. Even as he scanned the deck, Fatang and the other bodyguard hopped out of the car. The armed men from Aruch's personal security detail swarmed in from behind.

With shouts and threats, the soldiers quickly cleared the area of curious onlookers. Running, they returned to the car. When Nossur Aruch stepped out into the warm air, he was surrounded on all sides by a living wall. Guards crushed protectively around his rumpled form. Within the mass of human flesh, Aruch's shoulders slumped.

"Let us get this over with," he grumbled with an impatient lisp.

Amid the thunder of stomping feet, his men hustled the schlumpy PIO leader up the boarding ramp to the deck of the moored ship.

"HE'S HERE!" Bryce Babcock said urgently. "How do I look? Too casual?" He stretched his arms out wide. He'd torn the plastic off his dry-cleaned khaki outfit five minutes before. His dove-fir Earthpeace pin was affixed to his lapel.

"It rook fine," Dr. Ree Hop Doe replied.

Behind his thick, Coke-bottle glasses, Doe continually winced and blinked. The natural light streaming through the bridge windows was blinding. He had stayed belowdecks for the entire trip. Many of the crew had only just seen the Asian scientist for the first time.

"How's the bomb?" Babcock asked. "Is the bomb all right?"

"Bomb issa okay, Mr. Secretary."

"You haven't armed it?"

Doe shook his head. "Not without you terr me."

"Good. Good, good. *Excellent.* How do I look?"

After summoning Doe, Babcock had banished the rest of the crew below. The ragtag Earthpeacers would be a distraction during this momentous meeting.

Babcock peeked anxiously out the side bridge window. The familiar tingle touched his bladder.

Nossur Aruch was just stepping off the gangplank. PIO soldiers quickly secured the deck as the ex-terrorist climbed the steps to the bridge.

When Doe reached for the door, Babcock let out a horrified shriek.

"You're not here to open doors," the interior secretary hissed. "We used you people as slave labor to build the railroads, for Christ's sake. Is it too much to ask for a little less polite and a little more moral-outrage-inspired rudeness?''

When the door handle rattled, Babcock's eyes went wide.

''Chop-chop, Hop Sing,'' he snarled, shoving the Los Alamos scientist aside. The interior secretary flung the door open grandly.

''I bring you peace,'' Bryce Babcock announced.

Nossur Aruch was framed in the doorway, an unshaved troll in rumpled fatigues. He looked like a trick-or-treater whose Halloween costume had gone horribly awry.

''May peace be yours, as well, Mr. Secretary,'' Aruch responded in his lisping, almost feminine voice.

As the men exchanged handshakes, Bryce Babcock's bladder tingled with watery excitement. He shifted his weight.

''I assume, Mr. Secretary, by your message and the manner in which we meet that this is a rendezvous of secret significance?'' Aruch asked Babcock as he and a few of his guards were ushered onto the bridge. The former terrorist took special note of the subservient Ree Hop Doe cowering in the corner.

''Call me Bryce,'' Babcock chirped. ''After all. We are to be partners in peace together.''

Peace, peace, peace. The man was like a broken record.

Nossur had been right. This meeting was all about

the Mideast peace process. Babcock was here at the behest of the American President.

It was an insult to send someone of lower rank than the vice president or the secretary of state to meet with him. In the old days, he might have shot the interior secretary. At the very least, Nossur would have turned right around and marched out the door. But Nossur Aruch was a politician now, and politicians were not allowed to shoot people. And, lamentably, politicians never, *ever* walked out on foreign dignitaries. No matter how lowly their station.

Holding his more violent impulses in check, Nossur smiled politely at Bryce Babcock.

"As you wish," Aruch said, deliberately not using the idiot's name.

For a moment, Babcock just stood there. Grinning.

"I'm sorry, Nossur," he suddenly gushed. "I really am. But I just *can't* wait. I'm like a kid at Christmas. Sorry. Christmas is probably verboten, right? Well, whatever the Muslim gift holiday is? *That's* what I'm like a kid on right now."

As the lunatic babbled, he moved over to a map table. Something large had been placed on it, with a sheet draped over to obscure. Babcock grabbed a corner of the material and gave a yank. The sheet fell away, dropping to the metal floor.

"Ta-dah!" Bryce Babcock chimed. He held both

hands out to one side. A game-show hostess displaying a brand-new washer-dryer set.

The falling sheet revealed a gleaming stainless-steel object. So big around was it, Aruch could have taken it in a bear hug and not touched fingertips on the other side. A small pad with glowing multicolored lights was affixed to its side. A few of the small lights winked hypnotically.

"What is this?" Nossur Aruch asked, a catch of intrigue in his soft voice. Eyes wide and unblinking, he took a hesitant, reverential step toward the device.

"The solution to all the world's ills," Babcock intoned. He beamed through his jowly face.

The former terrorist looked at the interior secretary.

"It is a bomb of some sort?"

"It is *the* bomb," Babcock explained. "The last bomb *ever* needed."

"It is atomic?"

Babcock glanced at Doe. The scientist nodded.

"Ye-es," Babcock replied vaguely. "Technically it does work on the atomic level. But it's far more sophisticated than your garden-variety nuke. You must know that Earthpeace would *never* have anything to do with a *common* nuclear device."

Aruch didn't seem interested in the moral distinctions the environmental organization drew between one bomb and the next. His fascinated gaze was leveled on the bomb before him.

"They are supposed to be available on the black market," the Palestinian commented as he stared at the stainless-steel casing. He reached out a tentative hand. "Former Soviet warheads are alleged to be popping up the world over. I have yet to see one, however. Radioactive junk is all one can get these days. This is the genuine article?"

"No, actually," Babcock admitted, frowning slightly. Aruch seemed a little too interested in the bomb. "As I told you, it's not a typical nuclear device."

"It will level a country?" Aruch asked hopefully.

Babcock retreated a step. The glimmer of cunning in the PIO leader's eyes was unexpected and disturbing.

"Not in a standard way," the interior secretary offered slowly.

"Oh." The former terrorist's shoulders slumped. Hope instantly returned. "A city?" he asked.

"Maybe," Babcock admitted. "Listen, I'm not quite sure I like the way this is going."

"How big a city? Like Tel Aviv? Or Jerusalem? Do you have more than one? Where did you get it? Can you get more?" The questions came out in a flood.

Aruch didn't even wait for an answer to any of them. He wheeled to the men who had followed him onto the *Grappler*'s bridge.

"Load it in the truck," he commanded.

"Now wait just a goldurned minute there, Nossur," Bryce Babcock warned. He slid protectively between Aruch and the bomb. "I don't know what you have in mind, but—"

Without a look at the secretary, Nossur Aruch snapped his fingers. Guns instantly rattled up.

The interior secretary's sagging jowls locked in midprotest. His face registered utter shock.

Silent now, Babcock was shoved roughly aside. Helpless, he watched as two PIO soldiers hefted the prototype neutrino bomb off the console, carting it out into the sunlight.

Babcock cringed when they accidentally banged it on the metal door frame.

"He knows how it works?" Aruch demanded. He aimed a stubby finger at Ree Hop Doe.

When Babcock nodded dully, Dr. Doe's hooded eyes opened wide.

"I onry hera for cash," the scientist pleaded. "Rawyer costa much money. Appear process taka rong time. China no foot birr anymore." He wheeled on Babcock. "Terr him I no wanna be stuck with clummy Mexican marr rawyer!"

Aruch ignored the man's pleading eyes. Fatang stood near the door. Turning to the soldier, Aruch pointed at Doe.

"Bring him," the PIO leader commanded.

The guard directed two men to drag the whimpering scientist outside.

"What of this one?" Fatang asked, indicating Bryce Babcock with a jerk of his automatic rifle.

Sudden, intense fear gripped the secretary. Babcock's bladder reached critical mass. The warm release flooded down his legs and into his leather boots.

"He may yet be of use," Aruch admitted with some reluctance. "Bring him, as well."

There was no time for relief. Fatang grabbed the stunned Babcock by the arm, shoving him outside.

A military urgency seized the *Radiant Grappler*. Aruch quickly deployed his men around the ship, instructing them to look for other bombs. The first was loaded by soldiers onto Aruch's canvas-covered truck on the dock far below.

"There *aren't* any more," Babcock pleaded as PIO soldiers swarmed down into the bowels of the Earthpeace ship.

"We will see," Aruch said, big nostrils flaring.

A muffled popping sound was audible beneath their feet. Gunshots.

Babcock and Doe exchanged sick glances.

Standing in the warmth of the soft Mediterranean breeze, the pops seemed to go on forever. One for each Earthpeace crew member.

At first, Babcock's trousers clung wetly to his inner thighs. By the time the PIO soldiers returned to the deck, the same white sun that had browned the skin of pharaoh and bedouin for thousands of years had begun to dry the damp material to salty stiffness.

The soldiers cried ululations of triumph. Above their heads, they carried a lumpy bundle. Running, panting, they dumped their prize at the feet of Nossur Aruch.

The PIO leader raised an unhappy eyebrow beneath the great peak of his checkered kaffiyeh.

It was a man. He was lying on his side, his face turned away from Aruch. It was unclear if he was dead or alive.

"What is this?" Aruch scowled, nudging the body with the toe of his black boot. The man plopped over onto his back.

When the face became clear, Nossur Aruch's eyes sprang wide. His mouth formed a shocked O.

"It cannot be," he breathed. Arms flailing, he whirled on Bryce Babcock. "It cannot be!" he sang, delighted now.

Babcock shrank from the grubby, ecstatic little man.

"I thought it'd be poetic." The interior secretary shrugged, afraid. "He was always a warmonger."

The PIO leader's wild eyes flew to the slumbering form of the elderly former United States President.

He was the devil. A saber-rattler who had set back the cause of terror a generation. At least. A man whose time in office had put people like Nossur Aruch virtually out of business. To finally have this hated creature. *Here.*

It was a dream come true.

Joy bloomed like a desert flower on Nossur Aruch's face.

"He lives?" Aruch hissed.

"Pumped full of tranquilizers," Babcock admitted. "But, yes, he's alive."

"Take him," the terrorist ordered Fatang with growling delight.

As the ex-President was hoisted into the air, Babcock's eyes took on a look of wild helplessness.

"You want him? You can have him. He's yours. No fuss, no muss. Signed, sealed and delivered. Bomb, too. Hell, I'll even throw in the Chink, no charge." He stabbed a shaking finger at Ree Hop Doe. "Just let me go."

Nossur Aruch turned slowly to Bryce Babcock. The Arab was a crushed beer can in wrinkled khaki. A demonic smile split his stubbly face.

"Do you not wish to see the peace you have brought?" he asked with soft menace.

"Me? Nah. Not really," Babcock dismissed. "I really should get back to America. The department's got this new program where we're gonna be releasing grizzlies into Central Park. I really should be there to head off the protests. But, hey, don't let me stop you."

He spun. A rifle barrel was aimed at his face. He turned back to Aruch.

"*Or* I could go with you. See how this plays out." He nodded agreeably. "You know. Whichever."

Aruch ignored Babcock's panicked rambling. With a crisp nod, he turned away. PIO soldiers shoved Bryce Babcock and Ree Hop Doe forward.

With Nossur Aruch leading the way, the entire group hustled down the long gangplank of the *Radiant Grappler*.

Admiral Harris saw to it that the USS *Ronald Reagan* brought them as close to the maritime boundary of Lebanon as possible.

Concerned for Chiun's safety, the Navy man offered to have them taken ashore under cover of darkness. It was Remo who refused the assistance. He had the carrier's crew throw the smallest inflatable life raft they could find into the gently chopping waters.

Chiun climbed down onto the reinforced rubber seat in the front of the boat. Remo took to the rear with a paddle.

On the way to shore, they managed to avoid all boat traffic. Remo beached the raft in the rocks north of Tyre. Once they were on land, he grabbed the raft by its slippery rubber skin and tore it apart at the seams. It quickly became a flat yellow stain, washing back out to sea.

The two Masters of Sinanju scurried up the rocks. A sun-bleached road ran parallel to the shore. Side by side, they began the long trek down to the port city of Tyre. The sun beat hot on their faces.

''I know what you were doing back there,'' Remo commented as they walked along the empty roadway.

The Master of Sinanju was taking in their surroundings. ''Isn't it a lovely day?'' he said, ignoring Remo.

''Don't change the subject. I finally figured out what that act was you were playing with your pal, the prince of the sea. *And* why you've been doing the nice-nice thing so much lately.''

''Act?'' Chiun queried, all innocence. ''Do not presume you know everything about me, Remo. I have had a love of the sea ever since my childhood in Sinanju. I was merely engaging in polite conversation with a fellow maritime enthusiast.''

''Baloney,'' Remo said. ''You were cozying up to him just to bug me.''

''What?'' Chiun frowned.

''Don't deny it,'' Remo cautioned. ''I know what the last few days have been all about. You're trying to piss me off. This Abu ben Bubbie bullshit is just the latest installment.''

''You are babbling nonsense,'' Chiun said. ''I have always had an abiding love for the sea. It is the pool from which all life sprang.''

''Aha! Aha!'' Remo exclaimed triumphantly. ''You don't believe *that,* either. Koreans think man was crapped out by some big hairy bear.''

''Trust you to reduce the miracle of human creation to an excretory function,'' Chiun said blandly. ''*And* get it wrong.''

''Don't change the subject,'' Remo countered. ''You're being deliberately weird just to annoy me. And I know why. Even though you're claiming you're not, you're ripped at this whole Mr. Chin thing. But everyone you want to go after in Hollywood is already dead, so you're doing the next best thing. You're trying to bug *me* with all this nice and agreeable malarkey. You wanna put me on edge by making me think that every minute you might explode. Well, it's not gonna work, so you might as well cut it out. You're not bothering me one bit.'' He clenched his jaw accusingly.

''I do not know which I would prefer this to be a product of,'' Chiun said, shaking his head, ''dementia or stupidity.''

''Har-de-har-har. And don't even bother. I'm on to you,'' Remo announced. He outpaced the Master of Sinanju, marching with angry determination up the road.

Behind him, a barely perceptible smile crinkled the cobweb vellum corners of the old Korean's mouth. The smile remained fixed to his face the rest of the long walk to Tyre.

WHEN THEY GOT to town, Remo decided to find the Earthpeace ship before making his call to Smith.

According to the histories of Sinanju, Alexander the Great conquered the ancient city of Tyre by constructing a causeway that extended the mainland to the island on which the city was built. Once they had reached what had once been ancient shore, Remo and Chiun crossed the causeway and found their way to the docks.

It didn't take long to locate the *Radiant Grappler II*.

The Earthpeace vessel was berthed alongside a flat expanse of concrete. Its huge steel hull loomed high above them. The shadow cast by the *Grappler* was enormous, stretching across dozens of smaller ships docked nearby.

A single stenciled word on the prow of the ship identified her as the *Mykonos.*

"If they were trying to disguise it, they should've picked up a couple hundred crates of Renuzit," Remo commented. "The crate stinks like a floating bong."

They took the long gangplank up to the deck.

"Blood," Chiun said, the instant his sandals touched metal plating.

Remo was already sniffing the air like a dog on a scent. "This way," he announced.

Taking the lead, Remo stepped across the deck. The two men slipped through an open door that led into a narrow passageway.

The air conditioning was off. In the merciless Lebanon sun, it hadn't taken long for the interior of the boat to become oppressively hot. The warm-blood scent grew stronger the deeper they traveled inside the ship. A spiral staircase at the end of one hall led down another level. Both Masters of Sinanju climbed down to the lower deck.

The blood stench was thick here, intermixed with the stale sweat of old fear.

"It is coming from the hold," Chiun commented gravely.

Remo nodded, his face etched in lines of deep concern.

During their journey through the *Grappler's* bowels, neither man had sensed even a single, faint human life sign.

After a few labyrinthine turns in the corridors, a final straight passageway brought them to the hold. They spied the bodies from the catwalk.

The Earthpeace crew had been shot. Coagulating blood—a blackish-purple after so many hours—clung to tie-dyed clothes and torn jeans. The human corpses had been dumped onto a pathetically small pile of rotting tuna.

Adding a surreal edge to the grisly tableau, a few of the Earthpeacers had apparently surrendered their hammocks to the largest tuna. The fish swayed ever-so-gently in their final resting places, pennies over their dead eyes.

Remo ignored the bizarre scene. His worried eyes had alighted on the steel zoo cage in the center of the hold.

They took a ladder to the floor.

The stench was powerful. They picked their way

past Earthpeace corpses and rotting fish to the solid-metal cage. When he nudged the door open, Remo wasn't sure if he should be relieved or even more concerned.

The cage was empty. Just a few handfuls of hay tossed on the rusting floor.

"Looks like someone else has him," Remo commented, looking up from the empty cage.

Chiun didn't respond. Bent at the waist, he was examining the cage door. Remo was about to ask him what he was looking at when he was distracted by a sound behind them.

A cough. Wet and feeble.

Turning from both Chiun and the cage, he trained his senses on the field of Earthpeace dead, quickly isolating a single, thready heartbeat. Hurrying over, Remo found one of the men near the base of the tuna pile still clinging to life.

Lying in Remo's shadow, Bright Sunshiny Ralph's lip twitched. His eyes fluttered beneath ashen lids. Blood gurgled from a sticky wound in his abdomen.

Remo stooped next to the dying Earthpeacer.

"Who did this?" Remo pressed.

Sunshiny's eyes rolled open. They were distant, unfocused.

"Murderers," he gasped. Fresh pain made him wince.

"I gathered," Remo said, with arid urgency. "Who? Who's the murderer?"

Sunshiny sniffed blood. *"Us,"* he wheezed. "All these fish. Our ocean brothers. We murdered them in cold blood." His eyes grew teary. "And even worse, I participated in dolphinicide. *I* killed *Flipper,"* he wailed.

His life signs were ebbing.

"Who shot you?" Remo insisted.

"Oh. Nossur Aruch," Sunshiny wheezed. "His PIO soldiers." He was fading fast. A final thought seemed to come to him. "Are there dolphins in heaven?" he asked.

Remo nodded tightly. "Three meals a day," he replied.

Sunshiny Ralph carried the look of horror that blossomed on his face over to the afterlife.

Remo left the body, returning to Chiun's side.

"Looks like Nossur Aruch's our party crasher," Remo commented to the Master of Sinanju.

"I heard," Chiun replied. He had completed his examination of the cage. His wrinkled face was gathered into a frowning mass.

Remo knew the old man's expression could bode no good.

"Okay, what's the latest bad news?" he asked.

"The man imprisoned in this cage has been attempting to escape." He extended a long nail to the side of the door near Remo.

Following Chiun's finger, Remo felt his stomach clench. There were fresh silvery scratch marks all around the lock. Someone had been trying to pick it. The heavy hinges bore similar marks, as if the prisoner had tried to pry the fused bolt. Dumbfounded, Remo stared at the scratches.

"They cracked him over the *head,*" he insisted. "*And* doped him up."

"He is stronger than his enemies suspected," the Master of Sinanju replied gravely. "He has recovered."

As Remo stared at the empty cage, a creeping realization slowly replaced the numbness of discovery.

The kidnapped President had been taken hostage by yet another group, this one more radical than the first. And the veil of safety afforded them by unconsciousness had been lifted. When he spoke, Remo's voice echoed hollow off the faraway walls.

"I better make that call to Smith."

The former President of the United States had to admit it. The past couple days had sure been a mixed blessing. That was perhaps too genial a thought for a man who was bouncing in the back of a terrorist truck along some pothole-filled Lebanese road.

They'd dropped him to the floor, which was coated with a thin film of desert sand. Something cool and metallic pressed against his right cheek.

All around was joyful shouting.

The President was a prize. A spoil of war. Something to be waved over their heads like a captured flag.

As the whoops of joy fill the old President's ears, there came another, displeased shout. A sharp burst of angry Arabic. Afterward, the men grew silent.

The President was grateful to whoever had admonished the jubilant soldiers. Their screaming could get on a fella's nerves.

The truck continued to bounce along the road.

A turn? Were they heading up another street?

It didn't really matter. While the President knew the country he was in, even before the onset of Alzheimer's he'd been fuzzy on the geography of the country's interior.

Opening his eyes a sliver, he could just make out a pair of boots. Beyond them, the gaps in a dark burlap flap revealed a sun-drenched yet barren desert landscape.

Careful not to move his head, he strained to see with his peripheral vision.

The object that pressed against his face was silver. A stainless-steel casing as smooth as glass. The coolness was dissipating in the transfer of heat from his flesh.

He knew what the object was.

Thinking he was still unconscious, his Earthpeace captors had talked freely about it during his captivity aboard the *Radiant Grappler*.

The neutrino bomb.

The former President's administration had pressured Congress into funding preliminary research into the device. After he was out of office, his immediate successor had caved in to the unilateral-disarmament contingent on Capitol Hill and defunded the project.

As far as the President could remember, the work had proceeded only to the early-prototype stage. If memory served, he was cheek to cheek with the only weapon of its kind in existence. And it was now in the hands of the PIO.

The President knew that he was frail. During his long, murky twilight, therapists had made certain that he was kept as physically fit as his condition allowed. He was in exceptional shape for a man of almost nine decades, but the years had clearly taken their toll.

Obviously, he couldn't possibly hope to fight the whole gosh-darned PIO all by himself. But he also knew that he couldn't sit idly by and allow a fellow like Nossur Aruch to control one of the most dangerous pieces of military hardware ever developed.

Jostled on the floor of a PIO truck smack in the middle of a bunch of hostile black hats, the President made a decision.

When life deals you a lemon, well, make yourself some lemonade.

If push came to shove, in spite of his failing body, the ex-President would do what he'd always done. He would act. Whether it meant his own death or not.

After all, he had died in his mind years ago. If he tried now and failed, alone and forgotten in the dusty wastelands of arid Lebanon, his body would finally catch up.

''Oh, and add this to the crappy-news pile. He's awake now.''

The shocks were coming so rapidly Smith was no longer even trying to keep up.

''Are you certain?''

''At least he was when Earthpeace had him. The PIO could have clouted him again when they picked him up.''

Smith pushed his rimless glasses up off his nose. ''The PIO,'' he said, rubbing his eyes wearily. ''So they have taken possession of the device, as well.''

''Device?'' Remo asked. ''What device? And what's with me not being able to call you with Navy equipment? You've got me phoning from some dump of a restaurant in Tyre.''

An offended shout from the background indicated that the restaurant's proprietor spoke at least some English.

Smith took a deep, steadying breath. ''This has gone far beyond your original assignment. From what I have learned, Earthpeace has transported a neutrino bomb to the Mideast.''

Remo hesitated before speaking. ''I hope this is a bad connection, Smitty,'' he said evenly. ''Did you just say Big-Nose Aruch has a neutron bomb?''

''No, *neutrino*. A neutron bomb is a small battlefield or tactical hydrogen bomb. We encountered one once before. Remember the incident outside of Palm Springs?''

''How could I forget?'' Remo asked bitterly.

Smith heard the sound of distant glass breaking. A muffled shout in a foreign tongue.

"*I* possess the darkest memories of that time," Chiun's squeaky voice protested.

"Okay, so you do," Remo called back, peeved. "Did you have to throw my rice on the floor?"

"It slipped."

Smith forged ahead. "With a bomb of the type we encountered before," he persisted, "man is susceptible to neutron irradiation due to the abundance of hydrogen in the human body. Neutrons are able to travel great distances through matter until they are stopped by collision with these light atoms."

"You're losing me, Smitty," Remo warned. "A neutron bomb kills people, leaves buildings. What's the difference between it and this other cockamamy thing?"

"They are basically the same in design. However, the neutrino bomb, when detonated, is the inverse of the neutron bomb. The type of radiation released attacks a more specific type of heavy atom. It is harmless to light atoms."

"So people are safe?" Remo asked slowly.

"Essentially," Smith agreed.

Remo exhaled relief. "Dammit, Smitty, you had me worried."

"And rightly so," Smith said ominously. "One neutrino bomb could trigger events that might destroy the entire Middle East. Although the initial explosion is small, the aftereffects are the real danger.'' He closed his eyes as he explained. ''The bomb acts on the atomic level. It has a plutonium charge triggered by a standard chemical explosive.''

''Atomic. So it's radioactive,'' Remo said.

In his shadow-drenched office, Smith nodded. ''Yes. But it is only lethal within the blast zone. The fallout beyond that limited area is within normal tolerance levels. When the bomb is detonated, it releases a charge of magnetizing ions in a widening ring around ground zero. I have seen only theoretical models, but they indicate this zone could be vast enough to encompass many miles. Light atoms, and thus humans, will be safe. But the magnetizing ions will render metal-based mechanical objects as useless as slag.''

Remo had been listening with growing interest. ''It melts metal?'' he asked once Smith was through.

''Only literally in some cases. It depends upon the density of the atoms. But the practical upshot is the same.''

''*All* metal?''

''Yes,'' Smith said, nodding. ''Everything metallic within the enhanced radiation field would cease to function. This would include all industrial, residential and governmental devices. As well as military.''

''The peace bomb,'' Remo intoned softly.

''What did you say?'' Smith asked, surprised.

''It's what one of the Earthpeacers back in San

Francisco said,'' Remo explained. ''It just sounded like more goofball-fueled mumbo jumbo to me.''

''Not in this case,'' Smith said. ''I have learned that as a public-relations matter, the neutrino bomb was to be dubbed the 'peace bomb.' The name was thought to be more palatable for public consumption. Since the project was defunded years ago, the name is not known outside of Los Alamos.''

''Los Alamos?'' Remo demanded. ''They're the ones responsible for this?''

''The neutrino-bomb prototype was stolen from that facility,'' Smith admitted.

''Figures,'' Remo snarled. ''Somebody wheel it out past a guard while he was watching the head of the Energy Department on TV claiming that nothing was ever stolen from there?''

Smith's voice was deadly serious. ''The weapon was apparently taken from Los Alamos by none other than Dr. Ree Hop Doe during the phase when he was conducting espionage for the Chinese. According to his e-mail records, although he at one time attempted to sell it to China, they were unable to meet his demands. Apparently, he had forgotten it in his garage for the bulk of the past few years. He discovered it when he was searching for items to offer at a yard sale to raise cash for his legal defense.''

Remo was amazed. ''What, did he run a for-sale ad in the *Penny Saver?*''

''It did not get that far. Dr. Doe has been a member of Earthpeace for years. When he offered to sell the bomb to them, word reached Interior Secretary Bryce Babcock. He is the one who negotiated the purchase with Earthpeace funds."

"Another screwball cabinet secretary," Remo said. "Doesn't surprise me with that bunch. Isn't Babcock the guy who had his department release piranha into Lake Michigan a couple years back?"

"That is he," Smith said. "According to my information, both Babcock and Doe couriered the bomb to your location."

"I look forward to catching up with them," Remo said, a cold edge to his tone.

"That can wait," Smith insisted. "Your first priority is to find Nossur Aruch before he is able to detonate the bomb. If he succeeds in doing so, every last weapon in the region could be rendered inoperative."

"Hmm," Remo mused. "Imagine the Mideast without weapons."

"Yes," Smith replied gravely. "It would be a disaster of incalculable proportions."

Remo sounded surprised. "Are you kidding?" he asked. "People over here *live* to beat the snot out of each other. Maybe if they can't shoot at, blow up or launch missiles at each other, they'll finally have to sit down and figure out how to get along."

Smith shook his head. "I see the situation much differently," he said, his tone serious. "I envision chaos on a colossal scale. Remember, Remo, there will be no radio contact with the outside world. Telephone and any other communications devices will also be rendered inoperative. Isolated from their neighbors in the region, suspicions will ignite. Everyone will blame everyone else for what has happened. Clan fighting will erupt. There will be looting and rioting. Fires will be unstoppable due to lack of working equipment. Armies and police forces will be helpless to stop the anarchy. It is a nightmare scenario. If Aruch has gotten hold of the neutrino bomb, it is imperative that you retrieve it from him before he is allowed to set it off.''

''Fine,'' Remo said. ''I'll pick it up when I get the President. But I don't necessarily agree with all your doom and glooming.''

''About the former President,'' the CURE director said crisply. ''The neutrino bomb is now your dominant concern. If it comes to it, the President cannot be allowed to become a distraction.''

There was a familiar flatness to his voice. Smith had used that tone every time he had sent Remo on an assignment against a potential CURE security risk. To a man, they had all wound up dead.

Remo's voice took on a cautious edge. ''I don't like the sound of this, Smitty,'' he warned slowly.

''Nor do I,'' Smith replied levelly. ''But if it is detonated by Aruch in a strategically sensitive location, the neutrino bomb could destabilize that entire region of the world. The former President was already a liability before the bomb was added to the mix. If he becomes any kind of distraction at all, remove the distraction."

"Whoa, Smitty," Remo protested quickly. "Do you even *hear* what you're *saying?* You're asking me to kill a United States President."

From out the echoey depths of the Lebanese restaurant, Smith heard a whoop of sudden joy. The sound of breaking dishes and the crash of an upended table were followed by the rattle of an extension being lifted.

"How I have longed for this day, Emperor Smith," the Master of Sinanju sang jubilantly. "We will return to America in haste to dispatch the corpulent pretender to the throne. Once his deceitful head has been separated from his bloated body, the two of us will sit down and plan your coronation."

"Hang up, Chiun," Remo demanded, annoyed.

The Master of Sinanju ignored his pupil. "The patience you have displayed is remarkable, Emperor. In fact, I may now admit there were times when Remo and I had my doubts about your sanity. *Mostly* Remo," he said quickly. "But you have proved yourself a cunning and stoical man. Now, there are several options for assassination available. If you wish it to appear an accident, that can easily be arranged. A heart attack while jogging would be accepted by all. Especially with that flabby specimen. I, however, would recommend something loud and fun. Something that the public would enjoy. Something that says, 'I am me. Smith the Persistent.' A televised beheading would do the trick nicely. Prime time, of course."

"We are not talking about the current President, Master Chiun," Smith explained with weary patience.

The old Korean's voice sank in confusion. "Who, then?"

"It's the guy we're already looking for he wants us to ice," Remo supplied. "And I won't do it, Smitty."

"I agree with Remo, Emperor Smith," Chiun insisted. "If you wish to assassinate a President, why not the distended lummox who currently squats atop the Eagle Throne?"

"Chiun, please—" Smith began.

"If you feel we need first practice on past rulers, you may rest your regal mind. Our skills are as sharp as ever they were. Years of toiling on your behalf in the farthermost reaches of your kingdom have not diminished our abilities in the least. Our eyes are keen, our hands swift and deadly. We are fleet of foot and sharp of mind. Sinanju waits to aid your ascendancy to the seat of power of the new Rome, the Eagle Throne, O Smith the Patient."

"Will you hang up the freaking phone!" Remo shouted into the recesses of the restaurant.

"Think decapitation," Chiun intoned craftily. "We will talk later."

With that, he was gone.

"I'm not doing it, Smitty," Remo said once they

were alone on the line. "I might not know much about politics, but I know who I'd like to bump off. And this guy wouldn't be my first, second or *hundredth* choice."

"Remo, be reasonable," Smith pleaded. "You know that he represents a liability to begin with. The presence of the neutrino bomb makes the situation even more dire. If he knew what was at stake, the President would agree with me."

"I am not killing a United States President, Smith, and that's that."

"Of course he is not," Chiun called. He was nearer now, listening in on every word of their conversation. "That honor must go to the Reigning Master, not his apprentice. Sinanju has not assassinated an American President for two centuries. We cannot allow Mr. Bent Elbow to taint such a momentous event."

"Will you calm down?" Remo said hotly to Chiun. To Smith, he said, "I'll call when this is all over, Smitty."

"People love a good disemboweling! Always give the people what they want!" the Master of Sinanju could be heard shouting as Remo hung up the phone.

Smith's face didn't even register a single twitch as he leaned across the black surface of his desk. His features could have been carved from solid granite.

The blue phone made a plasticky clatter in its cradle.

The crisis was huge. On several different levels and on multiple fronts. All out of his hands. All he could do now was wait.

Shifting his feet from beneath his desk well, Smith spun his creaking chair to face the big picture window at the rear of his office. Breathing deeply, he stared at the gently lapping waves of Long Island Sound.

Besieged by the soothing image, the CURE director was overcome by exhaustion before he even realized it. Within minutes, Harold Smith was sound asleep.

"Khaddafi wouldn't treat me like this."

Bryce Babcock jutted his chin defiantly. His jowls flapped back against his neck like empty saddlebags.

"That is true. He would have cut out your tongue by this time," Nossur Aruch replied blandly. He was inspecting the exterior of the neutrino bomb.

Babcock and Dr. Ree Hop Doe had been brought to the PIO leader's Lebanon satellite office. As a sign of disdain, their captors hadn't even bothered to bind their hands. A pair of PIO soldiers stood sentry by the door.

The interior secretary stood to one side, helpless, as the PIO leader tapped at the stainless-steel shell of the bomb. A hollow sound greeted Nossur's finger.

"Hussein," Babcock challenged. "What about *him?* I'll bet *he* would have known what to do with me."

"Yes. He would have shot you."

"Khatami, then. Iran would have helped me."

"An American cabinet member? They would

have tortured you on videotape and mailed it to your State Department."

"Mujahideen."

"Bullets are at a premium in Afghanistan. They would probably have simply slit your throat. And you are going far afield with them, are you not?"

"The Middle East is the best place to set off the neutrino bomb," Babcock said, pouting. "A bunch of warring countries bunched closely together. I would have set it off in the United States, but the damage would have been too localized. The whole country wouldn't have been within range. I needed someplace that would feel the effects. Someplace that would be attention-getting."

From his half crouch, Aruch looked up.

"Oh, it will draw attention," he assured Babcock.

The interior secretary glanced angrily at Dr. Doe as if this turn of events were all his fault.

"Don't rook at me," Doe whispered. "I onry in it fora cash."

Babcock turned away in disgust.

His eyes—now those of a prisoner—dragged across the unconscious form of the former President. Soldiers had dumped him on the floor behind Aruch's desk.

The old man's chest rose and fell rhythmically.

The fact that he was still breathing made Bryce Babcock sick. *He* was to blame for all this. Him and his homespun warmongering. Of course, there hadn't actually been any wars, technically, for the eight years he'd been in office. But he *had* been responsible for building the bomb Doe had stolen. When it came right down to it, none of this was Bryce Babcock's fault. It was the former President who had delivered Babcock into the deceitful, violent hands of the PIO. Angry, he tore his baggy eyes away from the hated old man.

The dirty windows through which the desert sunlight spilled were built of a heavy Plexiglas. Even so, they seemed to have suffered damage fitting to a war zone. Chips and holes from bullets and ricochets riddled the thick panes.

Babcock noted that the walls opposite the windows were speckled with holes, as well. Some were so deep he could see straight through to the next room.

As he was peering through one of the larger holes, a sudden squeal of tires from the street out front caught his attention. Inside, Nossur Aruch and his men reacted instinctively to the sound. Eyes angry, they flung themselves to the floor, plastering hands over heads.

When Babcock glanced at Doe, the confused scientist was joining them. With perplexed reluctance, Babcock started to get down, too. He had just knelt to one knee when the first hail of bullets exploded through the wall.

Babcock and Doe collapsed to their bellies.

The attack was fast and furious. In a single, terrifying instant, a swarm of bullets ripped the office air. Screaming lead pocked walls and desk. Concrete dust and paperwork rained down upon them.

On the floor, a terrified Bryce Babcock felt a small puddle of warmth pool at his crotch.

When the shooting stopped as abruptly as it had started, Babcock didn't even notice. The furious shriek of gunfire still echoed in his ears.

Outside, more tires squealed, then faded in the distance.

Nossur Aruch scampered to his feet.

"Lousy teenagers!" he yelled. Bounding across the floor, he stuck his head out the window. "Why are you not in school!" he shouted after the rapidly speeding car.

He had to duck back inside to avoid another spray of automatic-weapons fire.

Muttering Arab curses, he stepped over the prone secretary of the interior and returned to the neutrino bomb.

Climbing unsteadily to his knees, Babcock blinked dust from his eyes. "What was *that?*" he panted. Concrete powder formed a clumpy paste near his damp zipper.

"That?" the terrorist said dismissively, as if nothing had happened. "My poor building suffers for the peace I have made with Israel. Or perhaps it is the Internet or music lyrics that causes them to act out. With kids, who knows?"

Expression dull, Babcock looked at the front wall.

Many more holes now marred its surfaces. One

of the windows had nearly been blown from its casing. It seemed ready to topple into the room.

He turned woodenly back to Aruch.

"May I go now?" Babcock asked numbly.

"Quiet," the terrorist snapped. He looked to the Los Alamos scientist. "*You.* Explain to me how this device works. Is it nuclear?"

Ree Hop Doe glanced quickly at Bryce Babcock. Gulping audibly, he turned back to Nossur Aruch.

"You pay, we talk," he said, licking his lips. "Money order or cash. No personar check, prease."

Very nearby, he heard the click of a bolt.

Out of the corner of his eye, Doe saw the hollow end of a rifle barrel aimed at his temple. Far down at the other end of the weapon was Fatang's eager young face.

The hope that he'd be able to hire even halfway decent legal representation for his espionage trial evaporated for the treasonous Dr. Ree Hop Doe.

"Yes, it nucrear," he admitted, shoulders slumping.

"This one said that it could blow up a city," Aruch said, nodding to Babcock. "Could it destroy Tel Aviv?"

Doe shook his head. "Inner brast zone onry extend about two mires," the scientist answered.

Aruch's stubbly face grew fierce. "Bah! Not good enough," he snapped. "What of the fallout?"

"That be much greater," Doe replied. "Test moder not clear, but incrusive range of two hundred mire possibre. Maybe more. From here could go far as Turkey and Saudi Arabia. Definitery Iraq and Syria."

"It would kill people that far away?" Aruch asked.

"No, no, no," Doe insisted. "For human to die, they need be in brast zone. But moder show bomb *could* break down the quadruple bond between adjacent atoms in transition metal compound far away as Pakistan." Sweating, he smiled hopefully.

Doe had obviously lost Nossur Aruch somewhere during his explanation. The PIO leader turned to Babcock.

"What is this nonsense?" he demanded.

"That's the whole point of the neutrino bomb," the interior secretary explained. There was pleading in his eyes. "It was built to render metal inoperative, not kill people. It's a weapon of peace."

Aruch shook his head. "There is no such thing," he spit. "A weapon has but a single purpose."

"Not this one," Babcock argued.

Aruch caressed the stainless-steel bomb casing with one stubby hand. "We will see," he said cryptically. "You will arm it. *Now,*" he commanded Doe.

This time, there was no talk of bank checks. Dr. Doe stepped obediently over to the bomb. The PIO leader watched in distrust as the scientist popped the side panel. A row of user-friendly buttons and an LED panel were visible beneath.

It took less time than programming a VCR. Once the bomb was armed, Doe glanced at Aruch.

"What time I set for?" he asked.

Aruch's eyes danced. "How far is the border to Israel?" he shouted over his shoulder to his waiting soldiers.

"Thirty minutes by land," Fatang replied sharply.

"Set it for one hour," Aruch ordered.

Doe did as he was told. The time now entered, he clicked the steel panel shut. A red digital timer counted down the time to detonation—59:47...59:46...59:45...

As the seconds ticked down, a thin trickle of drool appeared at Nossur Aruch's lip. Delighted eyes flashed to the two men who had brought him his prize.

"Who knows how to disarm it?" the terrorist asked.

"Onry me," Dr. Ree Hop Doe answered.

Both Babcock and Doe were shocked by the ensuing gunshot. Only when Dr. Doe fell away—hands clutching at the crimson stain that was already seeping across his white shirt-front—did Babcock see the gun in Aruch's hand.

As Doe dropped, gulping, to the floor, the terrorist slipped the weapon back into his black leather hip holster.

"Put it in the truck," Aruch commanded.

Fatang and another soldier strode forward and

collected the neutrino bomb. Stepping over Doe's lifeless body, they carted the bomb out the door.

"Come," the terrorist said to the still stunned Bryce Babcock. "Let us usher in peace together." He extended a hand to the open door.

Babcock took an uncertain step. "What about him?" he asked, nodding dumbly to the sleeping President.

When Aruch glanced at the former chief executive, a wicked smile split his prickly stubble. "We will save that one for later. Some of the men you mentioned earlier would pay a handsome price for him, don't you think?"

Cackling, Nossur Aruch left the room.

Bryce Babcock didn't know what else to do. His feet lead weights, he stepped past the former President. He trailed the PIO leader out into the baking light of the Lebanese day.

AFTER THE DOOR clicked shut, the President waited for the engine sounds to fade into the distance before opening his eyes.

When he was certain they were gone, he climbed unsteadily to his feet.

Bones creaked with age and muscles protested the sudden movement after so many hours of inactivity. Head woozy from the blood rush, he had to rest for a moment, propping a big hand against the desk. His leathery face was flushed.

They were taking the bomb to Israel. He'd *have* to follow. Would *have* to try to stop them.

But he was old now. Just the simple effort to stand had seemed a great challenge.

His head began to clear. No time.

Hobbling, the President made his way to the door.

He opened it a crack, peering outside.

Clear.

Opening the door wider, he slipped outside.

Quiet for a moment.

All at once, a shout in Arabic. A single gunshot.

Intense silence.

A second gunshot.

Followed by the whispering sigh of the desert wind. And nothing more.

Remo stole a rusty old Buick LeSabre from the roadside in Tyre. The owner of the restaurant where he'd placed his call to Smith had given them directions to the offices of the Lebanese PIO branch. He spit on the floor as he did so.

The four side windows of the big blue American car were open wide as they bounced their way down the rutted road.

In the passenger's seat, Chiun hummed a merry Korean tune. For the first time in days, Remo didn't get the impression he was faking it. This time, it seemed like the real deal.

"Smith does *not* want you to ice the President, Little Father," Remo insisted as he drove.

Chiun was breathing dry desert air and basking in the brilliant sunlight shining through the filthy windshield.

"You are young," the Master of Sinanju said, patting Remo's hand paternally. "When you have seen as many winters as I, you will know better how to judge the mind of an emperor." He stroked his wisp of beard pensively. "How do you think Smith feels about public scourging?"

"Look, Chiun," Remo said reasonably, "even if he *does* want you to kill the President—which he absolutely does not—how would it change your life one jot?"

"If Smith finally ascends to the throne of America, *I* will be at his side," the Master of Sinanju replied. "At long last, I may finally cease skulking in the shadows of anonymity where I have languished lo these many years and step out into the glorious light."

"And this couldn't possibly be motivated in part because you missed your fifteen minutes of fame when your movie tanked," Remo commented dryly.

"It did *not* tank, O crass one. It was not even released." He tipped his head. "Although now that you mention it, the notoriety I receive as official presidential assassin *could* boost rentals."

"Do you even get a cut?" Remo asked.

"No," Chiun admitted. "But I would. As a boon from President Smith for my many years of faithful service."

"Well, don't say I didn't warn you, Little Father," Remo said. "The best you can hope for is to bump off the guy who held the job two Presidents ago."

As they drove along the potholed road, a serious expression wrinkled Chiun's aged face. "He was the old one, was he not?" he asked.

"He was older than the other ones we've worked for."

Chiun folded his hands in his lap. "I liked him," he said, nodding. "He had the bearing of a true leader."

"Does 'leader' translate to 'despot' in this context?" Remo asked. "'Cause I don't think so."

"No," Chiun said. "While despots and tyrants provide sustenance for the babies of Sinanju, and so are much coveted as clients, only a handful have been great men. Many men lead, Remo, but few of them are leaders."

A particularly deep rut threw the front of the car to one side. Remo bounced the right rear tire through the furrow. The Buick rolled down, flew through and launched up out of the hole, landing in a cloud of dust. Undamaged, the sturdy old car soared down the road.

"Smith is certain the Emptying Basin technique has reversed?" Chiun asked, referring to the Sinanju term for the type of selective amnesia they employed.

"According to Smith, he remembers everything he was supposed to forget. Just like that conspiracy-theory movie director we dealt with a few years back."

"Hmm," Chiun mused. "This has happened before."

Curious, Remo pulled his eyes away from the flat road. Signs of life had begun to spring up alongside the highway. Rough vegetation signified a nearby source of water. Trees sprouted in the distance.

"There were others?" he asked, surprised.

"Not *others,*" Chiun said, perturbed. "We are the most feared house of assassins on Earth, not some family of blundering nincompoops. There was only *one* other."

"What undid it, surgery or a smack on the head?" Remo asked. These were the only two techniques he knew of that had thus far reversed the Emptying Basin.

The old man's reply surprised him.

"It was love," Chiun intoned somberly.

The Master of Sinanju sounded so serious when he spoke the words that Remo resisted the urge to crack wise.

"Have you never wondered, Remo, why Smith's desire for secrecy extends to the assassination of all who learn of his silly organization—friend and foe alike?"

Remo frowned. "Not really," he admitted. "He's always had a hard-on for security. I figured that was all."

Chiun shook his head. "When first I entered into his employ and learned of his paranoia, I told Smith of the Emptying Basin technique. He was pleased to know that it was possible to make someone forget about his existence rather than eliminate them. However, when he asked if it was possible for the Emptying Basin to come undone, I responded truthfully.

One time, many years ago, it did. Although there was only this single instance, Smith decided that the risk was too great for his precious secrecy. This is why, Remo, we only use the amnesia technique on your retiring Presidents and no others."

"I didn't know that." Remo nodded thoughtfully. "I guess from Smitty's viewpoint, it makes sense, too. It'd sure as hell raise more than a few eyebrows if every President who leaves office up and drops dead on January 21. So who's the one it stopped working on?"

"It happened in rather recent times," Chiun began, "in what inferior Western dating would call the thirteenth century. You know of the Mamelukes?"

Remo looked sheepish. "Big dog in the funny papers?" he ventured.

"I only wish I could be certain you were joking," Chiun said, eyes hooded. His voice took on the cadence of instruction. "The Mamelukes were a powerful aristocracy of landowners who ruled throughout the Muslim world for seven hundred years. Their influence was felt in India and Persia, as well as other nations, though to a lesser degree. But nowhere was their strength felt more than in Egypt.

"Now, the Mamelukes originally descended from slave stock. Their ancestors had been plucked from the ranks of non-Arab slaves to serve in the households of Muslim rulers and soldiers. But it did not take long for their masters to grow fat and lazy. The

Mamelukes soon subverted power from their owners, seizing control for themselves."

"Good for them." Remo nodded.

"And for us," Chiun agreed. "To consolidate their power, the former slaves imported more military slaves."

"Wait a minute," Remo said. "The *slaves* had slaves?"

"It was customary and quite proper at the time."

"It's also repulsive," Remo said.

"I agree," the Master of Sinanju replied.

He glanced around, as if someone running at sixty miles per hour beside the speeding car might hear what he was about to say. When he again spoke, his voice was conspiratorial.

"Slavery is not a good thing, Remo."

"I know that, Little Father," Remo said dryly.

"The only specimens in all the human race worthy of slaves are Masters of Sinanju, and we no longer keep them."

"I don't agree with that," Remo said, shaking his head firmly. "I don't think we're any better than anyone else just 'cause of all the stuff we can do."

Chiun gave him a baleful look. "I agree that you do not think. I will ignore the other nonsense."

Eyes flat, the old Korean looked back out at the dusty desert road. He resumed his tale.

"The influence of the Mamelukes grew as time went on. Eventually, their power became so great that they were able to afford the services of Sinanju.

"Now the Master at that time was named Suo-Lok. Traveled he from the sunny shores of Sinanju to the Egyptian seat of power of the Mamelukes in Cairo. From this ancient city did these sons of slaves wield influence from Syria to Arabia, from Libya to Sudan in far-off Africa. A mighty empire had they built, these slaves, and powerful they were, but they did not see trouble on the horizon."

"Another slave uprising?" Remo asked hopefully.

Chiun shook his head. "Mongols," he intoned. "Although this was after the time of the mighty Genghis, the Mongol hordes were still a feared enemy to much of the known world. Word had come to the Mamelukes that forces of Kublai Khan intended to invade Syria."

"Wait a minute," Remo interrupted. "We worked for the Mongols. Wouldn't it have been a conflict of interest for Suo-Lok to hire out to the other side?"

Chiun shrugged. "Contracts expire. Emperors pass to dust. It is the way of things."

"Okay," Remo said, nodding, "so we double-dealt the Mongols."

The Master of Sinanju forged ahead. "The Mamelukes were always fighting amongst themselves. Though it is thought that they eagerly united when threatened by an outside enemy, this is not so. However, the sultan who hired Suo-Lok, as well as the neighboring sultans, feared so greatly for their kingdoms that they grudgingly put aside their differences to repel the invaders. But unity alone does not a victory make. Only with Suo-Lok's aid were the Mameluke horsemen adequately trained to fend off the army of attacking Mongols."

"Where's the whole Sinanju amnesia thing figure into all this?" Remo asked, feeling they'd gone far afield.

"I am coming to that, impatient one," Chiun droned. "The sultan was so pleased with the Master of Sinanju's training of the Mameluke horsemen that he did hire him to the full-time position of royal assassin. While occupying this post, Suo-Lok did befriend the son of the sultan.

"Now, the sultan's son was a vile and cunning creature whose eyes were firmly set on the throne of his regal father. Many nights he did plot against the one whose seed did give him life. Always in the company of a servile concubine."

"Uh-oh. I smell a femme fatale," Remo said.

"You are correct," Chiun agreed. "One day, after he had failed to compliment her hair or give her a bauble to commemorate a particular date or smiled when he should have frowned—who knows what motivates women?—this young wench turned against her prince, fleeing to his father to report his treachery. Fearing for his own life, the prince did beg the Master of Sinanju to stop the girl before she could inform the sultan, thus sealing the prince's fate. However, he pleaded that she not be killed, for the faithless harlot was a favorite of his whom he loved deeply."

"Sounds like a job for selective amnesia," Remo said, growing intrigued. "Did he do it?"

Chiun nodded. "As a personal favor to his friend, the treacherous prince, Suo-Lok did intercept the consort and perform on her the technique of the Emptying Basin."

"Suo-Lok gave the guy a freebie?" Remo asked, surprised.

"Of course not." Chiun scowled, as if Remo were an idiot. "He was paid handsomely by the prince."

"Whew," Remo exhaled. "My universe nearly collapsed. I thought for a minute a Master of Sinanju had opted for friendship over cold hard cash."

"I implore the gods that such a thing does not happen in my lifetime," Chiun intoned. "In any event, Suo-Lok had created a dilemma for himself. He was already under contract to the father when he was hired by the son. To provide service to an enemy of the crown while in service to that crown—even if it was a prince of the realm—not only had the appearance of impropriety, but it was bad business."

"So what happened?"

"The hussy lived in blissful ignorance until one day she was kicked in the head by an ass. Memory returned to her and she did report the false heart of the prince to his father. Enraged, the sultan slew his son at once. Afterward, Master Suo-Lok was discharged from the Mameluke's service with only partial payment—this for subcontracting to the prince."

"So I was right," Remo challenged. "It was a smack on the head that brought back her memory."

"Essentially," Chiun admitted.

"So why'd you tell me it wasn't?"

"You might not have listened otherwise," Chiun sniffed, "and thus missed a riveting tale. We have arrived."

The Master of Sinanju tapped the slender fingertips of one hand to the dashboard. Annoyed, Remo glanced ahead.

The road from Tyre had taken them to Nahal Litani, a river northeast of the port city.

Settlements like border towns in an old Western grew among the trees alongside the road. They had just reached a sprawling collection of simple tenements and flat houses.

Using the directions given to them by the restaurant owner, they located the headquarters of the PIO. When they arrived at the dilapidated building, there were already several vehicles, mostly trucks and jeeps, parked in front. Angry men with coarse beards, automatic rifles and sloppy military garb stomped around the vehicles.

"Front door or back?" Remo asked, eyeing the men as he slowed the car. The men, in turn, looked on them with shock.

"This is Lebanon." Chiun shrugged. "Neither is safe."

"Front door it is."

Remo parked the Buick next to a jeep. The Arabs were like jackals on a carcass. The Buick was surrounded before he even shut off the engine.

Rifle barrels jammed through open windows. Wild eyes glared hatred at the two obvious foreigners. As he stabbed his gun muzzle against Remo's chest, the closest man let out a furious torrent of unintelligible Arabic.

Remo looked blandly from gun to Chiun. "What's he saying?" he asked.

"He wishes us to get out of the car," the Master of Sinanju replied. He was looking disdainfully at the multiple gun barrels jutting through his own window.

"You still in an accommodating mood, Little Father?"

The old man's nod was so subtle only Remo saw it. It was all Remo needed.

Remo's hand flew to the door handle. At the same time, Chiun's bony fingers flashed forward. They popped their respective handles simultaneously.

Doors flew open at speeds nearing Mach 2. Metal slammed flesh with meaty slaps. PIO soldiers were launched from the sides of the Buick like scattered seeds. Before the bodies struck dust, Remo and Chiun were already springing through the open doors.

The doors had taken out a total of seven men. They hadn't even crumpled to the ground before another thirty were flooding in to fill the void.

Automatics exploded to life, riddling the Buick with bullets. Tires erupted in coughs of dust and rubber.

Even as the old car was settling like a deflated balloon to the ground, Remo and Chiun were swirling into the midst of the furious PIO soldiers.

Remo snagged two kaffiyehs, one in each hand, yanking them together in a simple forearm snap. Skulls cracked open, popping squishy clumps of fat gray brain into the crystal-clear Mideast sky.

On the other side of the car, the Master of Sinanju's hand flashed up to the barrel of an extended rifle. A push popped the gun free of its owner. Unfortunately for the PIO soldier, his arm popped loose, too.

The rifle soared back, arm in tow. The gun became a missile unto itself as it pierced the chest of another PIO man. Shedding the excess baggage of its human appendage, the rifle continued straight through the soldier. It screamed in and out another advancing man before coming to a quivering stop in a third.

As the three men fell to the dust, Chiun was finishing off the original one-armed soldier with a sharp toe to the forehead. It had happened so quickly, the PIO man hadn't had time to mourn the loss of his arm before the blackness of oblivion overcame him.

Spinning from the body, Chiun whirled into the thickest cluster of men, catching up to Remo at the front of the car.

A mound of bodies decorated the ground at Remo's feet. Though their weapons were raised, the PIO soldiers seemed hesitant to use their guns in such close quarters.

"How many you get?" Remo asked Chiun as he worked.

The Master of Sinanju sprang off the ground, twisting in midair. Pipe-stem legs swirled into the throng of armed men. Two heads snapped around with brittle spine cracks.

"Six," he announced, kimono skirts settling around his ankles.

"You're slowing down," Remo chided. "I'm up to nine."

As he spoke, he launched an elbow back, catching a PIO soldier in the Adam's apple. When the man fell, clutching his throat, a heel kick collapsed his face into an angry smear of crimson.

"That is because *I* allowed *you* to work without distraction," Chiun retorted.

Sharpened fingernails slashed forward, ripping the throats from a pair of soldiers. Even as the first men were dropping, the old Korean threw his hands out to either side, catching two charging men in the chest. They stopped dead, quivering on the ends of extended index fingernails. When he pulled the nails away, the men collapsed.

The rest had gotten the message by now. The tattered remnants of the small PIO platoon decided to disperse. Abandoning their cars, they opted to leave on foot. Obviously, they thought screaming would somehow accelerate their pace. A theory not entirely unjustified given the speed at which they were flying down the street. They waved hands over heads as they shrieked.

"We're even," Remo announced, coming up beside Chiun. "Ten for you and ten for me."

A tie was apparently not good enough for the Master of Sinanju. Bending quickly, he wrapped one bony hand around the bumper of their Buick. With a painful wrench, he tore it free and hefted the heavy, rusted strip of metal high above his head. With a whoosh, it vanished from his fingertips.

Remo tracked the bumper as it flew end-over-end down the sun-cracked street. It soared only twenty yards before it lopped off the head of one of the fleeing PIO men. The body continued to run a few more steps as the head and bumper thudded to the road.

After brushing a cloud of imaginary dust from his palms, Chiun replaced his hands inside his kimono sleeves. He smiled triumphantly at Remo. "I win," he proclaimed.

"We'll settle up later," Remo said. "Let's go."

On the way inside the building, they found a

crumpled body lying facedown in the dirt. Remo toed it over.

Ree Hop Doe's glasses were askew, but his Asian features were unmistakable.

Remo's thoughts at once turned to the former President. "I smell a Los Alamos rat," he commented thinly as they viewed the body.

Leaving Doe to the desert sun, he pushed open the door.

There were PIO men inside, as well. These ones seemed to be more high-ranking than the corpses outside. Instead of rifles, they wore side arms. Once Chiun had liberated a few arms from a few sides, the initial anger they had displayed at the sudden appearance of the two men was replaced with intense agreeability. All around were nervous smiles.

"Where's Aruch?" Remo demanded of the man with the biggest epaulets.

Like the rest of the PIO membership, he wore a scruffy beard and fatigues.

"Gone." The man grinned, sweating.

"Did he take the bomb with him?"

The PIO soldier nodded. Terrified eyes darted beyond Remo to the pile of arms the Master of Sinanju had stacked near the door. The old Korean stood impassive beside them.

"Dammit," Remo growled. "Where'd he go?"

"Israel."

"*Where* in Israel?"

"I do not know."

"Chiun, this guy wants to shake hands."

The Master of Sinanju took a step forward.

"I swear I do not know!" the man begged.

Remo frowned. The PIO soldier was telling the truth.

"What about the President? He take him with him?"

"No," the soldier said. "The old devil is loose."

"What do you mean loose?" Remo demanded. "Where is he?"

"He escaped. Two men were killed."

Remo couldn't believe what he was hearing. "Where did he go?" he snapped.

"I do not know," the PIO man replied. His pleading eyes showed how hard he was straining to be helpful. "He left not long after Chairman Aruch. With his dying breath, one of the men he attacked said that he was going off in the same direction as our beloved leader."

"Perfect," Remo snarled.

With an angry slap, he smacked his palm into the man's forehead. Twin geysers of blood spurted from the soldier's ears. Spine snapping audibly, he folded back over Nossur Aruch's desk at a perfect right angle. Remo wheeled on the others, furious fire burning in his eyes.

"Get outta here," he ordered.

Rats escaping a burning building could not have fled faster. Using door and windows, the remaining PIO men dove out into sunlight. Remo followed.

"We better hurry, Little Father," he said tightly.

"We do not know *where* to hurry to," the Master of Sinanju noted as he trailed Remo out the door.

"Doesn't matter," Remo said gravely. "We've got a President as old as George Washington's grampa out trying to fight the bad guys, and a bomb that's about to melt every gun from here to Damascus." His face was dark. "We'd better drive like hell until we find one or the other."

The brittle door swung slowly shut behind them.

The ground had been broken on the planned Israeli settlement during the tenure of the previous prime minister. Houses had not yet been built, but the plans had been laid out for the tiny Jewish community just outside Nablus, a town north of Jerusalem, in the mostly Arab West Bank.

Protests against the planned construction had been ongoing, some violent. Although the new Israeli government was wavering, its citizens who had bought the land were not. The land would be settled. It was just a matter of time.

Nossur Aruch had other plans.

"This is perfect," the PIO leader announced to Fatang as his car crested a stone-covered hill. "Stop here."

The three PIO trucks trailing the big sedan came to squeaking stops along the hillside road.

Aruch didn't wait for his phalanx of bodyguards to run up the hill and surround him. He jumped excitedly from his car, hurrying to the lead truck.

Bryce Babcock got out after Aruch, his drooping face hanging in fleshy sheets of fear. With great reluctance, he trailed the terrorist down the hill. By the time the interior secretary caught up with the PIO leader, Aruch was already overseeing the unloading of the neutrino bomb from the rear of the truck.

"Careful!" Nossur lisped angrily. "Do not damage it."

When the men finally slipped the bomb from the shadows in the rear of the truck, Babcock saw that the timer was down to twenty-seven minutes.

Like an anxious child, the interior secretary tugged at the back of Aruch's sleeve.

"Uh, we should hurry," the secretary suggested.

"We are, we are!" Aruch snapped. "Get out of the way!"

Shaking Babcock away, the PIO head herded his men up the hill. They huffed beneath the weight of their heavy burden.

The Jewish settlement was to be built at the hill's plateau. String tied to posts that had been driven into the rocky ground indicated where the future foundations would be. Aruch brought his men through the field of scrubby green brush and white-and-gray boulders to the very heart of the future development. Snapping the string with a thick boot heel, he ushered the men into the living room of a home that would never be built.

"There," he ordered, pointing. "That flat rock."

Aruch climbed down to his knees, helping the men balance the bomb on the rock. Babcock grew more ill when he looked at the timer. Four more minutes had drained away.

"A statement to those who would steal Palestinian land," Aruch was saying to his men. "If only this area was inhabited..." There was disappointment in his wet eyes.

"Would you like a Kleenex, sir?" Fatang asked quietly.

"Hurry," Babcock pressed.

This time, Aruch didn't resist. When the PIO leader got to his feet, the interior secretary's relief was obvious. With one last longing glance at the neutrino bomb, Aruch led the charge back to the waiting cars.

When they cleared the edge of the flat hilltop, a vision more terrifying than an endangered condor-egg omelet greeted Bryce Babcock.

Down the slope, an Israeli convoy had parked behind the PIO vehicles. Curiosity had led them to investigate, but when the armed PIO contingent burst into view, the spark of alarm charged through the Israeli forces.

"Halt!" an Israeli colonel shouted. He raised his Uzi the instant the PIO soldiers appeared atop the hill. His men followed suit.

The PIO soldiers skidded to a stop, reflexively aiming their weapons down the hill.

"We don't have time for this," Babcock warned Aruch.

The PIO leader's eyes darted from the Israeli soldiers to his own men. The Palestinians didn't look at their leader. Their collective gaze was fixed on the hated soldiers below.

For a moment suspended in time, nothing happened. Tension in the Mexican standoff grew to a pounding drum of fear in Bryce Babcock's ears. All at once, the head of the Palestine Independence Organization drew in a deep breath. When he spoke, he did so loudly and clearly, so there would be no misinterpreting his meaning.

"Fire! " Nossur Aruch screamed, wild-eyed, at his men.

And as the PIO leader and the American interior secretary dove for cover, the peaceful, rock-strewn hillside erupted in gunfire.

REMO HAD STOLEN a PIO pickup to replace his crippled Buick. The truck flew south.

Keeping the gas pedal flat to the floor, Remo drove like mad for the Israel border. He prayed Nossur Aruch wasn't taking the scenic route to the Jewish State.

At speeds in excess of ninety miles per hour, they reached the border in less than fifteen minutes.

The soldiers on the Lebanon side wished to detain them. Two foreign nationals driving in what was likely a stolen Lebanese truck cried out for arrest. Remo convinced them to look the other way by breaking all their noses. Faces gushing blood, they waved the two men through.

"Has Nossur Aruch been through here?" Remo asked on the other side as the young Israeli border guard checked his and Chiun's phony passports. The guard was all of eighteen years old.

"He passed through a few minutes ago," the soldier replied.

"Did you search his car?" Remo asked, shocked. He hoped Aruch hadn't ditched the neutrino bomb somewhere.

The soldier looked up, his face bland. "There were four vehicles in his motorcade. We let them all go without inspection."

"Are you nuts?" Remo asked. "The guy's a terrorist."

"We have standing orders from the new government. We are not to create an incident with him."

"What if I told you he plans to blow up your country?" Remo snapped.

"He would have to get in line," the soldier said, not even looking up. He handed back Remo's and Chiun's passports. "You may proceed."

"Jesus, Mary and Joseph," Remo muttered. As the soldier headed back to his shack, Remo stuck his head out the window. "You at least have any idea where he might have gone?" he called.

The soldier shrugged as he walked. "He has an office in Hebron. In the West Bank."

"You know where that is, Little Father?" Remo asked the Master of Sinanju.

"Yes," Chiun replied, bored.

Remo gunned the engine. As they sped past the guard shack, he yelled, "And if you see a mushroom cloud, I'd suggest you duck and cover."

They raced down the road into Israel.

BRYCE BABCOCK FELT like one of the precious crocodiles his department had released in a downtown Kansas City park back in '97. *They'd* been shot at, too.

Bullets zinged all around.

The Israeli soldiers fired relentlessly, unleashing efficient, controlled bursts from their Uzis. The PIO's return fire was sloppy and impassioned.

Bullets whizzed crazily in every direction above the interior secretary's head.

Babcock and Aruch had taken cover behind a pear-shaped boulder. Endless ricochets sang off the rock. Chunks of stone and clouds of pebbly dust pelted their heads and backs.

The PIO leader had deliberately not unholstered his side arm. If push came to shove and his side lost, he intended to claim that his men had gone trigger-happy at the sight of the Israeli soldiers. He could probably make it stick. The current government in Jerusalem had already signaled great willingness to accept every cock-and-bull story Aruch pitched at them.

Beside the PIO chairman, Bryce Babcock was shaking visibly.

"We *can't* stay this close to the bomb!" Babcock

screamed over the gunfire, his fingers stuffed in his ears.

Uninterested, the Arab brushed dust from his kaffiyeh.

"Your colleague said it had a short range. This will be over soon. We are safe."

"*No,* we're *not*!" Babcock cried. "There could be a radiation-leakage problem before the bomb even goes off! It has a plutonium charge. If the shell gets pierced by a bullet while we're still in range, we could all end up with radiation poisoning!"

"I had not thought of that." Aruch frowned. "I suppose we *could* attempt escape."

To Bryce Babcock, sweeter words had never been spoken.

"How?" the interior secretary pleaded.

Aruch considered. "My car," he said finally. "It is closer than the trucks."

With saucering eyes, Babcock peeked around the side of the boulder. When he dropped back down beside Aruch, he was shaking his head violently.

"That's got to be a city block away," he said.

"An eighth of a mile. Perhaps a little less," Aruch said, reluctantly unholstering his handgun. As he was rising to a squat, Babcock grabbed his arm.

"We'll both be *killed,*" the secretary whined.

Aruch's smile was thin. "Do you know how to drive?" he asked, cocking his automatic with calm assurance.

"Yes," Babcock admitted, momentarily confused.

"In that case, do not talk. Run."

With that, Nossur Aruch ran out from behind the rock. Keeping low, he raced for his big bulletproof car. Bullets screamed all around him.

Babcock gasped. He had no desire to follow, but he was more terrified of dying alone. Shaking in fear, he made an instant, albeit reluctant decision. Jumping out from behind the rock, he followed the terrorist at a gallop through the deadly cross fire.

REMO ASKED the first Arab they passed if he had seen Nossur Aruch. The scowl that appeared on the old man's face told Remo that he had.

"The traitor took the road to Nablus," the man snarled, spitting on the ground. It seemed to be a common Arab reaction to Aruch's name. "He thinks we do not know him in his bulletproof car."

The man was leading a rag-covered donkey down the lonely road. From his stolen truck, Remo observed silently that his style of dress and the beast of burden trailing behind him were a passport to another time. The man could have been transported to the same road two thousand years before and not attracted one second's worth of attention.

"Nablus. You know where that is?" Remo asked Chiun.

"Am I now a walking atlas?" the old Korean complained.

"Please, Chiun," Remo pressed.

The Master of Sinanju frowned. "Yes, I do," he admitted. "But I am getting you a globe for your next birthday."

"Beats pasting Stan Ronaldman's ratty wig in my scrapbook," Remo said. "And you're assuming any of us is *having* another birthday."

Tires spun, spitting clouds of dirt around the Arab and his donkey. With a desperate lurch, Remo launched the truck down the road.

BY FAVOR OF THE BLESSED Earth Goddess herself, Bryce Babcock managed to survive the Israeli-PIO cross fire.

Bullets ripped the air around him as he ran the final few feet to Nossur Aruch's waiting car.

Arabs screamed curses down at Israeli soldiers. Some of the PIO men had already run out of ammunition. These were gunned down as they tried hurling rocks down the hill.

The PIO leader had dived for cover in the back seat of his sturdy sedan. Through the partially open window, fur-lined lips screamed encouragement to Bryce Babcock.

"Run, you fool, *run!*" Aruch yelled.

Panting from panic and exertion, the interior secretary's shaking hand grabbed the silver handle of the driver's door. Before he could pull, he felt something hard press into his back.

Babcock froze.

"Do not move."

The words came from a young Israeli soldier. The man had sneaked up around the PIO vehicles in order to get behind the firing Palestinian soldiers.

As his bladder drained down his leg once more, Bryce Babcock raised his hands numbly in the air.

An angry hiss issued from the rear of the car. Through the crack where a moment before Aruch's lips had been, there came a flash of white.

Babcock's ears rang from the nearness of the explosion. The soldier hopped back, a fat red hole in the center of his forehead.

Hands still raised numbly in the air—trousers soaked through—Babcock watched the soldier drop to the ground.

Aruch's automatic vanished from the window. His fuzzy lips reappeared.

"Get in, fool!"

Heart pounding, Babcock scrabbled for the door handle. Springing the door open, he fell behind the steering wheel. The keys were still in the ignition.

The engine started with a rumble.

Aruch was hanging over the back seat. "That way," he commanded with a sharp flip of his gun barrel.

Obediently, Babcock steered the car in a wide arc. They headed back down the road toward the waiting line of Israeli soldiers. Babcock winced as the Jewish troops opened fire on the runaway car.

"Do your worst!" Aruch shouted gleefully.

"You will not pierce the skin of this mighty Palestinian beast!"

They plowed through the line of soldiers. Although the men continued to fire from every direction at the escaping car, their weapons had no effect.

Aruch bounced giddily from window to tinted window. Even though the men couldn't see him through the dark glass, he stuck out his tongue at them.

In the front seat, Bryce Babcock's eyes were sick as he watched the display in the rearview mirror.

"How can you *be* so calm?" he asked in horrified wonder.

Nossur shrugged, settling back in his seat. "Welcome to the Middle East," he replied.

With bullets pinging off its rear windshield, the sturdy car raced down to the main, winding dirt road.

And on the rocky hill high above them, the red digital timer on the stainless-steel casing of the neutrino bomb continued to count remorselessly down to zero.

THE TRIO OF YOUTHS, each barely in his teens, carried old Russian AK-47s.

Remo was getting sick of having to ask for directions, but he didn't have much choice. He pulled alongside the teenagers.

"You guys seen Nossur Aruch?" he shouted across the seat, out Chiun's open window.

The name brought a reaction. The three boys raised their guns to Remo.

The Master of Sinanju was quick to react. Bony hands a blur of motion, Chiun snatched hold of each of the weapons, twisting barrels to useless angles.

The youths blinked. They looked at Chiun. They looked at their guns, which were now bent to boomerang angles and inexplicably pointing at the arid ground.

As if connected to a single brain, three frantic hands stabbed simultaneously in the same direction.

"When are you gonna take that job counseling troubled teens?" Remo asked as he pulled away from the trio.

They hadn't gone much farther down the road before Remo felt a sudden strange sensation through the tires of the truck. Whatever it was, it was new to him. And *huge.* Face a granite mask, he glanced at the Master of Sinanju.

Chiun had felt it, as well. Expression grave, his gaze was fixed on the distant hills. When he saw the look on his teacher's face, tension thinned Remo's lips.

"It was too big for conventional explosives," he commented worriedly, his own eyes trained on the far-off landscape.

Chiun nodded. The yellowing white tufts of hair above his ears were ominous thunder clouds framing a troubled parchment face. "If it were nearby, we would have seen the flash,'' the old Korean replied in a subdued tone.

Although both Sinanju Masters were trying to gauge the direction from which the vibrations were coming, it was difficult to tell with an explosion of the magnitude they'd just felt. All the earth beneath them seemed to be trembling. It was Remo who came first to a tentative conclusion.

''South?'' he ventured, unsure of his own deduction.

Chiun nodded slow assent. ''The vibrations *appear* to be coming from that direction,'' he agreed.

At the moment, they were driving south. Fast.

''Hang on!'' Remo yelled.

He slammed on the brakes, at the same time wrenching the wheel left. The truck squealed a shriek of protest as the pickup's brakes caused tires to tear road. A thin film of desperate dirt rose from beneath the empty bed as the truck whipped around in a 180-degree turn.

Remo didn't wait for the pickup to complete the turn around before slamming on the gas.

The truck lurched forward, spinning out against the shoulder of the road before roaring back in the direction from which they'd come.

And as they fled, the cloud appeared over the darkening horizon. An unaccustomed tug of fear took hold of Remo the instant he saw it in the rear-view mirror.

It rose above the spinout cloud the truck had

made. Expanding across the pale desert sky, the fat blob of thick thrown-up dirt was balanced atop a heavy stalk of pulverized earth. Until he saw the mushroom cloud, Remo had hoped he and Chiun were wrong. But they were right.

Someone had detonated the neutrino bomb.

No escape. Too close. Screaming forward, the shock wave would reach them any second.

In the side-view mirror, the Master of Sinanju was watching the cloud rise higher in the sky. His weathered face betrayed awe and worry.

"Faster!" Chiun commanded over the growing wind.

"I've got it flat out!" Remo yelled in reply.

A sudden gust of wind burst forth across the desert. A violent artificial sandstorm. The cloud rushed forward, swallowing up the truck. The road before them vanished.

Remo felt the truck pulling away from him. The wind had taken control of the vehicle. In an instant, they were being propelled ahead of the gale at speeds in excess of the indicator. The needle jumped impossibly to the farthest point on the speedometer and locked there. Remo felt like Dorothy caught in the twister. He fought to keep the truck under control.

The wind seemed to cut away all at once. For the briefest of moments, it appeared the storm had stopped.

All at once, they were struck from the front with the force of a solid moving wall of air.

"Hold on!" Remo yelled, just as the windshield shattered across them.

The wind had turned around, rushing in to fill the vacuum created by the exploding bomb.

Even a Master of Sinanju was no match for so awesome a man-made force.

The truck was lifted off its tires. Sand blew in through the vacant windshield.

The truck hit something—a hill, the road. It was impossible to know.

Hit, roll. Hit, roll.

Horrible metallic crunching noises rose over the monstrous wind. Fenders buckled as if beneath a mighty fist. The hood ripped away and was flung into the depths of the roiling dust cloud. Through half-squinting eyes, Remo caught sight of the Master of Sinanju.

The old Korean was being thrown around the cab. From what little Remo could see, he appeared to be weathering the storm. Until the section of seat he was holding unexpectedly gave way.

Chiun's parchment face registered a brief instant of surprise. That was the last thing Remo saw before the violent wind grabbed hold of him. The Master of Sinanju disappeared out the window and was swallowed up by the sandstorm.

Just like that. He was gone.

"Chiun!" Remo yelled, the words inaudible in

the terrifying gale. Remo felt his mouth fill with gritty sand.

The twinge of fear he'd felt before exploded fully.

Chiun was gone.

And in that moment of panic for his father in spirit, Remo allowed his concentration to lapse.

He did not feel the steering wheel coming loose. It popped free without a sound. When he realized what had happened, it was already too late to do anything about it.

The howling wind plucked him from the cab, lifting, flinging him roughly through the air. There was no time to think of Chiun or of his own safety. Remo flew face first through the open windshield.

And in a screaming whisper that issued from the very mouth of Hell itself, the swirling, ferocious sandstorm consumed him utterly.

Baghdad's elite Republican Guard, pride of the Republic of Iraq, was on maneuvers in the Tigris-Euphrates Valley in the land once known as Mesopotamia.

It was a special day for the highly trained soldiers. President, Prime Minister and Chairman of the Revolutionary Command Council, Saddam Hussein himself was on hand for the latest military exercises.

Hussein sat in an open Jeep above the field of battle. A frozen smile gripped his face beneath his bushy mustache as he reviewed his mighty troops through his field glasses.

Hundreds of massive tank treads kicked up huge plumes of dust as the armored vehicles rumbled across the arid plain.

Beyond them, a network of cunningly deceptive trenches had been dug by foot soldiers for this battlefield mock-up. From his vantage point, Hussein could see the men lined within the trenches awaiting the attack.

The Gulf War had done much to deflate the confidence of the Republican Guard. Convinced that they were invincible, the soldiers had been stunned by the rapidity, as well as the severity of the United States-led operation. It had been necessary in the years since for Hussein to rebuild the morale of his once feared army.

Between the soldiers in their trenches and the approaching line of tanks, another group of men stood out in open desert. Tiny in comparison to the mechanized beasts, these soldiers bravely awaited the approaching vehicles.

Hussein ran his binoculars along the ragtag collection of men, pitifully small in the vastness of the Iraqi desert.

His smile broadened.

Kurdish rebels. *Hundreds* of them.

The men hailed from the mountainous north of the Mideast nation. Hussein had slaughtered most of them several years before, but he had kept some alive for special occasions. Like this one.

The Kurds had not been given guns. They were armed only with knives. This was a sensible precaution, for only a fool would arm a Kurd. Even for a battle simulation. After all, someone could get hurt.

Ragged in their surplus Republican Guard uniforms, the Kurdish soldiers stood, bravely awaiting slaughter.

The president of Iraq was dressed identically to all of the men below him, with one great, unseen exception.

In the war with America, any strip of white cloth

available to the Iraqi troops had been employed as a flag of surrender. This included one uniform item in particular. That problem had been addressed by Saddam Hussein himself. In the newest incarnation of the elite Republican Guard—no underwear.

Right now, Hussein's Fruit of the Looms were riding up on him as he shifted his ample rump on his hot leather seat.

Tugging at his backside, he kept his binoculars as steady as possible. He didn't wish to miss one moment of the action.

The tanks were rumbling close. Only a few yards from the helpless men.

The Kurds stood their ground. There was no point in running. They would be shot from behind if they tried.

The great thundering rattle from the massive metal machines could be felt throughout the valley.

Watching through his field glasses, Hussein chewed his mustache in gleeful anticipation. But as he watched, something odd seemed to happen.

All at once, the air in the valley shimmered. It was as if the world for a moment turned slightly out of focus. As quickly as it had come, the disturbance passed.

The desert wind picked up, blowing from the field of battle the plumes of smoke that had been rising from the treads of the approaching tanks. Hussein's olive skin was pelted with a fine spray of sand.

A normal desert wind. That was all.

No. Not all. Something below him had changed.

His precious tanks had stopped moving. All two hundred of them were now frozen in place.

Nothing seemed to happen for a long time.

After a pregnant silence, a tank lid sprang open. It was followed by another, then another. Soldiers began to scurry out into the sunlight.

"What is happening?" Saddam Hussein demanded of his coterie of subordinates. "Why are they not grinding those Kurdish dogs beneath their treads?"

Haste was made to learn the reason for the lack of tank movement in the field of battle.

Far below, the Kurds were hesitating, unsure this wasn't some kind of trick.

When the lack of movement continued for another handful of minutes, Hussein knew that it had gone on too long. Something was desperately wrong.

The Kurds sensed it, as well.

There came a fearsome cry from the belly of the great valley. Hundreds of Kurd mouths let flow whoops of explosive rage. Knives raised above their heads, they swarmed toward the row of inert tanks.

Behind the Kurds, the armed men in the trenches didn't act. They were a safety measure to keep the Kurds in line, yet they did nothing to stop them. When Hussein swung his binoculars over, he saw that the men in the trenches were struggling with their guns.

"Shoot them!" Hussein shouted into the valley.

He wheeled on the men nearest him. "Order those fools to fire!"

The man nearest him slammed the portable phone with his fist. "The radio does not work, my president."

Hussein whirled back around.

The slaughter had already begun.

Men fell to the sand. *His* men. Saddam Hussein's vaunted and feared Republican Guard.

Men clutched bellies and throats. Blood flowed into the sand of their forefathers.

The soldiers in the trenches still had not fired. Hussein realized with a horrid, sinking feeling that the only reason they would not shoot was because they could not shoot.

The Kurds finished with the tank soldiers in less than three minutes. Charged with the thrill of victory—knives dripping blood—they raced back for the men in the trenches.

The Republican Guard soldiers had already stripped off their trousers. Naked from the waist down, they waved their pants in the air atop the barrels of their useless guns.

The Kurds did not recognize their surrender. They had for too many years been victims of Iraq's celebrated Republican Guard.

It was a massacre. In minutes, pools of dark blood stained the powdery sand in the trenches.

Sickened by the spectacle, Hussein turned to his men, his face ashen.

"Let us leave," Hussein intoned hollowly.

"The jeeps do not work, my President!" a frantic aide announced.

Hussein's head whipped to the valley.

Below, the Kurds were almost finished with the slaughter. There was only one place left for them to go. And with a sinking feeling, Hussein knew where that was.

Throwing his binoculars to the sand, Chairman of the Revolutionary Command Council Saddam Hussein spun from the field of battle and ran like a jackrabbit for home. In his haste to run back to Baghdad, he did not even bother to pick at his wedged underpants.

THE TWO SOVIET-BUILT MiG-23s raced along the sticky black tarmac of the Syrian Arab People's Airport in the low-lying hills south of Damascus.

Fuselages shuddered as the cooler mountain air grabbed the swing wings of both planes. With a piercing cry, the airport fell away and the powerful jets screamed into the heavens.

At one time, the Syrian air force had seventy of the aircraft. But in the wake of the Soviet Union's collapse came a serious equipment shortage. Parts were being scavenged from donor planes just to keep the dwindling aircraft of the Syrian air force aloft. These were two of the last complete multirole all-weather fighters of this type still in service.

The MiGs left Damascus far behind, soaring

along the lower hills of the Anti-Lebanon Mountains.

In the distance, Mount Hermon rose majestically from amid the lesser mountains. At more than nine thousand feet, it was the highest point in the country. According to the history of the area, Hermon was the site of Christ's transfiguration before his disciples.

Of course, the Syrian pilots did not believe such nonsense. Hermon was a mountain that, along with the rest of the Anti-Lebanon range, separated the Syrian Arab Republic from its geographical neighbors. That was all.

Hugging the mountains to the east, the MiGs soared in the direction of the disputed Golan Heights. Sunlight glinted off the cockpit domes.

In spite of speeds nearly exceeding fifteen hundred miles per hour, Mount Hermon seemed not to move. It stayed patiently beside the roaring fighters as they flew, an ancient, watchful sentry.

The routine patrol continued south as far as As Suwayda, then looped north for home.

As the bleak terrain raced beneath the bellies of the twin planes, one of the pilots thought he saw something in his peripheral vision. He glanced over his shoulder in the direction of Mount Hermon.

The mountain seemed to shiver.

Behind his goggles, the pilot blinked his eyes. When he looked back, Hermon was stationary once more, as if nothing had happened. But something *had.*

Perhaps it was a problem with his goggles. Or perhaps there was fog on the interior of his cockpit dome. At this height and in this climate, ice should not have formed on the exterior of the craft, but that was a possibility. It might have even been an earthquake. Whatever had happened, there had to be some explanation.

The pilot thought to report the strange phenomenon once he landed. He would never get the chance.

All at once, a stiff breeze blew in out of the west, engulfing his aircraft.

The nose of the MiG seemed to wobble. Just as Mount Hermon had.

The wind passed.

Another bizarre occurrence to report.

The pilot adjusted the stick slightly.

It failed to move.

Concerned, he tugged harder.

Nothing. It was locked in place.

Checking the other systems, he found to his horror that they were all the same. Frozen solid.

The MiG began to lose altitude.

Looking over, the pilot saw that his sister craft was in the same predicament. Nose dipping forward, it had begun an inexorable screaming dive for the lowland mountains.

No way to pull out of the dive. Controls frozen.

Nothing more he could do. The plane was going down.

The pilot hit the eject switch.

Nothing happened.

He hit it again. Still nothing.

Ground racing up now. Faster, faster.

Pounding the switch. Banging hands against the dome above his head.

Nothing moved. Everything fused.

Ground visible on the other side of the dome. In front of the nose.

Too fast…too fast…

The two MiGs impacted against the rolling base of Mount Hermon twenty seconds later. Twin explosions of yellow and orange gouted a spray of metal and stone.

And though the crashes and ensuing fires were fierce, through it all Mount Hermon stood. Unchanged.

THE SCENE PLAYED OUT the same way from Cyprus to Saudi Arabia, from Egypt to the west of Iran.

Afterward, some claimed they had felt something. All said they saw something. A strange shimmering of the land, followed by a warm wind.

Guns seized up at a rally in Lebanon. King Abdullah's plane nearly crashed during takeoff in Jordan. Elevators, automobiles, kitchen appliances, construction equipment—indeed all metal-on-metal hardware within at least a seven-hundred-mile radius around Israel's disputed West Bank—became inoperative. As if clenched in a powerful, invisible fist.

And around the world, stunned governments nearly tripped over one another as they sprang to sudden action. All of them with the same goal: to gain a foothold in the suddenly powerless region.

29

Their car suddenly seized up on the road into Hebron.

Behind the wheel, Bryce Babcock desperately turned the key, at the same time pressing his foot on the gas.

Nothing happened. Not an engine struggling sound, not a feeble click. Nothing.

"The peace bomb," Babcock exhaled, nodding anxiously.

Nossur Aruch leaned over the front seat.

"Give it more gas," he instructed angrily.

"I already did."

"You flooded the engine," the PIO leader accused.

"How could I?" Babcock whined. "We were driving fine. It just *stopped.* It must be the neutrino wave."

Aruch growled, dropping back in his seat. "*Now* what am I supposed to do? I cannot walk back to my office. They will slaughter me in the street."

"What about this stuff?" Babcock suggested. He

lifted a few articles of clothing that had been left on the seat by Fatang and the other bodyguard.

Aruch's facial stubble gathered into a prickly frown. Reluctantly grabbing the clothes, the PIO head improvised a disguise.

Aruch abandoned his beloved checkered family kaffiyeh for a more traditional, less cumbersome head wrapping. A pair of dark sunglasses obscured his crazed, unblinking eyes. That was it. On another man, two minor changes like these wouldn't have mattered, but on Nossur Aruch they managed to obliterate his two most distinctive features.

"I shame my ancestors to dress like this," Nossur Aruch complained as he stuffed his beloved head covering inside his wrinkled fatigue jacket.

Disguise in place, he grabbed the door handle.

The door refused to budge.

"What is this devilry?" Aruch demanded, furiously rattling the handle.

"The neutrino wave would have fused virtually all metal on metal," Babcock grunted from the front seat. He, too, was attempting to open his door. It was stuck fast.

The shatterproof windows refused to power down.

"So how do we get out?" Aruch snapped.

It took twenty more minutes and the removal of the back seat. On their backs, both men were able to kick open the sedan's trunk. Sweating profusely, they climbed out the back and onto the rock-strewn street.

"What's that noise?" Bryce Babcock panted when they were safely outside the car. His khaki shirt was drenched.

Aruch tipped his head. "It sounds like a mob," he replied, puzzled. "But if it is, it is not like any I have ever heard before."

The two men headed off into the city, threading their careful way to Aruch's Hebron office.

They had not gone far before they found the source of the noise.

Aruch had been right. It was a mob—and it was also unlike any he had seen in his lifetime.

"They are not using guns," Aruch breathed to the interior secretary, his voice a hoarse lisp.

"They wouldn't work, either," Babcock explained. "Metal on metal, remember?"

The crowd had formed a semicircle around a short, garbage-strewn alley. The center of attention, an emaciated old man stood at the far end of the lane.

Men had gathered up chunks of crumbling buildings and roads. Laughing and shouting, they hurled the rocks at the cowering, bleeding old man.

"*He* has a gun," Aruch hissed, indicating a man who had just joined the crowd.

The man aimed his weapon. Aruch watched in interest.

As soon as the new arrival depressed the trigger, there was an explosion. However, it didn't come from the barrel.

The gun blew up in the man's hands, ripping them to shreds. Screaming in pain, he fell to his knees.

The crowd didn't notice. Their stone throwing had reached a fever pitch. The pathetic old man surrendered to the jagged rocks without so much as a sigh. He died in a bloody heap at the rear of the alley.

Aruch turned to Babcock. When he peeked over his sunglasses, there was sad understanding in his eyes.

"No guns?" he asked, disappointed.

"I *told* you," Babcock replied nervously.

"But this was to be the Great Holy War," Aruch complained. "The Jews have lost their teeth. Detonating that bomb was a symbol for my people to rise up for a free Palestine. How can we have a proper *jihad* without arms?"

"*Please,* Nossur," Bryce Babcock begged. He was thinking of all the peace bomb was supposed to have done. It was supposed to be a shining example to the rest of the world. Not a prelude to chaos. "It wasn't supposed to be this way. This was supposed to be for the *good.* Like when I set those leopards loose in Pennsylvania. If you'd only surrender to the loving embrace of peace, all will be well." His attempt at a benevolent smile made him look constipated.

Aruch's expression fouled to disgust.

"Peace is for those who have not the stomach for war," the PIO leader proclaimed. He raised a stubby, threatening finger to the interior secretary. "And for *your* sake my beloved missile had better work," he menaced.

Whirling from Babcock, he hurried from the mob, heading deeper into the city. Casting a last, frightened look at the bloodied dead man, Bryce Babcock hustled in Aruch's wake.

The desert storm screamed off into the arid hills where it had been born, and was gone.

Remo had concentrated on weightlessness during his time hurled through the air and so was featherlight when he finally landed softly on his stomach, a quarter of a mile back from the spot where the forward rush of air from the neutrino bomb had caught his truck.

The wind had not yet died away before he sprang up. Unharmed, his worried eyes scanned for the Master of Sinanju. He found him immediately. The old Korean was up and padding across the desert toward him, his face a stony frown.

"Your driving skills are appalling," Chiun accused as he approached. "If you wish me dead so that you may assume Reigning Masterhood, please tell me. I would rather send myself home to the sea than participate in any more of your one-man demolition derbies."

"Don't start on my driving again," Remo warned, masking his intense relief. "Even *you* can't possibly blame me for *that.*"

At Remo's side now, Chiun puffed out his chest. "Perhaps," he admitted. "Nevertheless, you are crashing carriages with alarming frequency of late. When we return home, I am enrolling you in a driver's-education program."

As before, Remo detected a light undertone—very faint. He now suspected he knew why.

"Look who's talking," he replied. "Ted Kennedy laughs at your driving."

He looked back to the point they both knew to be ground zero.

The mushroom cloud was dissipating into thin smears of puffy lines above the hills. Even the wind was dying down.

"I guess we were far enough away to avoid the radiation," Remo commented.

"It is in the air," Chiun pointed out.

"Not bad," Remo said. "The sun on a weak ozone day."

"Nonetheless, we should leave this area."

Remo nodded.

They walked a half mile down the road when they came upon what was left of their truck.

The roof was crushed as if beneath a dinosaur's foot. The bed was twisted to a right angle from the cab. One axle had snapped. Half of it—along with the attached tire—was missing altogether.

"I guess we don't really need it anymore anyway," Remo commented. "It's pretty obvious we won't be bringing the neutrino bomb back with us."

"What of the emperor-in-exile?" Chiun asked.

"Yeah, the President," Remo said, exhaling. "He was going after Aruch. If we're lucky, we'll find both of them together. Assuming we can scrape up transportation."

"Ye of little faith," Chiun replied, eyebrow arched. He nodded down the road.

When Remo turned, he saw that a group of men on camelback was riding in from the north. They had seen the cloud and survived the terrifying gust of wind and were now coming to investigate the cause of the strange phenomenon.

When Remo turned back to Chiun, he was shaking his head.

"I am *not* riding one of those things," he said emphatically.

"We haven't a choice," Chiun insisted.

"They could probably give Ronaldman's wig lice lessons," Remo groused. "And I thought thanks to Master Na-Kup that you didn't like Mountain Monsters or Hill Humps or whatever the hell the Sinanju scrolls call camels."

"Hush," Chiun admonished. "I am about to negotiate with bedouins—the most crafty and avaricious hagglers in the world—and I do not need your constantly flapping lips as a distraction."

"Yeah? Well, I hope you have a plan," Remo muttered.

"Of course I do," Chiun sniffed.

The old Korean waited patiently for the men to

arrive. Remo stood beside him, tapping his foot on the road.

There were nine of them, all dressed in traditional robes and kaffiyehs. They slowed their beasts near the pair of strange pedestrians.

Faces dark as a desert night, their suspicious eyes peered out over sand-coated veils.

"Greetings!" the Master of Sinanju called up to the Arabs. "My son and I require two of these fine animals. Remo, pay the nice men."

"Some plan," Remo griped. Grunting, he dug in his pocket, removing a wad of bills.

Apparently, the bedouins didn't have a problem with American currency. Remo peeled off several hundred dollars, handing the bills to the eager men.

Two camels were separated from the rest. The Master of Sinanju scampered quickly onto the hump of the larger beast.

"Try not to crash this, Lead-Footed One," Chiun announced to Remo. With a twist of the reins and a kick of his heels, the camel began to trot down the road.

"I'll crash you," Remo grumbled. Grabbing a fistful of fur, he pulled himself up onto the hump. Grinding his heels into the animal's sides, he sent his camel after that of the Master of Sinanju.

31

Though the media liked to think he had slept straight through his eight years in office—save, of course, the single time he managed to pad, yawning, down to the Oval Office to approve a secret arms deal to a fundamentalist Islamic nation—the former President of the United States had been as attentive as his post would allow. As luck would have it, he remembered from White House briefings that the main office of the Palestine Independence Organization was in Hebron. Problem was, it was miles away across hostile terrain.

A stolen robe and headdress had gained him anonymity after his harrowing escape from his PIO captors in Lebanon. The features that peeked out around his veil had not brought unwanted attention. His dark tan and weathered skin were common enough for men in this part of the world.

A stolen jeep and dumb luck helped him slip across the border from Lebanon into Israel. His biggest problem came once he was inside the Jewish State.

His jeep ran out of gas. Carrying his disguise in

a lumpy bundle beneath one arm, he was forced to continue on foot. He hadn't gone far before he was spotted by a border patrol.

Fortunately, in another lifetime, the President had been a bit of a thespian. His acting skills had come in handy when he was being questioned by the soldier.

The former President claimed to be an American tourist who was visiting Israel with his wife. He said he had become separated from the rest of his bus tour.

The soldier was very young. So young, he failed to recognize the old man standing before him.

After admonishing the tourist for his carelessness, the soldier drove him back to within a few miles of the disputed West Bank where the President claimed his tour bus was scheduled to arrive any minute.

After the soldier had gone, the President donned his Arab disguise once more and headed into the West Bank.

As he made his way through the busy streets, the former President caught a few curious glances from passersby.

In his robe, with head and face covered, he was dressed rather formally for the disputed zone. Most Arabs in the area were comfortable wearing a simple open shirt and slacks. However, in spite of the interest some might have had, they left the President alone.

Aruch's office...Aruch's office...

He wasn't quite sure where to go. For some reason, he seemed to think it was on the south side of Hebron.

The buildings were all at least three stories tall and set directly on the roads. They lent a feeling of intense claustrophobia to the narrow streets.

The President pushed himself forward. He felt the strain of labor burning in his lungs. His heart pounded. Muscles ached from effort.

He was exhausted. Ten years before, this would have been a grueling test of endurance. But at his age and after all he had recently been through, it was nearly too much for him.

It was a struggle to move on.

But he *had* to. Nossur Aruch had the neutrino bomb. The PIO leader *had* to be stopped.

As he trudged on, puffing ragged breaths through his sweat-and-saliva-soaked veil, the President thought ruefully how much easier it would have been for him fifteen years ago.

Back then, all he would have had to do was pick up the red phone in the White House. Smith would have answered, and within minutes his men would be deployed. Aruch, Babcock and the neutrino bomb all would have been stopped.

But he could not live in the past.

Smith's men were doubtless looking for him. The President himself had seen to that. But they might not know where he had ended up. They could still be wandering around the California hospital. No, the

President was here, *now.* The only man who knew what was going on. The *only* man who could make a difference in time.

Panting, trying to run. More a hobble.

A rumble in the distance. Thunder?

The buildings around him seemed to shimmer. For a moment, it looked as if they might flicker away altogether, fading into the desert, joining the dust of countless civilizations that had squatted for a brief time beneath the same heartless sun, only to be absorbed by the sand.

Wind followed. Strong, but not fierce. Kicking up great clouds of dust in the narrow passageway between the tightly lined buildings.

The dust began to settle moments later. Even before it had, the President knew he was too late.

Tiny battered cars stopped dead on the street around him. Their drivers could not get them to start again.

Shouts from buildings.

Confusion. Fear. *Panic.*

The anarchy would come quickly. He was too late. There was nothing more he could do here.

The President turned, hurrying back the way he had come. He would get back to Israel. To safety.

Aruch hadn't brought the bomb to Hebron. The wind had been to the President's back. He had planted it somewhere closer to the border with Lebanon.

After forty-five minutes of running back and forth

in this squalid city, he was growing dizzy from his exertions. The frustration of failure piled atop the strain of effort.

An old man. He never should have tried. Never should have taken the risk.

Even as he thought the words, he knew they were wrong. They were foreign to him. Not what he expected from himself.

He had tried. He had failed, but he had *tried.*

Sweating profusely. The chaos in the streets growing around him with each tortured step.

Gangs grabbing strangers. Fearful shouts. Sudden bursts of anger. Somewhere nearby was a cheering mob.

His heart pounded. Mind swirled.

Couldn't breathe. Too much effort.

Have to stop. Have to rest. If only for a minute.

He paused against the side of a building at a quiet intersection. Panting, he leaned against the hard wall. A wrinkled hand pulled the veil from his face only for a moment.

Fresh air. He breathed deeply a few times.

The air was like sandpaper on his raw throat. Still, it felt good. Refreshing. Bracing.

Keep moving.

He pushed away from the wall, reaching to replace his veil as he did so.

The President took a step around the corner…

…and plowed directly into Nossur Aruch.

Colliding with the rushing figure, the PIO leader

was forced to take an awkward step back. He was slammed from behind by Bryce Babcock.

When he saw whom he had bumped into, the whites of Aruch's eyes became visible above his dark sunglasses.

"What is this!" the terrorist demanded, fumbling a curving dagger from a scabbard at his waist. He pressed the knife to the belly of the ex-President.

The President was too out of breath to reply. Wheezing, he allowed the veil—which he had not fully reattached—to drop from his hand. It swung down to his shoulder.

"No. Put it on," Aruch commanded.

Nodding weakly, the elderly man did as he was told. Once his face was hidden, the PIO leader nodded.

"I do not know how you got here, but you are coming with me, ancient one," Nossur Aruch growled. With a shove, he propelled his captive forward. All the while, he held the knife menacingly close to the older man's side.

The former President was too weak to resist. He allowed the PIO leader to guide him at knifepoint. Bryce Babcock fell in behind the others.

Together, the unlikely trio hustled off through the growing chaos of Hebron.

The Master of Sinanju rode into the ancient city of Hebron like a conquering hero, perched carefully atop his magnificent galloping desert-brown camel.

Remo's camel was struggling to keep up. The animal spit and hissed and made a general nuisance of itself as it clomped on broad-toed, furry feet into the chaotic streets. It would have stopped running altogether if not for the judicious coaxing Remo occasionally applied.

"Why is my camel so winded?" Remo complained as they waded into the surly crowds of Arabs.

"You are too fat," Chiun called back. "See how my beast accepts its precious feathery cargo with speed and grace."

"It's as graceful as a frigging camel, Little Father," Remo said. "We would have been better off saddling two pigs." His own mount wheezed suddenly. Remo grimaced at the sickly sound. "I think mine has asthma."

"Stop complaining. Camels all make similar noises."

"Wanna trade?"

"Why would I want your sick camel?"

They rode deeper into the city.

Packs of men with mischief as their purpose prowled the streets. Apartment windows had already been smashed on most buildings. Cars whose engines had been frozen by the neutrino wave sat abandoned in the middle of roadways. Molotov cocktails had been tossed into some of the vehicles. From the open car windows, orange flames licked up into plumes of thick black smoke.

Remo was nearly shocked by the speed at which the inhabitants of the town had descended into feral behavior, but then he realized that—at least according to the regular images on the nightly news—they hadn't been too far away from it to begin with.

Riding down a particularly ravaged street, a group of men took evil interest in Remo and Chiun. One Arab with a board in his hand separated from the rest. He ran over to the Master of Sinanju, screaming a torrent of unintelligible Arabic while waving the chunk of wood menacingly.

With a toe-kick to the nose, Chiun sent the man sailing backward onto the hood of a stalled car. After that, the crowd cut them a wide swath.

In the next three city blocks, they passed seven rock fights, five knife imbroglios, three immolations by fire, an impalement, six savage chain beatings and two stonings.

"It's nice these people haven't forgotten their

roots,'' Remo commented aridly as they rode past a group of Arabs who were pounding one another over the head with particularly thick copies of the Koran.

''Man has raised hand against his fellow man since the beginning of time.'' Chiun nodded. ''Be thankful it is so, for if it was not, we would be out of work.'' The old Korean's eyes narrowed. ''There,'' he announced abruptly.

He aimed a tapered finger down the road to where the street curved away between tightly packed buildings. A group of five Arabs was working near a jeep.

''What about them?'' Remo asked.

''They are of the Aruch clan,'' Chiun replied.

''How can you tell?''

''Do you not recognize the kaffiyeh?''

Remo looked over at the black-and-white-checkered headdresses some of the men wore. He shrugged. ''One dirty dishrag's the same as the next to me,'' he said.

Chiun fixed him with a hooded stare. ''Observe, O educated one,'' he said dryly.

Using his ankles, the Master of Sinanju gently pinched his camel's furry hump. The beast lowered obediently to the ground. Chiun had no sooner slid off the animal than he was marching over to the Arabs.

Remo's camel wasn't at all obliging. Even though he copied Chiun's technique exactly, the animal only spit and snorted. It even twisted its head around, trying to bite him. He finally gave up altogether and hopped to the ground. He trotted up beside the Master of Sinanju.

"I miss having a car," Remo complained as they walked.

"Cars are filthy inventions," Chiun replied.

"Camels are filthier," Remo said. "And I never had a Chrysler try to bite me on the leg."

The Arabs heard them talking. The men had been fussing about, attempting to figure out why the jeep would no longer run. But at Remo and Chiun's approach, they grew instantly alert.

AK-47s had been abandoned to the hood of the car. They grabbed them now, brandishing the weapons like clubs.

"Banu al-Asfar!" one of them screeched, at the same time swinging his gun toward Chiun's head.

There was a satisfying crunch of bone as gun butt met cranium. Unfortunately for the Arab, the rifle failed utterly to make contact with the intended skull.

The man watched in horrified wonder down the length of his gun as the side of one of his comrade's heads collapsed into a visible V-shape. Somehow the man had moved into the spot previously occupied by the ancient intruder.

As the first dead Palestinian fell to the ground, the man became aware of similar noises all around him. Horrid crunches of bones being irreparably broken. When the Arab wheeled, he thought he saw flashes of movement. Never in the same spot, and never resolving into human form. When the last of his companions fell to the ground at the front of the jeep, the Arab looked up, his eyes sick.

The old one was back in his original position. The young white stood nearby, ankle deep in bodies.

"We need a tour guide." Remo smiled. "You're it."

The Arab looked down at his dead companions. He looked back up. He gulped.

"I will lead you to the very portal of hell and beyond," the Arab enthused.

"PIO headquarters'll do," Remo said.

"Anything you wish," the Arab replied with a frantic nod.

Chiun's face was impassive. "Remo, lash this dog to the reins of your camel that he might precede us to the evil one's lair."

Nodding, Remo grabbed hold of the Arab and began to drag him back down the street. He took only two steps before he noticed that his camel was nowhere to be seen. Only Chiun's animal remained.

Remo stopped dead. "Hey, my camel is gone," he griped.

"Tether the Arab to your neck for all I care," Chiun said, breezing past him. "Just do not let him get away."

Leaving Remo to deal with their guide, the Master of Sinanju marched quickly down the street, lest Remo get any designs for his own mount.

THE DOORKNOB HAD FUSED to a solid mass on the front of the Palestine Independence Organization building. Luckily, a few of Aruch's men were loitering outside the building. They managed to pop the door open with a minimum of effort.

"Get out of my way!" Aruch commanded the instant the door sprang into the foyer.

He bulled his way through the mass of men and into the main hallway. The others followed him inside, propelling Bryce Babcock and the former President before them.

Aruch led the parade to his office.

"The day has arrived at long last!" Aruch sang merrily as he stomped across the room.

Passing his cluttered desk, he breezed onto the veranda. Outside, Nossur Aruch didn't seek the help of his men. This was a special moment. One he wished to keep for himself.

Like a selfish child with a birthday gift, he tore at the netting surrounding his precious rocket.

It was difficult at first. Much of the camouflage remained stubbornly attached to the uppermost portion of the long rocket. A final mighty tug brought the entire plastic covering tumbling to the balcony.

The missile was a slender white tube with two sets of wings—one halfway down the length of the assembly, the other, smaller pair near the tail. A stabilizing dorsal fin extended from the rear.

Two sustainable ramjets were fixed to the dorsal and ventral sides of the missile. In addition to these, four jettisonable rocket boosters were attached in a fan arrangement around the housing.

The menacing black nose of the Bloodhound pointed to the northwest.

At the base of the missile, Nossur Aruch glanced at his guests, tears of joy in his eyes.

"She is beautiful, is she not?" the PIO leader said, sniffling. He ran a hand lovingly along one of the slender boosters.

The former President of the United States remained silent. He stared at Aruch, a grim expression on his weathered features.

"That's a rocket," Bryce Babcock said, shocked.

"A Bloodhound Mk2. British long-range. It will strike Jerusalem minutes after launch."

"It won't work," Babcock blurted.

"Do not attempt to talk me out of it," Aruch warned. "I have waited years for this glorious day."

"That's not what I meant," the interior secretary said. "The *rocket* won't work. It's metal on metal. The neutrino wave would have neutralized its working components."

Aruch glanced in horror at Babcock. "You lie!"

Babcock shook his head. "Please, Nossur. You saw the evidence out in the street. With your own car. If you try to launch that thing, it will *not* go up. Worse, if some of its components survived the neutrino wave, it could detonate right here on the pad."

"It *could* have survived?" Aruch ventured hopefully.

"No," Babcock insisted. "It will never launch like it's supposed to. That's the whole point of the peace bomb. But some of the inner workings could have survived. Lead could have shielded some of the smaller metal parts. Silicon or plastic might have made it through. Enough might work in there to detonate whatever explosives are inside."

Nossur Aruch listened carefully to what was being explained to him. He made an instant decision.

"You," he announced, pointing to one of his men. "Fire this missile in precisely two minutes."

While the PIO soldier stepped dutifully onto the balcony, Nossur Aruch hightailed it back inside. Running through the halls of the headquarters, he led his entourage--which still included Bryce Babcock and the former President—into the courtyard on the far side of the building.

They had barely gotten outside when the ground was rocked by an explosion.

Leaves shook and fell from carefully tended trees. Birds took flight. The blast shook the three-story building behind them to its very foundation. The rear wall teetered for a long moment before finally crumbling inward. When it fell, it revealed a pile of rubble beyond it. The rest of the building had already collapsed in on itself.

Choking dust filled the courtyard. Thick black smoke poured up from the ruins.

Nossur Aruch took in the devastation with a look

of dull incomprehension. That expression slowly melted into one of pure, unadulterated horror.

With a shuffling deliberateness he turned, panting, to face the interior secretary of the United States. His insane eyes were as wide as saucers.

"You blew up my headquarters!" Nossur Aruch yelled at Bryce Babcock.

"I warned you," Babcock whimpered, shrugging fearfully. He cringed as if waiting to be hit.

Aruch turned back to the smoking remains of what had for years been the home of his beloved PIO.

"You blew up my headquarters!" he screamed again.

"Sorry," Babcock offered weakly.

"Even the accursed Jews never did that!" Aruch screamed.

Babcock said nothing more, fearful that he might inspire more anger in the PIO leader.

Head shaking in disbelief, Aruch stared at the ruins of his headquarters. Only the back steps remained. He kicked at a piece of shattered brick.

"What made this happen?" Aruch demanded.

"The peace bomb lets off a powerful magnetic force," Babcock said. "It would have fused the missile to the platform. I explained all this to you before."

"Yes, yes, yes." Aruch waved impatiently.

Although he had heard the words, he had found

them foolish and, consequently, had disregarded much of what was said. But now...

"What is the effective range of your bomb?"

"No one's really sure," Babcock admitted. "Could be a couple of hundred miles."

"This would be the same in all that area?" he asked, flapping an arm to the destroyed building.

"Yes," Babcock said, relieved that Aruch seemed to finally be getting the whole point of the peace bomb.

"So whoever gets weapons into this region of the world first will rule it," Nossur Aruch said. A wicked smile began to form within the graying stubble on his wrinkled face.

"Um—" Babcock began warily.

Aruch cut him off, a smile appearing in full bloom. "We need guns, bullets, explosives. And a radio. One that will have survived your peace bomb."

"None of them *would* have," Babcock insisted.

Aruch's response to this was a knowing smile.

"I will need money," the PIO leader continued. He walked around Babcock to stand toe-to-toe with the President. "What do you think, old one? I am certain Iran would be interested in having you as a prize. Libya would also pay a handsome price. For that matter, a dozen countries in this region. Many more around the world. You will make me the last great monarch of all the Mideast."

He spoke it as a challenge.

The former President looked down at Nossur Aruch. His sun-creased face held an expression of bland contempt.

"Why is it that little fellas like you always have such big mouths?" he said in his soft-spoken, aw-shucks twang.

The PIO leader's smile vanished into his whiskers, replaced by a scowl. Wheeling to his men, he snapped a thumb to the President.

"Take him," he barked, at the same time marching for the gate at the rear of the courtyard. "His worthless hide is as good as gold. We ride this hour to my ancestral land. And to glory."

"I PAID GOOD MONEY for that camel," Remo groused.

"You should have watched it better."

"I think that bedouin ripped me off. Is there such a thing as a homing camel?"

Remo was trudging morosely beside the Master of Sinanju, who was seated grandly on the hump of his camel. Up ahead, leading the two of them through the streets of Hebron, was their captured PIO soldier.

"Do not complain to me because you cannot be trusted to care for pets," Chiun said. "You should have started with something smaller. Perhaps a hamster."

"Yuk it up," Remo muttered. "I'm glad *one* of us is having a good time."

Truth be told, despite the long walk beneath the hot sun and his own complaints to the contrary, Remo found that his mood, like Chiun's, was lighter than it had been of late.

After a miserable, self-indulgent three months, the Master of Sinanju seemed to finally be putting his movie deal behind him. This little jaunt around the world had turned the Korean back into his old self again, and in spite of all the kvetching and insults, Remo was happy to have him back. Of course, he kept his own mood masked, lest Chiun, sensing complacency in his pupil, revert to being the pain in the neck he'd been since last spring.

"I just hope the President is with Aruch after all this," Remo commented.

From the distance, they felt a sudden rumbling. It was a much smaller explosion, nowhere near as powerful as that from the neutrino bomb.

"What was that?" Remo asked as the aftershocks rolled away beneath their feet.

As if in reply, a thin finger of black smoke began to rise in the pale blue sky above the distant rooftops.

"Whatever it is," the Master of Sinanju intoned, "it comes from the direction in which we are headed."

It took another fifteen minutes to wend their way through the maze of streets to the spot where the explosion had originated. When they got there, they found the pile of smoking debris that was all that remained of the West Bank offices of the PIO.

"This was the headquarters?" Remo asked their Arab companion.

"It is the home of the Palestine Independence Organization," the guide replied.

"You think Aruch was inside?" Remo asked Chiun.

The Master of Sinanju had dismounted from his camel and was walking around the brick and mortar rubble with his pupil. He paused in the rear courtyard.

"No," Chiun said. He pointed at some footprints, recently made in the dusty earth. "Several men escaped injury. And look," he added, "the former occupant of the Eagle Throne was with them."

"The President?" Remo asked. "Are you sure?"

Chiun gave him a baleful glare.

"Okay, so he went with him." Remo nodded reasonably. "Now we've got to figure out *where* they went."

"There is no figuring necessary," Chiun explained. "Aruchs are born of the desert. That is where he will return."

"How can you be so sure?"

Chiun folded his arms matter-of-factly. "A dog never tires of smelling the same mound of excrement," he replied.

"Since I'm lousy with pets, I'll have to take your word on that," Remo said. Surveying the damage, he exhaled in annoyance. "Well, if we're going into the desert, I'm not hoofing it."

"There is a stable nearby," the PIO guide offered hopefully.

This sounded good enough to Remo.

"Scrounge us up four horses and I'll consider letting you live," he said to the soldier.

Face brightening, the man spun, hurrying from the rubble-strewn courtyard.

"Let's hope the President can keep his mouth shut a little longer," Remo said to Chiun as they followed the man out to the street. "If he spills the beans this late in the game, Smitty'll have a stroke."

A few hours of untroubled sleep at his desk had faded into a waking nightmare for Harold W. Smith.

Remo and Chiun had failed to halt the detonation of the neutrino bomb. That much was painfully obvious.

The world had been turned on its ear following the events in the Middle East.

Beep. Beep. Beep.

The sound came from Smith's computer. More raw data.

Scanning it quickly, he filed it. It was like spooning out the ocean. Another bulletin raced in to fill the space.

Beep. Beep. Beep.

The CURE director was looking at one of the greatest crises he had ever faced.

The range of the neutrino bomb's magnetizing wave was far greater than even the wildest guesses of the scientists at Los Alamos. Even though the small plutonium bomb had been set off in the north of the West Bank, it had caused a technological catastrophe nearly eight hundred miles away in some instances.

Due to the effects of the bomb, Israel, Lebanon, Jordan and Cyprus were totally cut off from the outside world. Nothing technological appeared to be working in any of the small nations nearest the blast site. Much of Iraq was similarly affected.

Saudi Arabia, Egypt as far as Aswan, Izmir, Turkey, on the Aegean, Syria—all had experienced the devastating sweep of the magnetic neutrino wave. The invisible wall of heavy atoms had even reached as far as Abadan, Iran—some 780 miles from the blast zone.

It was a cataclysm of incalculable proportions.

The only information coming out of the region was that available via satellite.

Smith had shifted his focus almost immediately. At that point, the neutrino bomb was the old news. What was happening in the rest of the world as a result of the blast was what worried the CURE director now.

The situation was grim.

As he had secretly feared, other nations viewed the incident as an opportunity.

Smith was in the process of reading the latest report, this one from Cuba.

Castro had acted on the news out of the Mideast with surprising speed. The head of the former Soviet client state was in the process of rounding up weapons to ship to Arab sympathizers. A fleet of three banana boats had been assembled to sail the arms to the Mediterranean. For Castro, it was both a moneymaking scheme and an attempt by the forgotten dictator to gain a toehold in the region.

While Castro's eagerness to take advantage of the situation was almost laughable, the actions of other nations were far more serious.

Smith dumped the terse Cuban report back into the growing file of international opportunists. He pulled out an update of one of the more troubling cases.

Russia was involved in a massive collection of arms. Even as Smith read the report, he knew that crates of guns and ammunition were being airlifted to ships in the Black Sea.

The former superpower clearly saw the events in the Mideast as an opportunity to regain some of its past glory. Smith had even intercepted a private memo to the United Nations that had originated somewhere high up in the Russian Duma. Before the end of the day, there would be official condemnation from the Russian government for the actions of the United States in the West Bank. At the same time, the vessels would already be on their way to the Middle East.

America would be helpless to stop them.

The Sixth Fleet was in disarray. The aircraft carrier that had brought Remo into Lebanon was out of commission. At present, it was unknown whether it was damaged beyond repair. Smaller battleships in the vicinity had been similarly affected.

The Russians would have no interference entering the region. There would be no objection from the helpless U.S. ships nor from their impotent crews. They would be forced to watch in silence as the Russian flotilla sailed with its deadly cargo into the silent ports of terrorist nations.

And the United States would not be alone in silence. The navies of virtually every nation in the area had been crippled by the neutrino wave. At the moment, hundreds of vessels were floating helpless in the sea, targets to be boarded or blown out of the water by hostile forces. The crews did not even have arms to resist.

While the Russians presented the greatest threat, they were by no means alone. Libya and Iran were involved in an air war—limited at present—to see who would have the pleasure of annexing the entire affected region.

The French saw an opportunity to retake some of their former possessions.

China was thrilled with the chance to spread its military influence into a new region and, if anyone attempted to stop them, perhaps employ some of the American technology they had obtained with Dr. Ree Hop Doe's aid.

Even the British—worried that others would get there first—were preparing arms shipments. A force was already on its way from those western areas of the Mediterranean not overcome by the neutrino blast. More were heading in from the Atlantic.

America was also responding.

Worried that some hostile nation would be first to lay claim to the wide-open oil fields of several of the countries in the magnetized zone, task forces from the Second Fleet were already being pulled out of the western Atlantic and sent into the Mediterranean. Ships from the Pacific were being spread thin into both oceans to compensate. But the repositioning would take two days at best.

Fortunately, it seemed that, at least for now, everyone was experiencing the same disarray. Smith dreaded the moment that someone realized the real opportunity was not in the Mideast, but elsewhere in the world. Many nations were so eager to race for the pot of gold they saw in the Mediterranean they were leaving their own territorial waters nearly undefended. It was a blind feeding frenzy, the likes of which the modern world had never before seen.

Smith watched it all from his Folcroft office, helpless to do anything about it.

Hopefully, Remo was nowhere near the bomb when it went off. If he had survived the blast, he was somewhere in the area. Even though he had failed to stop the bomb, there was still the matter of retrieving the former President.

At this point, Smith would have liked more than anything to send CURE's enforcement arm after whoever had set off the neutrino bomb. It appeared to be Nossur Aruch and his PIO. Bryce Babcock was not alone in this; that much was certain. But there was no way to contact Remo in the field. If he found the President, Remo might just bring the former chief executive back without going after the PIO leader.

In the end, the villain in this might get away. Smith would have to satisfy himself with the fact that having the former commander in chief returned to American soil might be the only resolution to this dire situation.

And the tinderbox that was the Middle East would have to decide its own fate.

As he worried over this inescapable conclusion, Smith's computer emitted a sudden electronic beep.

Typing rapidly, he brought up the latest information the CURE mainframes had culled for him.

Behind his rimless glasses, his gray eyes scanned the newest lines of text.

Spain was now in on the act. The European country was sending several naval vessels to the Mideast. At present, the data on the latest nation to join the growing tide of warships was incomplete. Intelligence sources had yet to determine how much weaponry the Spanish State was shipping to the region.

Smith dumped this latest report in with the others and backed out of the system. Before shutting off his computer, he disabled the automated beep that alerted him to incoming information concerning the region. It had been sounding almost nonstop since the detonation of the neutrino bomb.

Smith was only one man. There was nothing he could do from his Folcroft office that would remedy this crisis.

Even Remo and Chiun, with all their abilities, would be unable to stop the situation from playing out in whatever manner was destined.

One way or another, it was already over.

With this thought in mind, Smith got up from his computer and climbed wearily from behind his desk. With both hands, he rubbed his aching lower back.

The Folcroft cafeteria had received a shipment an hour before. He had heard the truck back in behind the building.

The cafeteria director was supposed to have gotten in some of the prune-whip yogurt he enjoyed.

Smith left his office in search of his guilty little pleasure. The only one in his dour life.

34

The army had grown from a handful of ragtag PIO soldiers to a mighty force of shouting, triumphant Palestinians. By the time they passed through the Ghor depression through which the Jordan River flowed to the north of the Dead Sea, they were five hundred strong.

Horses panted and frothed, propelled by frantic kicks from jubilant Arabs. They screamed the war whoops of their ancestors as they passed the border of Israel into Jordan. Two meaningless names. Both nations would soon be one. Along with many others.

At the front of the army, Bryce Babcock struggled to stay in his saddle. The horse between his legs pounded forward in spite of its rider's limited equestrian skills.

Beside the interior secretary, the former President of the United States rode into the encroaching night, his body moving in perfect rhythm with the animal beneath him.

And, on his magnificent sleek black steed at the head of the victorious pack—sweat glistening off its muscled rump, hoofs digging half moons in the clayish earth—Nossur Aruch was a conquering god.

They had sensed his purpose, these sons of Palestine who followed him. Gone were the feelings of mistrust from the past few dark years. Gone, too, was the anger. The hatred. He was power; he was the future. And they were his.

To lead.

To govern over.

To send to their deaths if he so commanded.

He was their caliph. Their sultan. Their king.

Nossur Aruch was finally, at this late point in his life, the monarch he had always hoped to be.

He had tossed away his pathetic disguise in Hebron. There was no longer a need. He wore his white-and-black-checkered kaffiyeh proudly once more. Many others in his band wore the same headdress. The new mane of power in the Mideast. Symbol of a dynasty that would last longer than the pyramids themselves.

Although he had declared himself president-in-exile of Palestine years before, he was not actually of the region. He was Jordanian, born to Palestinian parents. The land of his forebears was east of the Jordan. It was to this spot—this haven—that Aruch and his army now rode.

The day was growing short. Night was sweeping in upon them, brushing the last of the white-hot desert day from the sky by the time they reached the oasis of the Aruch family.

In his youth, he had always thought of it as a place of coolness and shade. A sanctuary in the fire that was the desert. In his adulthood, he saw it for what it was. A pitiful lump of washed-out green in the Jordanian desert between As Salt and Madaba.

The sun was gone. Melted into fat blobs of orange as they rode into the oasis. Long shadows cast from ill-watered trees became specters of black across the sand.

The army pounded to a thundering halt.

They had no sooner stopped when the ragged tents that were speckled between the trees began to disgorge hordes of pitifully filthy men and women. Inhabitants of the oasis. The family of Nossur Aruch. They crowded around the army, pawing at boots and trouser legs, all the while wailing pathetically.

Aruch kicked at the faces of any who came near him. There were at least a dozen of his sisters jostling them. Even more nieces and nephews.

"Leave me, wanton trulls and whoresons!" Aruch shouted, viciously booting his older sister, Shaboobatez, in her fuzzy jaw. It would have knocked out her teeth had she had any left.

Hands raised in supplication, his family backed away.

Aruch slid off his horse.

The women of his clan were notoriously ugly, snagging as mates men who floundered at the stagnant end of the gene pool. The homely children they produced wouldn't have surprised anyone with a passing knowledge of genetics. The world would have been shocked to discover that Nossur Aruch had gotten the looks in his family.

The PIO head was like a movie star at his high-school reunion as he pushed his way through the sea of grabbing hands.

A filthy nylon tent checkered in white and black to match his kaffiyeh stood out in front of the rest. Aruch made it to the rear of the crowd, slipping through the closed tent flaps.

Inside was bare. It was no surprise. Years ago, on his first trip to the outside world, he had returned to find his tent completely stripped. His family had a tendency to steal anything that wasn't nailed down. Fortunately, their avarice was matched only by their laziness.

Dropping to his knees in the center of the tent, Aruch used his palms to push away the powdery sand that was the floor. A few short sweeps revealed a trapdoor. At one end was a wrought-iron loop.

Clawing for the handle, he pulled. At first it was a struggle, but soon the fused trapdoor hinges popped. He lifted the door.

At once a generator hummed to life. Fluorescent lights flickered on a moment afterward, revealing a steep staircase that ran down into an unseen chamber.

Aruch hurried down the stone steps.

Another metal door was at the bottom—a necessary precaution just in case his family found the heavy lead trapdoor above. A key hung in perpetuity around his neck. Aruch stuck it in the lock, saying a quick prayer to Allah that the neutrino wave hadn't somehow damaged the bolt.

With a satisfying click, the door rattled open.

Aruch exhaled relief.

The lead construction of the upper door had shielded down below. And if things in the stairwell worked, that meant everything beyond did, as well. Including his radio. His conduit to the outside world. The thing that would make him king of all the Mideast.

Heart pounding a thrilling chorus in his ears, Nossur Aruch pushed open the door that led to his great destiny. With a devilish smile, he slipped inside the dimly lit chamber.

IF REMO WAS NOT POSSESSED of the ability to unerringly judge direction by attuning himself to the gravitational force of the Earth, he would have been convinced they were riding in circles.

Every inch of desert they passed since riding across the Jordan looked exactly the same.

They were stopped now. Their horses whinnied, kicking up clouds of dust.

The sun had fled. The world around them had taken on shades of pale blue. Above them, the burning stars were close enough to touch off spot fires in the desert sand.

A cold night wind blew across their backs, sending up minicyclones of dust in the vast tracts of empty space before them.

As Remo and their PIO guide sat waiting on their mounts, the Master of Sinanju walked a few yards ahead. He was bent at the waist, staring thoughtfully at the ground.

"This sand is shifting so much you can't tell anything," Remo called to him. His horse gave an angry snort.

Chiun did not respond.

"It'd help if *you* knew where we were going," Remo accused the PIO soldier.

The Palestinian shook his head in apology. "I am from Hebron. I do not know the desert."

When Remo again looked to the Master of Sinanju, Chiun was kicking lightly at the sand. Puffs of dust swirled away from the toes of his sandals.

Turning back to the PIO man, Remo shook his head. "You're a sorry excuse for a guide, you know that?" he said. "Hit the road. But leave the horse."

He nodded to a second, riderless mount next to the Palestinian's.

The man eagerly unlooped the reins from his saddle, handing them over. Before Remo could change his mind, the soldier gave the ribs of his own horse a sharp kick. The animal began to beat a hasty retreat back toward Israel.

As the PIO soldier rode off in one direction, the

Master of Sinanju came padding back from the other.

"Any luck?" Remo asked.

"They rode this way several hours ago," Chiun said as he pulled himself up into his saddle.

"How many?"

"It is difficult to tell. The tracks have degraded. Perhaps twenty-five score." His wrinkled face was troubled.

"Old Nosehair has pulled together quite a little army for himself," Remo said with a thin frown. "Whatever he's got planned, I say we nip it in the bud."

There was no disagreement from the Master of Sinanju. Nudging their horses with their heels, they rode off side by side into the silvery desert night.

THE STATICKY VOICE on the radio spoke English, but with a distinctly Russian accent.

"It will be our delight to aid the Palestinian people in this time of difficulty," the Russian colonel said.

"How soon?" Nossur Aruch asked furtively into the radio microphone. For some reason, he felt compelled to whisper.

It was cold in his bunker. He shivered in his artificial cavern far beneath the sand.

"The *Pa-Roosski* is off the coast of Lebanon now. We can airdrop you a shipment within four hours."

"What of the Americans?"

The Russian's smile was nearly visible across the empty miles that separated them.

"Their Sixth Fleet is drifting helpless at sea," the colonel said. "Some of their vessels have run aground They are of no consequence to either of us."

Relieved that his one concern had been allayed, Aruch gave the Russian his coordinates in the Jordanian desert.

"Several packages will be arriving at your location shortly," the colonel said. "I know that you will use their contents wisely. Russia intends to enjoy a long and mutually beneficial relationship with the Palestinian people and their president. Good night, sir." With that, the Russian was gone.

The deal was struck. Just like that.

Aruch slipped the receiver into the hook on the side of the large square box.

He had not even had to offer the former American President as payment. Money wasn't necessary now. The Russians only wanted to establish a new client state. Their first in years.

For Nossur Aruch, it was all too good to be true. He would get his guns *and* he would receive payment. After all, the ex-President was of no use to him. He would auction off the old one to the highest bidder.

Aruch lifted the phone once more. With a single, stubby digit, he began dialing the long code that would connect him to Tripoli.

Remo heard the dull hum of the plane engine before the Master of Sinanju. It was coming from the north. Chiun's ears pricked up a microsecond after his pupil's. As they rode through the desert, they turned their faces to the sound.

The fat shape of a low-flying transport plane appeared as a dark shadow above the desert expanse.

It was a Russian Antonov An-26 Curl. A popular light tactical transport craft. The drone of its twin turboprops grew to an earthshaking bellow as the plane roared over the desert only a few miles from where Remo and Chiun were following Aruch's tracks. Falling in line far ahead of them, the aircraft began to track the same course as the two Masters of Sinanju.

"I think it's safe to assume they're not delivering copies of your movie to the Assam Blockbuster," Remo said tightly.

The Master of Sinanju didn't reply. His narrowed eyes were trained on the Antonov's distant shuddering tail.

Desert wind pelting their faces with grains of fine sand, they raced after the plane.

EXCITEMENT HAD PREVENTED Nossur Aruch from sleeping. Although night was nearly gone, the PIO leader was still wide awake when the growing thunder that was the Russian plane reached his thrilled ears.

He leaped eagerly to his feet, racing through the tent flaps and out into the patchy green island of the oasis.

Most of his army was still awake. Men sat around open fires at the edge of the oasis. A corral for the horses had been roped off in the adjacent desert. Near it, Bryce Babcock sat glumly. Beside him, sleeping lightly, was the former President of the United States.

Although Babcock was free, the President was not. The ex-chief executive's wrists had been lashed together.

Aruch's army had heard the plane, as well. They rose expectantly to their feet, eagerly following their leader into the desert just beyond the edge of the oasis.

Along the horizon, predawn streaks had begun to bleed into the smothering veil of night. The massive shape of the Antonov—visible as a gray shadow against what remained of midnight's twinkling alabaster stars—was like some great primordial bird.

Running lights off, the plane flew in low. It

seemed to drag daylight in its wake as it closed the distance between them. The Antonov bellowed over their heads, its great belly clearly visible to five hundred upturned Arab faces.

Aruch saw the cavernous black opening of the rear ramp just up the fuselage from the huge tail section.

When the Russian plane had cleared the far side of the oasis, something big and blockish slipped from the blackness of the open ramp.

The huge shipping crate tumbled through the air only a few seconds before a perfect white mushroom shape blossomed behind it. The parachute snagged eddies in the chill air, slowing the descent of the massive crate. The box hit sand a few seconds later, and the nylon chute collapsed, spent.

A cheer went up from Aruch's army. His men swarmed from the oasis, racing up to the big crate.

Crowbars were jimmied into the sliver of space between the wood on one side. Nails creaked in pain as the crate was pulled apart. The side dropped away with a sudden slap, disgorging contents at the feet of Nossur Aruch.

The AK-47s that spilled out had not been packaged as they would have during the glory days of the old Soviet Union. These guns were fully assembled. They had been piled in the crate with only torn sections of moth-eaten surplus Red Army blankets wrapped around them. Yellowed ten-year-old shredded copies of *Pravda* had been shoved in to fill any vacant space.

There were fifty guns in the case. These were hastily snatched up by the nearest PIO soldiers.

The Antonov was making another pass. In the desert a half mile distant, it began to drop a series of smaller crates. These floated to earth more slowly, touching the sand at about the time Aruch and his men reached them.

When they were split open, the boxes revealed hundreds of smaller cases of ammunition.

Like starving men on a shipment of food, the Arabs dove for the ammo. This was distributed to those with guns.

By now, the sky had lightened.

Far across the vacant plain, the Antonov was turning back for another run. In it was the future of the Mideast. The future of *King* Nossur Aruch.

His plan was set. They would take back the West Bank by force. Organized, his men would swarm through Jerusalem and into Israel. From there, he would secure his seat of power, striking out into the region in all directions. Like the relentless magnetic wave of the neutrino bomb, he would sweep across the Middle East until everything—from the Mediterranean to the Persian Gulf, from Turkey above to Egypt in northern Africa—fell beneath the trampling hoofs of his unstoppable Palestinian army.

The Antonov was nearly upon them once more. The desert shook with the violent force of sound flowing from the mighty turboprops of the impossibly large aircraft.

All at once, the big Russian plane seemed to make another, separate noise. A high-pitched shriek of rapid deceleration. Almost simultaneous to the appearance of the new sound came a blinding flash of light from the fuselage of the big plane. The Antonov appeared to jolt to one side as a crackling plume of flame and smoke erupted from her starboard nacelle. The engines exploded an instant later, ripping most of the right wing from the craft.

The crash came almost too quickly to be believed. At one moment, the Antonov was burning and airborne; the next it was plummeting earthward. It hit the sand with a thunderous boom, tearing a furrow of flame through the desert.

As the nose of the crashing plane barreled toward them, flaming out of control, Aruch and his men split apart. Screeching in panic and confusion, the soldiers raced into the desert, into the oasis, anywhere that would get them out of the path of the Russian plane.

As they ran, a pair of jets appeared up out of the growing dawn. The new planes screamed forward, ripping across the lightening sky.

Even as he ran, Aruch recognized the familiar flag painted on the tails of the two Mirage F-1s. It was a plain green, the traditional color of Islam. The flag of the Socialist People's Libyan Arab Jamahiriya.

Libya had blown the Russian plane, as well as Nossur Aruch's precious cargo, out of the sky.

"Sons of dogs!" Aruch bellowed, shaking a balled fist at the jets as they flew over his family's oasis. In the desert behind him, the crashed Antonov exploded and burned. "The infidel Khaddafi did not pay for this!"

The jets took a wide arc over the Jordanian desert before circling back around. Holding formation, they raced toward the oasis.

The Palestinian army dispersed before the Mirages.

Aruch slowed his pace as the jets flew toward him. Even as he noted that the Sidewinder missile was missing from the port wingtip rail of the right plane, the left plane was loosing its pair of similar missiles.

They detached in a cloud of trailing white smoke, rocketing toward the oasis. Eyes wide, Aruch dove for the sand and covered his head.

When the missiles struck an instant later, it was as if the desert floor had turned to flame.

Hundred-year-old trees exploded to smoking pulp. The plants were flung like matchsticks into the desert. Fire erupted from two smoking craters in the oasis. One heavy tree trunk crashed to the rope rail—the only thing that had prevented the terrified horses from running after the initial missile attack on the Antonov. The animals bolted now, racing across the desert.

By the time Aruch scampered back to his feet, the Mirage jets had circled again.

From the ground, rounds of automatic-weapons fire spit from the pitifully few guns the PIO soldiers had collected from the first and only Russian crate. The Libyan pilots returned fire on their way back to the oasis.

"He did not pay!" Nossur Aruch shouted as he bounded into the smoking ring that was his ancestral home.

Bryce Babcock greeted the PIO leader, grabbing him by the jacket. The interior secretary's drooping face was covered in grime. His eyes held a crazed, fearful look.

"What's going *on?*" Babcock begged.

"I am being *cheated!* That is what is going on!" Aruch screamed, shoving past the secretary.

Babcock dogged him as he hustled over to the seated form of the ex-President. The din had awakened the older man.

"Who are they? What do they want?" Babcock sniffled, a fearful eye on the sky. It had suddenly grown eerily quiet.

"I contacted several parties last night who I thought might be interested in purchasing the old devil," Aruch said, waving at the President. "Libya and Iran agreed to bid on him. But that beast in human form Khaddafi has decided to kill him without paying!"

Aruch again shook a fist at the empty sky. As if

in response, another rocket soared in out of nowhere, this one exploding in the dense greenery behind Aruch's tent. The PIO leader threw himself to the ground once more. Dust and rock pelted his back.

When he got to his feet, he found his tent had collapsed. Fire tore across the dry fabric. A few feet away, Babcock had crawled fearfully behind a shattered tree trunk.

With rage-twisted fingers, Aruch grabbed for the President.

"Looks like you should be trading up for a better class of friend," the old man commented, his weather-hardened face curled into the suggestion of a smile.

"Shut up!" Aruch snapped. "We will be safe in my bunker. I will get a fair bounty for you one way or another, old one." He dragged the President to his feet.

They had not taken a single step before an amused glint appeared in the eyes of the former chief executive. He was looking away from the burning tent. Toward the edge of the oasis.

"It's about time you fellas showed up," he said softly.

The voice that responded to the former President was new. And most terrifying of all, the words spoken were in unaccented English.

"Don't you remember? We always time these things for optimum dramatic effect."

Aruch whirled.

Two strangers had entered the oasis. A young white and an old Asian. As they slipped silently forward, Aruch stepped back, grabbing hold of the ex-President.

"He's *mine!*" the PIO leader screamed. As backdrop to his frantic shout, a new sound exploded in the sky above them.

A squadron of eight F-5s appeared out of the east. As they tore overhead, Aruch recognized the green, white and red flag of the Islamic Republic of Iran.

A demonic look of glee appeared in the eyes of Nossur Aruch. *Allies.* Fellow Arabs to help him battle these two men and the treacherous Libyan planes.

"They are here for him!" Aruch cried victoriously. Grabbing the rope that bound the President's hands, he tugged the old man's wrists in the air.

"I will get my pay! I will not be denied my rightful throne as ruler of all the Middle East!"

Far above, the Iranian planes began to fire on the Libyan craft, chasing the first arrivals away. The moment the Mirage jets broke formation and tore away across the desert, the F-5s turned their attention back on the oasis.

Nossur Aruch felt exaltation right up until the point the first plane fired Maverick air-to-surface missiles into the cluster of flaming trees and brush.

Shocked, Aruch cowered from the blast. When he straightened up, he saw that Remo was walking toward him. The PIO leader reacted with surprising speed.

A hand dropped to his belt, ripping his familiar automatic free of its leather holster. In an instant, the gun was pressed up against the President's temple.

"Do not move!" Aruch ordered.

In spite of the danger to the man who at one time had been the most powerful leader on Earth, the younger intruder did something that surprised the PIO head.

Remo smiled.

"Sorry, pal," he said, still walking. "You lose."

The leader of the Palestine Independence Organization had not expected his bluff would be called. But in a moment of shocking realization, he understood why this man hadn't stopped. His gun wouldn't work. It would have been rendered ineffective by the magnetizing wave of the neutrino bomb.

Desperate, Aruch flung his gun away, grabbing at the knife in his waist scabbard.

He had only brushed the hilt when he felt a sharp stab of pain in his gut. The wind instantly whooshed from his lungs. When he doubled over, a knee crashed into his forehead. As he fell to the sand, Nossur Aruch saw the former President of the United States staggering over to the young white stranger.

Reaching out, Remo snapped the President's bonds.

"I think you might have picked the wrong line of work, Mr. President," he said, nodding approval.

"Which time?" the former President replied with a fatigued, boyish grin.

Nossur Aruch struggled to his feet. "You will not take him!" he shouted. "He is *mine!* I need him for arms!"

All at once, the PIO leader felt a gentle displacement of air. The old Asian was suddenly beside him. Aruch had not even seen him move.

"But you already have arms, foolish one," the Master of Sinanju explained in a squeaky singsong.

Nossur Aruch felt a sudden wrenching sensation in his right shoulder. It was the worst pain the PIO leader had ever experienced in his life, as if a white-hot poker had been stabbed into the joint. And even as his shocked nervous system attempted to reconcile the horrid sensation with anything he had ever before experienced, the old terrorist's pain-flooded eyes detected something in front of his face.

It took a moment for Nossur Aruch to recognize his own right arm.

"You see?" Chiun said, waving the appendage before Aruch's horrified face. "And you are not only blessed with one, but two."

More pain. This time on the left.

Chiun held Aruch's other arm aloft. The white bone of the humerus jutted from the flesh. Muscle and tendons hung in ragged strips from the bloody end.

It was all too unreal. Reeling drunkenly, Aruch watched as the old Korean raised the inert arms high in the air.

With a violent snap, Chiun flipped the arms, now animated extensions of his own hands, toward each other. They swung around in two sweeping arcs, flat, lifeless palms eventually clapping with a terrific crack. However, in order for them to make such a sound, they had to first pass through the skull of Nossur Aruch.

The PIO leader's head exploded like a stomped-on water balloon. Brains and blood burst out in squishy red lumps across his ancestral land.

When he was finished with the limbs, Chiun dropped them atop the PIO leader's twitching body.

By now, there were more jets rending the sky above the oasis. Several more Libyan planes had joined the fray, replacing those that had fled. The *rat-a-tat* of autofire ripped across the warming sky.

"We should make haste," Chiun suggested.

Remo nodded. "Get the President out of here. I'll be with you in a minute."

As Chiun hurried the old chief executive to their frightened horses, Remo strode across the clearing. He had spied the familiar figure cowering behind a pulpy white tree trunk. He stopped before the shaking man.

"You're Bryce Babcock, right?" Remo's tone was cold.

Eyes screwed tightly shut, the interior secretary

had remained stock-still since Remo and Chiun's appearance, hoping that he would not be noticed. He jumped at the closeness of Remo's voice.

"Maybe," the secretary replied weakly.

"This is all your fault," Remo said. It was not an accusation, but a statement of fact.

His accuser's gaze was too unforgiving. At Remo's harsh stare, Babcock broke down whimpering.

"It wasn't supposed to be like *this,*" he wept. "It was supposed to bring peace. Peace to a region of the world that's never even known what real peace is. And if people here could finally get along, the rest of the world would have seen the light."

Remo's face was hard. "You're the one who had Earthpeace kill all those people in California just so they could kidnap the President."

Bryce Babcock sniffled. "You can't make an omelet without scrambling a few eggs," he offered timidly.

Remo's dark expression never wavered.

"Prepare to be scrambled," he said icily.

Hands flashed forward. Remo clamped firmly to either side of Babcock's head.

Babcock's bladder sensed before any other part of him that something was desperately wrong. It was splattering its final contents onto his boots even as the first hint of pure alarm appeared in his sagging eyes.

Remo's hands vibrated. And as the movement

worsened, the head between them shook with increasing fury.

It was as if the secretary of the interior had been hooked to a paint mixer. When Remo was through, Babcock's skull was filled with frothy gray sludge the consistency of a fast-food shake. Foamy brain overflow drizzled out nose and ears.

Dropping the lifeless body with its mushy pureed brain to the ground, Remo hurried from the oasis.

The dogfight above the desert had grown more frantic.

Rocket pods were firing all around the area. Bullets sang in every direction—in the sky and from the land. Bodies of PIO soldiers littered the field of combat.

More Iranian jets roared in over the Jordanian desert. The Palestinians on the ground assumed correctly that they were under attack from another hostile force. Before they had even been fired upon, they began shooting at the incoming Iranian planes. The Iranian F-5s responded to the hostile gunfire from the ground by launching wing-mounted missiles into the horde of Arab soldiers.

A few burning fighter planes had joined the Russian Antonov in the sand.

Pockets of fire erupted in the desert. Explosions ripped away at the oasis, at the remnants of Nossur Aruch's men and at the downed planes.

Running, Remo met Chiun and the former President a mile away from the worst of the combat. Both men were already atop their horses. Remo swung up into his saddle.

More Libyan jets had roared into view behind them. They immediately engaged the fresh Iranian aircraft. In their spare moments, they joined in the attack on the ground. Their purpose for being there was forgotten. Killing the ex-President had become secondary to blowing up one another.

Spurring their horses on, Remo, Chiun and the former President of the United States rode for several miles, eventually climbing an isolated dune far away. Turning in their saddles, they watched the combat rage, the field of battle awash now in the bloodred morning sun.

"Well, I suppose some things never change," the President said softly as they watched the dogfight. Echoing gunfire rose from the distant sand. He looked back to the Masters of Sinanju. "Speaking of which, I had a talk with your boss. You fellas were supposed to do that amnesia thing on me again. I was hoping you could work it this time so I'd be okay. You know, just forget what I'm supposed to, and so forth?"

There was a hopeful look on the old man's face.

It was the one question Remo hadn't thought to ask. "Chiun?" he said.

The Master of Sinanju shook his head sadly.

"Lamentably, no," he intoned. "It is rare, but for those who are affected as you by the Emptying Basin, there is no alternative."

The President took a deep breath. Turning from them, he stared off into the distance.

The battle raging far away was not even a distraction. He was staring beyond it, at the sky, at the land. At something unseen, far distant.

It was as if in that one moment he wanted to lock on to a small part of the world. Of *himself.* To try to hold on to something. When he finally looked back at them, his lopsided, youthful smile had returned. There was a hint of wetness in his tired eyes.

"I suppose now's as good a time as any," he said.

Remo returned the smile, a hint of sadness on his face. "It can wait till we get back," he offered gently.

The President nodded. "I suppose it can," he agreed. "As long as the two of you keep an eye on me until then."

"Sinanju will forever be by your side, noble one," the Master of Sinanju nodded.

The President's smile broadened as he appraised them both. "Well, what are you two lollygaggers waiting for?"

With a boyish energy that belied his years, the old man gave a wrench at his reins. For a minute, Remo thought he was going to fall backward off the animal.

The horse rose majestically onto its hind legs. Whinnying once, it dropped its front hoofs back to the sand, launching itself forward as it did so. The animal raced off across the desert. The President bounced expertly in the saddle, shoulders hunched, elbows raised like a Pony Express rider. A cloud of dust followed him.

"I reckon some people just have a knack for flamboyance, eh, Mr. Chin?" Remo commented, turning to the Master of Sinanju.

A smile toyed at the corner of Chiun's papery lips.

With a tug, his own horse repeated the maneuver of the President's, lifting its front legs high in the air. Chiun held the animal there for a moment, finally launching it forward before its front hooves had even reached the sand.

He raced off after the President.

"I hope I have half that energy when I'm a hundred," Remo muttered to his pony.

"You should live that long," Chiun called back.

Laughing out loud, Remo dug his heels into the sides of his horse. The three men rode off toward Israel, away from the rising sun.

GOLD
EAGLE

24

Anxiety had kept Harold Smith glued to his desk for hours. When the blue contact phone finally jangled to life, he grabbed for it with both hands.

"Report," he snapped.

"The President's been kidnapped, *again,*" Remo's somber voice announced. "And just so we get all the bad news out of the way up front, Nossur Aruch and his merry band of PIO minstrels have him now."

Alone in his office, Smith's lids blinked over bloodshot eyes. His sleep-deprived brain attempted to absorb this latest information. Shock alone dulled his natural urge to panic.

"When did he change hands?" he asked woodenly.

"Judging from the dried blood— What do you say, Little Father?" he called away from the phone. "Hour and a half?"

"*Two* hours, Emperor Smith," Chiun called from the nearby background.

"You get that?" Remo asked.

"Yes," Smith said, his tone hollow.